What Kind of Fool

What Kind of Fool

Rhonda McKnight

www.urbanchristianonline.com

Urban Books, LLC
78 East Industry Court
Deer Park, NY 11729

ISBN 13: 978-1-60162-818-3
ISBN 10: 1-60162-818-8

First Printing February 2012
Printed in the United States of America

10 9 8 7 6 5 4 3 2 1

Distributed by Kensington Corp.
Submit Wholesale Orders to:
Kensington Publishing Corp.
C/O Penguin Group (USA) Inc.
Attention: Order Processing
405 Murray Hill Parkway
East Rutherford, NJ 07073-2316
Phone: 1-800-526-0275
Fax: 1-800-227-9604

What Kind of Fool

Rhonda McKnight

Advance Praise for *What Kind of Fool*

"Rhonda McKnight is back with her special blend of Jesus, drama, and more emotional intensity than she's ever delivered before. *What Kind of Fool* is sure to satisfy readers from the first page to the last word."
-Sherri L. Lewis, *Essence* Bestselling Author of *Selling My Soul* and *My Soul Cries Out*

"Samaria is back with a bang! Rhonda McKnight delivers the surprises one after another in this fast-paced story that will keep readers at the edge of their seats."
—Tiffany L. Warren, *Essence* Bestselling Author of *The Bishop's Daughter* and *In the Midst of It All* and the founder of the Annual Faith and Fiction Retreat

"*What Kind of Fool* is an amazing story. It was so good, I could hardly stop reading. I loved it."
-Bettrena Williamson, Global Impact Ministries Daughters of Destiny Book Club

What People Have Said about *-An Inconvenient Friend*

"Rhonda McKnight has written a sizzling novel, full of jaw-dropping sexy drama and unexpected plot twists. I was captivated by this fresh, original story from page one."
—Victoria Christopher Murray, *Essence* Bestselling Author of *The Deal, the Dance, and the Devil* and *Sins of the Mother*

"Talk about scandalous! *An Inconvenient Friend* is full of drama and deception, but God's message of forgiveness and redemption are powerfully delivered.

Rhonda McKnight has quickly earned her place as a favorite in Christian fiction."

—**Sherri L. Lewis**, *Essence* Bestselling Author of *Selling My Soul* and *The List*

"A smoothly blended story line of the Bible and everyday life, *An Inconvenient Friend* will have you looking closer into your relationships."

—**Reviewed by Sharon Lewis of The RAWSISTAZ (tm) Reviewers**

Praise for *Secrets and Lies*

"Rhonda McKnight has written an emotional but inspiring story of faith, trust, and forgiveness as well as the importance of having God in our lives."

—*Jacquelin Thomas*, *Essence* Bestselling Author of *Sampson* and *The Ideal Wife*

"Rhonda McKnight is a fresh new voice in Christian fiction who writes with the skill and grace of a seasoned pro. Her characters seem like friends, and her prose flows effortlessly."

—*Stacy Hawkins Adams*, *Essence* Bestselling Author of *The Someday List*

"Rhonda McKnight's debut novel doesn't disappoint. It mixes appealing and relatable characters with doses of drama and mischief that kept me hooked until the last page."

—*Tia McCollors*, *Essence* Bestselling Author of *Steppin' Into the Good Life* and *The Last Woman Standing*

Dedication

For my father, Jimmy McKnight . . .
who encouraged me to dream, taught me to be
wise, and showed me how to take chances.

Love, Giant ♥

Acknowledgments

These acknowledgments are all about my readers, that is, right after I finish with family. My novels tend to be very serious, but I'm actually a fun-loving person thanks to people like Uncle Downing Kennedy, Elaine White, my late aunt Mary (Phena) Hilyard, Donnell Gardner (the culprit in every spanking I ever had), my sister, Cynthia (undercover hilarity), and my mother, Bessie McKnight, who's victimless sense of humor I surely inherited. Special hugs to my cousin Felicia White. You are so courageous. And my cousin Georgia Brockington—thanks for *reading* my books. Okay, I love y'all who buy and don't read too. ☺

My sons, Aaron and Micah, you make my world a better place. Love you!

If I don't say Margaret Brown, she might not babysit for me. Thank you, Margaret. I'ma break you off something real soon (wink).

My sister-circle of writers has expanded, but in some sense it has gotten tighter because there are those who are *always* there for me. Sherri L. Lewis, Dee Stewart (aka Miranda Parker), and Tiffany L. Warren. Thanks to Tia McCollors, ReShonda Tate Billingsley, Pamela Samuels Young, Zaria Garrison, and Shawneda Marks for sharing advice, love, and an expanded point of view. And then there's Victoria Christopher Murray,

Acknowledgments

my mentor, who imparts so much . . . Well, there are no words, not even from a wordsmith. You're the best VCM!

Pastor Eric at Stockbridge Assembly—your sermon on 4.11.2011—"Dying to Live"—confirmed everything I was writing in this story. Pastor Steven Hedgecoth, all your sermons are words from the Lord. Thank you both for being such awesome men of God.

Dee Stewart—You are a living example that the words *heart failure* don't mean it's over.

Maria Caraballo—Homey, thanks for hooking me up with the Spanish translation and Bettrena Williamson for giving me that final proofread and finding all those typos that I couldn't see.

I won an *EMMA!* Thanks to the Deatri Bey-King and the Romance Slam Jam Organization.

Now, I'm about to mess up because I crashed my computer and lost my calendar, so I'm working from memory (Big Sigh!). Book Clubs that showed me extra love: Tasha Martin and ALL the Sistahfriends, Global Impact "Daughters of Destiny," Majestic Bloom, Divas Read Retreat, Women of Character, Words of Inspiration, Sisters of Ruth, Page Turners BC of Atlanta, Divas Urban BC, Girl Fridayz BC, Word for Women BC, Sister N Ink, Proverb 31 BC, Diva Readers, Divas Read Too, Southern Divas BC, Doing Something Different BC, Soul Divas, Peace In The Pages, WEG BC, Readers' Paradise, SistaGirl BC, Distinguished Divas BC, Atlanta Urban League, Books N Beverage (shout-out to Shernita Alston), Sisters With Books BC, and Jazzy Sistahs BC. Readers giving out extra love: Cecilia Johnson, Patricia Woodside, Author Myra Rutledge, LaShaunda Hoffman, Yolanda Latoya Gore, Kimberly Knox, Sheryl Farmer, Phillis Adams, Priscilla Johnson, Apryl Orr,

Acknowledgments

Crystal Gamble-Nolden, Robbie Bowie, Sammi Matel, Beverly Harper, Erika Echols, Lisa DeNeal, Yvette Bentley, Michele Winstead, Nakeisha Brumfield, Angela Chatman, Angela Richards, Sharon Lewis, Etrina Atterberry, Chiquita Broadus, Sharon Jordan, Diane Hardy, Chevonne Frasier, Milbourne Stafford, Donyalla Manns, Beattie Beard, Yolanda Ervin, Cherlisa Richardson, Olivia Stith, Michelle Rayford, Angel Arnold, Monique Burkes, Makasha Dorsey, Kim Knight, Felecia Pressley, and author Leigh McKnight. Hugs to everybody else in my Facebook and Twitter family.

Thanks to all the reviewers and bloggers who took the time to review: APOOO; RAW; SORMAG; BooksALatte; and OOSA, thanks for adding me to your Best of the Best for two years in a row. Idrissa Uqdah and AALBC, Linda Fegins, Lyn Cote, Darlene Mitchell of Romance in Color, Tavares Carney of Echleon Reviews, Writer's POV, *Black Literature* magazine, Cheryl Francis, Literary Wonders, *Review* magazine, Cecelia Dowdy's Christian Fiction Blog, uh . . . Don't be mad if you're not here. I still got love for you; just nudge me and I'll put you in the next book.

My special stores and lit events: Waldenbooks, Sumter, S.C., and the staff, BooksAMillion, Columbia, S.C., and Urban Knowledge, Columbia, S.C. The Faith and Fiction Retreat and the Divas Read Retreat, both an amazing blessing.

Tyora Moody of TyWebbin Designs, Lisa of Papered-Wonders, Deb Owsley of Simply-Said—you ladies put the words *class* and *professionalism* in author services.

Thank you to Carl Weber and the entire team at Urban Books for keeping me in print and Carol Mackey for selecting both my novels for the Black Expression Book Club.

Acknowledgments

Joylynn Jossel—my editor—you have a good eye and a kind heart. Thanks again for letting me tell my story my way and for putting up with my comma splices. I'm going to do better. ☺

Sha Shana Crichton—my agent—I don't know how big you are, but you are worth your weight in gold for sharing good, sound advice.

Did I forget you? Forgive a sista. I'll catch you in the next book. Did I say Tasha Martin???

Now, let's turn the page. Samaria is back again, and the drama has become very . . . *inconvenient!*

Prologue

Samaria

My heart nearly pounded out of my chest as I said the words. "Yes, I'll marry you."

Mekhi Johnson slid an enormous princess cut diamond ring on my finger and the room that was filled with more than one hundred people we didn't know erupted into a deafening applause. I released the air in my lungs, smiled, and leaned forward to kiss Mekhi on the lips.

Familiar music began to play in the background; Mekhi stood from his down-on-one-knee position and pulled me from my chair to my feet. The recording artist, Ne-Yo, stepped onto the small stage near us and began to sing one of his older songs, "Stop This World."

"Time for a dance." Mekhi swept me onto the floor. Ne-Yo's voice massaged the words to his hit song, and I fell into step with Mekhi. He lowered his lips to mine and kissed me hungrily, almost too hungrily for the public. Our lips parted. "Surprised?"

He knew I was. We hadn't talked about getting married. Not really. We'd just reconciled a few months ago after being separated from each other for eight years. And there was the matter of my pending trial and prison term.

"You know I'm surprised." I raised my hand and placed it on his shoulder.

"But you don't look happy." Mekhi leaned away from me a little. "You look stressed, baby."

I was stressed, more stressed than a ring from Tiffany's could help. The light hit my diamond, and it caused a rainbow-hued sliver of light to slice the air in the room. I had to admit, the ring was a good effort. He had paid a fortune for this monstrosity. It had all the four c's and then some.

"Sammie," Mekhi pulled me closer and whispered in my ear, "what's wrong?"

Truth. Mekhi and I had made a solemn vow that we would always tell each other the truth. Aside from fidelity, it was the only promise we'd made, and yet, less than five minutes after he asked me to become his wife I was going to lie to him. "I ate some Chinese food today, and my stomach has been bothering me." His brow furrowed, and I changed the subject. "You must be some big shot getting Ne-Yo to sing for us."

We both looked at the singer. *Happiness like this can never last, can never last.* Ne-Yo nodded at us and smiled.

"I'll be an even bigger shot if I can get him away from his label," Mekhi said, and I almost laughed at the thought that he could steal Ne-Yo from Def Jam. But even the joke couldn't pull joy from my soul.

I looked out at the smiling faces in the crowd. My family, which consisted of my mother and two cousins, had come out, as had Mekhi's mother and brother and a few of our friends from high school. The rest of the audience consisted of Benxi, Mekhi's multiplatinum recording star, the only star on his fairly new, but quickly rising, record label, the *Real Housewives of Atlanta,* and every other celebrity and wannabe celebrity that called Atlanta home. I should have been thrilled. This was the life I had always wanted. Money, jewelry, parties, celebrity . . . But I wasn't. It was happening at the wrong time. This party was happening on the wrong day.

"I need to go to the restroom."

"Now?" Mekhi frowned. We were the entertainment for our guests, and I knew the least I could do was finish the dance, but I couldn't. I was going to throw up.

"Now." I pulled away, just enough for him to know it couldn't wait.

"Okay, baby." He let go of my waist. I smiled at the room full of people and quickly made my way to the ladies' room.

"Restroom break," Mekhi said, and I could hear laughter above Ne-Yo's crooning. *I've never felt a love strong enough to stop this world from spinning . . .*

I closed the door and turned the lock. My world was spinning, but not in a good way. I went to the sink and turned the faucet for cold water. Quickly, I splashed some on my face and in my mouth, then pulled paper towels, wet them, and wiped my chest and neck. When I was done, I dropped my upper body against the counter. My elbows rested on the porcelain lip of the sink, and through wet hands I choked back tears. Mekhi had done everything in his power to make tonight wonderful for me. He knew the stress I'd been under. Waiting for a trial that would likely send me to prison for stealing and distributing prescription drugs was hard, especially when I was guilty, but he couldn't make what I learned today right.

My doctor opened a file on her desk. "You're eleven weeks pregnant."

I sat back in my chair. The breath I'd been holding escaped my lungs.

She looked down her nose through aqua-blue reading glasses before she removed them. "You're not surprised. You took a home pregnancy test."

I stood to my feet, walked on shaky legs to the huge window adjacent to the chair I'd occupied, and peered out at downtown Atlanta. The hustle and bustle of traffic was at its midday high, but my world had just stopped. "I thought I had a period a few months ago."

"You likely had some bleeding from implantation, not a menstrual cycle."

"Eleven weeks." I turned away from the window to look at her. "I can't be that far along."

"But you are. The sonogram confirms it."

I shook my head, felt nausea engulf me.

"Samaria, is something wrong?"

A knock sounded at the restroom door, pulling me from my memory. "Samaria," I heard my cousin Ebony call. "Mekhi asked me to check on you. You okay in there?"

I returned my gaze to the mirror. I was not okay. As a matter of fact, everything was wrong. I placed my hand on the tiny mound that had raised my abdomen just enough for me to notice a change. The diamond on my finger caught the light and reflected off the mirror in front of me. Mekhi loved me, but he was marrying me because I was pregnant. I knew that. He'd said we'd do it eventually, but there was no point delaying it since the trial was pending and the baby was coming. What he didn't know was eleven weeks ago, I'd slept with not only him, but my ex-lover, Gregory Preston, and I had no idea which one of them was the father of this baby.

Part I
Angelina and Greg

The fool says in his heart, "There is no God." ~
Psalm 14:1 (NIV)

Chapter 1

Angelina

"I can't ever trust you again." I slid the divorce papers across the table. "It's over, Greg, just sign them."

I watched my husband sit back and slump in his chair. "But—" he began.

"Don't say it." I waved a hand to cut him off. "It won't matter."

"But, I do," he continued. "I love you. I want to work this out."

Our waitress crept past us. Our menus were still open, so she continued to the next table. I supposed she'd assumed we still weren't ready to order. Little did she know if any eating was going to happen, Greg would be doing it by himself. I wasn't planning to stay around long enough to dine. I just wanted to meet in a public place so I could end the conversation on my terms, and so I wouldn't be weak.

"Angelina, are you listening to me?" The velvety tenor of his voice pulled me from my thoughts. "I feel like this is more about Samaria than it is about me." He pushed the papers back in my direction. "If it hadn't been her—"

"It'd still be over."

"I don't believe that."

"Why? Because I put up with it before?" My mind went back to the other affair, an anesthesiologist at a conference. It was one weekend, but it cut me to the core. I remembered the pain in my heart, the months it took to stop crying, and what it took to rebuild trust. But nothing had compared to the way I felt when I'd found out about Samaria.

I'd suspected there might be another woman, but not somebody I knew, someone I considered to be a . . . friend. I closed my eyes to the pain that was still fresh. Then reopened them and met the sad gaze of my husband, soon to be ex-husband. I cut my eyes away from him before his good-lookingness melted my resolve.

Greg Preston was the most handsome man I'd ever known in my life, better looking than most actors on television. His looks were the gift of a Creole mother and a dark-skinned Cuban father. He had skin the color of a cocoa bean and hazel eyes so sharp in contrast to his complexion that it gave him an exotic look, almost animalistic, like a wolf dipped in chocolate.

"Talk to me, Lena," he pleaded. It was so unlike Greg to beg for anything. He'd been begging for months. "Punish me, but don't do this. Please, can't we try?"

I released a plume of air from my lungs and forced Samaria's face from my mind. "I wanted to work it out before," I said. "I wanted another child, so I thought if I just put up with you no matter what, I'd eventually get pregnant again." I pushed the thought of our deceased daughter, Danielle, from my mind and forced myself to take in a breath of air. "But now, I realize I've been a fool." I shifted my eyes away from him. "For years, I'd been a fool."

"So are you saying you haven't loved me for a long time?"

"No. That's not what I'm saying." My eyes met his. "I'm saying I compromised because I wanted a baby, but now I realize it was silly to try to have a baby with a man I don't trust."

Greg loosened his tie like he needed air to speak. "I didn't ask you if you trusted me. I want to know if you still love me."

"Greg," I said sharply, "what part of 'that doesn't matter' don't you understand?"

"Lena, It's not like I knew who she was." He leaned forward, raised his voice a little, and we both looked to the left and right to see if we'd drawn an audience.

True, Greg had not known that Samaria Jacobs, the woman he was sleeping with, was the same woman I'd befriended and had known as Rae Burns. Greg had not known his mistress was so devious that she'd joined my church and wormed her way into my life, all with the intention of gleaning enough inside information to wreak havoc on our marriage. But it didn't matter. I'd told myself the first affair was the last affair, and I was standing on that, no matter how much he begged, no matter what my heart said. It was time to use my head.

"What about my will?" I ignored the voice in my head and slid the papers that had now become a "hot potato" back across the table.

Greg lowered his head. When he raised his eyes, unshed tears shown in them. "I know—I know I was wrong, but I thought—I thought Christians were supposed to forgive."

It was me who sat back now. I was shocked he'd pulled the Christian card on me. Steam rose in my belly, and I was annoyed that he'd hit a nerve. I'd wrestled with the same thought all week, the thought or the voice that entered my head when I accepted the papers from my attorney.

"Are you sure you don't want me to just have these served?" Mavis Benchley, one of the top divorce lawyers in Atlanta, had asked as she peered suspiciously over her glasses.

"No. He's asked to meet with me this week, so I'll just give them to him myself."

"Don't do it." There was the Holy Spirit again. I felt an uneasy burst of perspiration, and my breath caught in my throat for a moment. But I shook my head, just as I was doing now. I didn't want to hear what that voice was asking me to do.

"Forgive?" My hand felt unsteady. I returned the glass to the table. "What makes you think I haven't forgiven you?"

Greg's face clouded over with confusion. He didn't really understand the doctrine of forgiveness, and he'd just played himself. "If you've forgiven me, why this?" He let his eyes fall on the papers for a second, and then returned his heated stare to mine.

"Because forgiveness doesn't always mean things will work out the way you want them to. Forgiving doesn't mean a happy ending." I raised my glass and took another sip. My stomach felt like it was in knots, and the same bead of perspiration was forming over my lip.

"I can read you. You still love me."

I hated that those words were true. I hated that I wanted nothing more than to reach for his hand, let him touch me, and take me home and make love to me again. I was such a fool for this man. And even though it had only been three months since we'd separated, celibacy wasn't wearing well, not after thirteen years of marriage and good lovemaking. I wanted . . . I needed . . . *No, be strong. You have to end this.* "I want a divorce." I looked him squarely in the eyes, prayed my waning confidence didn't allow him to read me.

Greg threw his head back and touched the papers as if my final declaration had made them real. He picked them up for a few seconds and lowered them to the table. He did not meet my gaze when he said, "I need my attorney to look at them."

"I'm not really asking you for anything."

That statement got his head up. "What does that mean?"

"I just want the house. I'm going to sell it and buy something smaller."

"That's ridiculous." Greg frowned. "I will not agree to give you nothing."

"I thought it would be easier—" I stopped, pressed my lips together, and then began again. "I thought it would be faster, and I'm willing to do anything—"

"To be free of me." He raised his hand and washed his face. "I won't let you walk away without a decent settlement. It wouldn't be fair."

I thought of Katrice, my new daughter or soon-to-be daughter, once the final hearing for her mother's parental rights had been held. They'd be severed, and then I would be free to adopt her. Having the extra money in the bank would look good on my adoption application, and I could use all the pluses I could find with the divorce pending. Single parents adopted children all the time, but having a strong financial situation could help the application.

"Can you see Phil right away?" I asked, knowing he'd give them to his fraternity brother, who, for many years, had been our personal attorney.

Greg put the papers inside the manila envelope I'd delivered them in. "In a rush?" He closed the metal clasp and let out a long sigh.

"Not really, but it's a good time to sell the house," I replied. "The truth is . . . I have a buyer."

He nodded absently, like he had emotionally checked out of our battle of wills. "Go ahead and sell it. You don't have to wait for the divorce if you have a buyer."

His eyes were so sad that I could barely stand to look in them. He dropped his head. He was looking down, at what I had no idea, but I could tell he was concentrating really hard. He raised his head, swallowed, and in the most desperate tone I'd ever heard, he moaned my name. "Angelina, it hasn't even been that long. Can't we—"

"Save your breath." I stood. "I'm not going to change my mind." I picked up my handbag. "Just have Phil send them to my attorney, and please, come get the rest of your things from the house. They're in the garage." I turned on my heels. I couldn't bring myself to say good-bye, so I didn't. The emotional roller coaster in my spirit moved me through the restaurant like a car on rails. Once on the street, I did a slow jog to the entrance of the parking garage, and impatiently tapped my foot as I waited for the parking valet. Not wanting to wait even a second for change, I overtipped him, slid behind the wheel, and gunned the gas. I was running, and I didn't know if it was from my husband, myself, or my God.

Chapter 2

Angelina

"You're making the worst mistake of your life."

"Mom . . ." I attempted to get a word in. My mother and I had been bantering back and forth about Greg for more than five minutes, and my mother's outrage over my decision was winning. "Would you let me talk?"

"You told me what you had to say, and it still don't make no sense. You're divorcing your husband so you can adopt somebody else's child?"

I pulled the telephone away from my ear and looked at it. I wanted to slam it into the receiver. Somebody else's child? I hate that my mother thought of it that way. I took a deep breath and put the phone back against my ear. "I'm not divorcing Greg because of Katrice, and you know that."

"I know you messing up your life." My mother's voice was shaking. "That man is begging you on his knees. He even said he would go to counseling."

"And you would know that how, Mom?" I asked. "I wish you'd stop talking to him. He has his own mother. You're mine."

"That man is like a son to me. He loves you, and he's a good husband. A good provider. You have no business even *thinking* about divorce."

"Mom, I've made up my mind." I started to perspire again. I carried the phone into the foyer to see what the thermostat was set at.

My mother continued to drone on. "So you gonna let that wretched gal win. You gonna let her have your husband just like she wanted all along."

"Greg and Samaria can have each other. I don't care." That was a lie. The thought of Greg with Samaria made me positively sick. But I was sure he was too angry with Samaria to think of continuing a relationship, or at least I hoped.

I'm not supposed to care, I thought, pushing Samaria's face from my mind. I closed my eyes to the image of the large tears that had spilled down Samaria's cheeks. *"You are a home-wrecking, backstabbing tramp, and I never want to see you again."* Those had been my last words to the woman. Samaria had called several times after. Even wrote me some letter apologizing and saying she knew forgiveness was not possible, but it was her Christian duty to accept responsibility for what she had done. New converts have an overzealous penchant for following the Word. I would ordinarily be pleased, but from Samaria, it was more salt in a wound that had come from battery acid the woman had poured all over my heart. I would never forgive her and never forget.

"You're crazy. You don't hand over your man to a mistress. If she's bad enough to take him, then let him go, but to hand him over when he's begging to stay . . ."

I pulled the phone away from my ear and peered at the number sixty-eight on the wall. I wondered if the thermostat was broken. The house was really warm. I'd never had it this low even on the hottest of days that Atlanta had to offer.

"Angelina," my mother yelled, "do I need to come there and talk some sense into you?"

"You don't need to come here. You're talking enough on the phone every day and honestly, Mom, if you don't stop this, I won't have a choice but to stop taking your calls."

My mother didn't say anything. That was a bad sign. She might really get on a plane and come from Charlotte just to knock me in the mouth. I needed to change the subject. "I've sold the house. I'm moving in a few weeks."

Once again, my mother was mute. She loved my house, and I know she thought I was insane to sell it.

"The buyer practically walked up to my door," I continued. It was true. My nosy neighbor, Joy, had knocked on the door last month expressing concern over having not seen Greg's car. I put her out of her curious misery and told the woman I was getting a divorce and probably selling the house. Joy expressed condolences for a moment and appropriately patted my hand, but none of it felt sincere. I knew why within seconds.

"You don't need to put a sign up," Joy had said, slapping her hands against her cheeks. "My best friend in the whole world is dying to buy your house. Every time she visits she says so. We want our kids to grow up together . . ." and Joy continued her brattle of celebration without regard for my feelings about the whole thing.

"Why, all you'll need is a real-estate lawyer. It'll save you a bundle." Joy clasped her hands together. "I'm so glad I came by. What good news."

I knew it was, in fact, good news. The market wasn't great, especially for homes in this pricey range, and I needed to sell. The house held too many memories. I wanted a fresh start without Greg lurking in the shadows and in every corner.

My BlackBerry began to ring. I pulled it from my pocket. "Mom, I have to go. I'm getting a call from the office."

"Think about what I said. Don't be a fool. Pride cometh before destruction."

"Bye, Mom." I pressed the END button on one phone and the TALK button on the other.

"Angelina, you have to come in!" Portia yelled before I could get my hello out.

I raised a finger to the thermostat and pushed the button until it went down to sixty-six. That had to kick the fan on and get a breeze going. If it didn't, I'd have a repairman come look at it tomorrow. "I have another appointment. What's going on?"

Portia paused, and I heard her clear her throat. "I hate to tell you this on the phone, but some government men are here from the IRS Criminal Investigation unit. They say they need to see our records."

I took a step back from the thermostat and tried to steady myself. I shook my head to clear double vision. Had I heard Portia correctly? *Criminal investigation.* I wiped my sweaty forehead, and then everything went black.

I didn't remember getting up off the floor or grabbing my purse or getting in my car. But I was in it, speeding down Peachtree Parkway to my small office on Holcomb Bridge Road and trying to figure out why I'd fainted like the heroine in a 1940s movie. I was also trying to figure out why representatives from the IRS's Criminal Investigation Unit were at *my* office. What in the world could they want with my records? The only person who handled the money was Don Conley, the accountant. He was a CPA, and I trusted him implicitly. That's why I'd called him as soon as I'd gotten in the car. Voice mail greeted me, and I left a desperate plea for him to call me back, which he was doing now.

"Don, there are IRS investigators at the office, wanting our records. Will you meet me there?"

He said of course and the knot in my stomach loosened a little.

It seemed like it took forever for me to pull into the small parking lot of the building I leased. Something Extra, my nonprofit foundation, was a three-person shop nestled near downtown Norcross. My building and the surrounding offices were converted Victorian homes clustered around a duck pond. The rent was more than I should be paying, but I couldn't resist the tranquility the quaint, historic location afforded me. Suburban Atlanta was a maven of newness, filled with architecture that was a compilation of glazed terracotta, mirrored glass, and steel. I desired to escape it all for a simpler, quieter location, so I preferred the wood, brick, and beveled glass that could still be found in downtown buildings in Norcross.

I took the three steps at a rapid pace and pushed the door open to the reception area. Portia flew from behind her desk. Her emerald-green eyes bugged like glassy volcanic rock, and her gelled red hair looked like lava shooting from a recent eruption. Her freckles stood out against the backdrop of pale skin that had become even paler since I had seen her a few hours ago. "I'm sorry," she said, "but I knew you had to come back for this."

Two men in ominous dark suits and white shirts stood from the small sofa on the far end of the wall. Like the *Men in Black,* they stepped toward me. I was almost expecting them to do impersonations of Will Smith and Tommy Lee Jones, that is, until they turned official on me.

"Angelina Preston?" one of them asked. I nodded, and he removed an identification badge from the inside of his jacket pocket. "I'm Agent Rod Crisp, and this is Agent Vince Lyons. We're with the Internal Revenue Service Office of Criminal Investigation."

Agent Lyons, the brother, reached into a gold business card case and handed one to me. "We've come to seize your financial records for our investigation."

My throat went dry. The words *IRS, criminal, seize, records,* swirled around in my head like frisky fish in a round tank. It took a few seconds, but I finally found my voice. "I don't understand."

"Something Extra Corporation is being investigated for the possible illegal activities of embezzlement and money laundering."

Tears burned the back of my eyes. "There's some type of mistake. I'm a small nonprofit. We don't see enough money for embezzlement and money laundering."

"Ms. Preston, we've conducted a general investigation that tells us otherwise. Now we need to continue our investigation with—"

"Do you have a warrant or something?" I interrupted him. I wasn't about to be railroaded by these guys. Before they could respond, I heard a noise behind me. Portia's metal pencil cup had hit the tiled floor with a ping.

"Here," Portia yelped out the word and extended a blue trifolded document. "They gave it to me."

I took it and let out the deep breath I'd been holding. It was a search warrant, but I knew they would have one. People like this always came prepared. At least in the movies they did, which was the only place I'd ever seen such a thing as an IRS criminal investigation. *What's happening?*

I dropped the search warrant on Portia's desk and reached for a tissue. I could feel perspiration rising all over my body. They had me scared, and I didn't want to go through this alone. "Would you at least wait for my accountant? He's on his way. He should be here any minute." I heard myself pleading, but my words fell on unsympathetic ears.

"We do not wait for *any* company official to begin our seizure. However, we will interview Mr. Conley, along with the other staff and volunteers once we've reviewed your records," Crisp replied.

A beat of silence, and then the brother said, "Please show us where you keep your records."

I fought the scream that wanted to escape my lungs and did as I was asked. They picked, prodded, and tore through every piece of paper and ledger stored in hardcopy and on the computers. In the end, they took all my financial documents and the hard drive to both the computers, leaving only the one on Portia's desk, because it had no financial records. How were we supposed to work with no computers? This was insane.

They left. I looked at my watch. It was five o'clock. I had to get to the daycare center and pick up Katrice. I had already promised her I would be early today, and now I would actually end up being late because I had been waiting for Don. Don, who the agents knew and paused upon saying his name; Don, who said he'd be right over, but neither called nor showed; Don, who's phone was ringing straight to voice mail. I slammed down the file folder I'd been holding.

"Angelina," Portia crept into the room, "can I get you something before I leave?"

I raised my pounding head. My eyes were so heavy I could barely see her. In fact, when I looked at Portia, all I could see was the fear that had been clenching my own heart for the last two hours. What had Don done? What was I going to do if my business, my baby, was in trouble?

I started Something Extra, a nonprofit organization that raised funds for foster children, three years ago. Their donors contributed to a pot of money that bought Christmas presents, school clothing and supplies, paid cheerleading and football team fees, graduation dues, vacations, even vehicles and college scholarships when I could finagle them. My volunteers and I were busy, all day every day, setting up fundraising events and begging for money to pay for them. It was a good organization. We helped so many children. Could Don have stolen from the kids? Don is a retired accountant who'd spent twenty-five years of his life making sure the books were correct for other companies. I felt bile rise. I pressed my lips together to keep from throwing up my lunch. "I'm fine. Go home."

Portia hesitated for a moment, bounced up and down on the balls of her feet, and then turned to walk out of the room. "I'm sorry, Angelina." She stopped in the doorway. "I'm so sorry that all of this happened."

I rolled my chair back and pushed myself to my feet. Nobody was sorrier than I was because Greg had warned me about Don.

Chapter 3

Angelina

"I'm not a criminal attorney, but it seems that the IRS's paperwork is in order." Mavis Benchley handed the letter and warrant from the Internal Revenue Service back to me.

Hope escaped from my lungs with the breath I'd been holding.

Mavis reached into her desk and offered a business card. "He's a criminal lawyer."

I read the name on the card. Bernard Hightower.

"He's very good, and he likes to fight the big bad government," Mavis added.

I tried to crack a smile, but my heart was breaking. I'd put years of time and sweat into building my little do-good nonprofit into a viable resource for foster children. No one was doing what I did on as large a scale as I was. What would the foster parents association do without Something Extra? I sighed again.

"I received the paperwork from your husband's attorney," Mavis told me.

I straightened my back with new interest. "That was fast," I said, thinking it had been less than a month since I'd met with Greg.

"It looks like you really are going to have an uncontested divorce." Mavis put her reading glasses on her nose and picked up a sheet of paper from my open file.

"He's offering a generous cash settlement, offered to pay all existing joint debts, and has given you 100 percent of the equity in the house."

I tried to smile again. That was a good thing, an easy divorce, but somehow it didn't feel that way. "I'm pleased."

Mavis removed her glasses and crossed her hands on her desk. "I have to say this, I rarely have an uncontested divorce. People just don't hire me unless they're anticipating a fight, but when I have had uncontested matters, the couples have had irreconcilable differences like children outside of the marriages, addiction problems, or someone is going or has gone to prison."

I could already feel the weight of the words that were about to come, but I asked anyway. "What are you saying?"

"I'm saying . . . that you and your husband haven't even gone to counseling. I sense you still care about him, and, well, based on this offer, he still cares about you. Why not give this more time?"

I threw my head back. My mother, and now my attorney, telling me I should think about getting over Greg's repeated infidelity.

Mavis continued. "If I file these papers as you requested, you'll be divorced from Greg in as little as thirty-one days. It'll probably be a little longer because family court is backed up, but not much. You've only been separated for a couple of months."

"Three months," I corrected her. "And that's been long enough to decide what I want to do."

"Three months after thirteen years of being together?" Mavis continued.

"I thought you worked for me." I rolled my eyes. "You seem to be working for him."

"I'm working for what's right. I may be a divorce attorney, but I'm also a woman who's been hurt. I recognize pain when I see it. I'm just not sure you've taken enough time to work through your emotions."

I stood. "I appreciate the contact information for Mr. Hightower." I picked up my handbag. "And, I appreciate your concern, but really, I can't live with Greg anymore. I've tried, but I can't forget what he's done."

"Forgetting slowly happens after you forgive." Mavis stood also. "Have you tried forgiving him?"

I turned off my car's engine, reached for my coffee cup, and pressed my body back into the leather seat. I took a sip, closed my eyelids, and reopened them, only when I was sure I could keep the tears I'd been fighting from falling. It had been hours since I left her office, but Mavis Benchley's words were still bothering me. I couldn't believe she'd had the nerve to diminish Greg's affair. Forgive him. Why was everyone assuming I hadn't forgiven him just because I still wanted the divorce when cheating was a deal breaker for most marriages? And it wasn't like it was his first time. He'd done it before.

With all the negative feedback from the people who were supposed to be on my side, I found myself constantly trying to bolster confidence in the choice I'd made. I shouldn't have to do that. They were my friends and family. They should be on my side. I pushed thoughts of Greg and all the other people in his cheering section from my mind. Not like that was my only problem. In fact, at the moment, my divorce was the least of my concerns.

I looked at the *Atlanta Herald* newspaper that had been riding around on the empty seat next to me like an unwelcome passenger for a week. Its headline screamed ugly words that cut me a little more every day.

CHARITY FOR FOSTER CHILDREN INVOLVED IN MONEY LAUNDERING SCAM!

And if that wasn't enough, I'd been on the television also. My picture splashed all over the local networks for the entire city of Atlanta to see and assign guilt to. I'd been judged before I'd been formally charged with anything. God help the innocent in the current media and legal system. I knew I'd never again assume anyone was guilty just because their mug shot was featured next to some reporter's talking head.

I climbed out of my car. As I rounded the front of my office building, the postman turned into my walkway. I reached the steps at the same time he did. "Good morning, Mr. Rogers," I said, greeting him.

"Morning," he replied, reaching into his mail cart. "You got a ton of stuff today."

He handed the mail to me, and my heart sank. It was more hate mail. I bit my bottom lip and managed a tight-lipped smile as I took the enormous stack from his hands.

"Hope it's checks in there," he said. "People still believe in you. I know I do." He winked.

Warmth spread through me. This time my smile was genuine, even though I knew better. People *did not* believe in me. People believed I was guilty of stealing money they'd donated to foster children. The first week it was the phone calls and e-mails. Now the disenchanted had taken to more traditional means of letting me know what they thought. I could just imagine the contents: *Thief, you'll burn for what you did,* or *I knew you were too good to be true,* and *I hope you go to jail.* Those were the general sentiments, but I thanked him, and we went our separate ways, he down the cobblestone sidewalk and I into my building.

Portia was on the phone when I walked in. I heard her whisper she had to go, right before she ended the call. Then she removed her headset and stood. I greeted her, and she followed me into the office, sharing the painful details of the many harassing phone calls she'd taken all morning.

"Why don't you let the calls go to voice mail and screen them from there?"

"I'm a receptionist. You pay me to answer the phone," Portia said, like she hadn't just made the task of taking calls seem like torture. She was such a character.

"Do it your way." I collapsed into my chair.

"You have a few calls to return. The messages just got buried under the mail." Portia pointed to the pile that had slid and was now covering my desk completely. "Do you want me to sort that?"

I considered it, but realized I didn't really want Portia or any of the few volunteers I had left seeing the mail I was getting. A voice on the phone was one thing, but an angry letter was worse. "I've got it," I replied.

"Any news about Don?"

"Not since you asked me at five o'clock yesterday." The question annoyed me, but I smiled as I answered. Portia was genuinely concerned. She'd been with Something Extra for three years now. This IRS thing was her problem too. She'd be out of a job if I had to close up shop.

"Oh, I was just wondering, you know," Portia paused, heightening the drama, "if the IRS or cops were looking for him."

"I imagine before this is over they will be. I mean, if anyone had access to money around here it was him, and his being MIA is certainly not helping any case he would try to make for innocence."

Portia didn't say anything. She just stood there looking confused.

"Would you close the door on the way out? I need to make a personal call."

"Oh, of course." Portia snapped back to herself. "Don't forget to unearth those messages." She left the office.

I picked up the pile of mail and fished out the three message slips Portia had been speaking of. Two were from local Family and Children Services offices, probably wanting to know if I was going to deliver summer camp monies, and the third was from the head of the board of Youth Services.

The first time the horrid story ran in the paper, I'd received a telephone call from Dr. Adams. He expressed his concern for my situation, and then asked me to explain what was going on. "This isn't going to come back to bite the board if we continue to allow you to serve?" he'd asked pensively.

I'd assured him it would not. But now, less than two weeks later, he was calling again, and I had to admit I was concerned about why. I had spent my entire adult life in service to children and families. I started my career as an entry-level case manager and worked my way up to directorship of the second-largest county office in the state. It was Greg who had insisted I step down from the stress. I'd been having trouble conceiving, so I'd given in to his moaning about my job, but that hadn't helped. We found out our problem getting pregnant was his, not mine. We eventually resorted to in vitro fertilization and were successful on the first try.

I reached into my desk and removed a framed picture of my beautiful baby girl. She'd lived six months before SIDS had taken her one afternoon. Greg had been home with Danielle while I was shopping. I'd returned and found him asleep on the chaise. It appeared that Danielle was napping, but I quickly realized our daughter wasn't breathing. It was a cruel irony, two people who fought to save lives every day, I in child welfare and Greg as a neurosurgeon, losing a life that was so precious to us. If I was honest with myself, I'd have to admit that had been the beginning of the slow death of our marriage. His affair with Samaria had just put the nail in our coffin.

I returned the picture frame to my desk drawer, shut out the emotions that thoughts of Danielle stirred, picked up the telephone handset, and dialed.

Dr. Wilfred Adams was a large man whose voice was full, masculine, and on today, deceptively calm. After greeting me he said, "This situation with the Internal Revenue Service . . . I'm afraid I'm going to have to ask for your resignation."

Talk about getting right to it. He usually made small talk. *My resignation.* No middle step, no investigation or suspension. I opened my mouth to speak, but found my words stuck in my throat.

"I know it seems drastic, but this really is a mess. I can't ignore the concerns of the community," he reasoned.

I could hardly lift my voice above a whisper. "I understand."

"Of course you can have your seat back once this is cleared up favorably. We won't fill it."

I nodded. "I appreciate that."

"Your service in this county is unmatched, and I'm sorry to have to dishonor it this way. But you know how it goes."

I couldn't deny that I did. I was just hoping . . .

"Fax me a letter, will you?"

"Of course," I said. "I'll let you know when everything has been worked out."

"You do that," he said. "And, Angelina . . ."

"Yes."

"Good luck with it all."

I sat there for a moment holding the phone. That seat on the board was my last connection to the work I loved. I needed to meet with the lawyer Mavis had recommended and find out how long this investigation could go on, because no matter what Dr. Adams said, when he started receiving pressure to fill my seat on the board, he would fold and fill it. I pressed talk on the handset, reached into my pocket, and pulled out the business card for Bernard Hightower.

Chapter 4

Greg

I paced the floor of the small apartment that had become a prisonlike home when Angelina put me out. It was Friday night, and I was alone, again. I thought of the invitations I'd received. A few of my colleagues were having drinks at the bar down the street from one of the hospitals. It was one of those places where the waitresses were half naked and provided service with a smile. Then I thought of the other invitation, one that was not so public. I removed my BlackBerry and looked at the text message that had just come in from a sexy female doctor I'd collaborated with on a procedure last week.

Greg, remember, the offer for dinner is open, anytime. I can guarantee dessert will be good.

I knew what that meant, and I was dying for dessert. I was way overdue for some sex. I looked at the text message again. Then I remembered the last time I hooked up with a woman on the fly. I'd ended up with Samaria. *Disaster*. I tossed my BlackBerry on the table. Ms. Dessert was going to have to serve it up for someone else. I wasn't going down that road again, not until I was divorced, and I was hoping that wouldn't happen.

I took the few steps necessary to reach the expanse of windows that provided a panoramic view of the city of Atlanta and let out a heavy sigh. Angelina. She wasn't budging. She wasn't even taking my calls. Not even about the IRS thing. I'd thought that was the perfect opening for me, but when I went to the house last week, she showed me a stronger woman than I was expecting to see.

The doorbell chimed that annoying song my wife had custom ordered. No one answered, but just as I was about to turn and leave, Angelina swept the door open. The motion produced a current of wind that picked up her hair and silk robe, giving her an ethereal glow against the dimmed light in the foyer of our home. She was not happy to see me. "What are you doing here?" she asked.

"I read the *Atlanta Herald*. I've been calling you. Why didn't you tell me about this?" I stepped into the house and closed the door.

"Because it's not your problem. It's mine." She was looking me straight in the eyes, like her problems hadn't been mine for thirteen years.

"You know anything that's hurting you is hurting me." I surprised myself with that line. I meant it, but more important, I knew it was something she'd want to hear.

She put a hand on her hip. "This isn't a good time. You should have called first. Katrice and I are having dinner."

"I did call first. You're ignoring my calls." I let out a breath. "Look, I'd love to see Katrice." Angelina's face said what her mouth didn't, and I knew that had been a mistake. Using the kid was not going to work. "I'm hungry. Can I have dinner with you?"

Angelina looked at me like I was crazy, and, in truth, I felt crazy for asking. I was desperate to spend some time with her. How else was I going to get her back?

"No. I don't want her thinking we're still together," she said. "I don't want her confused."

"Confused? I'm still your husband," I said, firmly, hoping she'd find a little macho bravo attractive. Begging was for punks.

She shook her head. "In name only." Her voice trembled, and her eyes filled with tears. She used her fingertips to stop them. "You came to see if I was okay. As you can see, I am."

"But this is really bad, Lena. How are you holding up?"

"It's tough. I'm embarrassed, and I'm worried, but I'm okay."

"I'm not here to tell you I told you so, but I knew you were putting too much faith in Don. One person should never have this kind of control." I let out a breath. "It's my fault too. I should have made time to help you or at least hired a consultant to go over the books." More of the truth that she'd want to hear.

Angelina relaxed some, as if my putting it on Don eased her anxiety. "I knew better. I learned about this in grad school. I was too busy raising funds and all the stuff I like to do to make sure the financials were okay." She shook her head. "I just trusted him, you know."

My heart broke for her. I reached out and pulled her into my chest. Angelina melted in my arms, but it was temporary, because I went too far when I kissed her temple. She jumped back like my lips had seared her skin. "Leave, Greg." She pulled farther away and opened the door.

"Honey, please."

"Get out!"

Now, almost two weeks later, I could still hear the door slam like she was trying to throw it through its wooden frame. I took both fists and banged them against the glass in front of me. I shouldn't have kissed her, but I couldn't help it. She smelled so good, like a cookie. I missed her.

I turned my back to the view, walked to the sofa, and fell down, face-first, into the cushions. Dr. Gregory Preston, handsome, accomplished, and already fighting off the sex kittens who'd heard I was living apart from my wife. For some men, my situation would be a dream come true, but all I wanted to do on this lonely Friday night was cry like a woman, because I hadn't realized how much I loved my wife when I'd had her.

Chapter 5

Greg

I looked at the divorce papers. It was going to be over if one of us didn't stop it. The problem was, Angelina really had to be the one to halt it; otherwise, I'd just be delaying the inevitable. It had been two weeks since Phil had sent the papers back to her lawyer. The judge would be signing off on them in a month or so. What was I going to do?

I ran my hand over my two-day-old stubble. Then I picked up the glass I'd been refilling for over an hour and took a long sip of vodka. I wasn't ordinarily a drinker, but I had nothing to do and nowhere to go. I was depressed, so depressed that I'd cancelled my afternoon appointments and come home. I didn't even want to play golf. If I didn't drink, I was liable to hang myself. I raised the glass again and emptied it.

At some point I had dozed off because the ringing of my cell phone woke me from an alcohol-induced sleep. I rolled over on the sofa. The vodka bottle that had been resting on my chest fell and hit the floor. I reached for my cell and recognized the phone number. "Just what I need. More drama." I pushed the TALK button and said a reluctant hello.

"Greg." My sister Catherine's voice came through the receiver. "I'm sorry to call with bad news, but Uncle Simon died." She delivered the message with such a curt, emotionless tone that she could have been telling me the battery in her car was dead. I wiped my face with my hand. I hated to hear that. I really liked Uncle Simon.

"When?"

"Yesterday."

I moved my body to an upright position on the sofa and looked at the digital clock on my desk. Seven P.M. I'd been asleep a few hours, and I still wasn't awake. I shook the cobwebs. "What happened to him?"

"What happened? You know he had a stroke, and then a heart attack a few months ago. He's eighty-three. His body couldn't take all that."

I stood and paced a bit. I hadn't thought about my family in a long time. It had been over two years since I'd seen my parents. They'd come to Atlanta for Danielle's funeral, but I hadn't been home since I'd volunteered after Hurricane Katrina.

"Greg, are you there?" Catherine's voice was shrill. She had an annoying pitch that she unconsciously released whenever she was running out of patience, which was often because she had none.

"I'm here. I guess I didn't realize Uncle Simon was in his eighties."

"That's because you never see anyone. You never come home. And there's another thing. Daddy was in the hospital for a couple of days. He's been drinking and eating bad. You need to talk to him. He's going to kill himself."

I could tell she was getting riled up. Catherine was a bitter, forty-year-old divorcee who had been left behind when our baby sister, Tiffany, and I had left Louisiana for college and never looked back. She was always angry, but she rarely exaggerated. If she was calling with a complaint about our father, it was necessary.

"The viewing is the day after tomorrow. I know you're not close to Uncle Simon, but you must come, because I can't do anything with Daddy. You're his . . . son. Maybe you can." The word "son" dripped venom. It told me that she was still salty about the fact that our father made it no secret that he loved his "son" best. Her voice broke through my thoughts. "Can we expect you?"

I guess I had to. "Yes."

"Good. I'll see you when you get here."

The phone went dead. It was just like Catherine to make her point and not allow anyone else to make theirs. Although I'd never say anything so cruel to her, I reckoned that nasty little habit was one of the ones that drove her ex-husband off.

I stood, stretched, and walked over to the windows. The sun had gone down, and the stars twinkled in the sky like tiny diamonds over the city. I wished I could enjoy the view. I wished I could enjoy anything, but all I could think about was Angelina. She would appreciate this view. She loved sitting on the balcony outside our bedroom at night. She'd sit there for hours taking in the night air and staring at the sky. She'd sold the house, but the one she'd moved into had a porch and a deck. I knew that because even though I hadn't had an invitation, I'd driven by one day and checked out the exterior. I felt like a stalker, but I had to know where she was. I needed to know what her new home was like. Oddly, it made me feel closer to her.

I wondered if Angelina was outside now. Was she seeing what I was seeing, or better yet, was she thinking of me?

"Not likely," I whispered to myself, pulled the chair out from behind the desk, and sank my body into the cushions.

I pushed the power button on the laptop and waited for the operating system to boot up. Once I had the Internet, I opened my calendar. I was booked pretty solid, but I knew I could get a colleague to cover for me. My father was drinking again. He knew better. He and I had covered this ground before. Angelina had just delivered Danielle, and she told him his granddaughter wanted to get to know him. He stopped drinking for more than a year.

Instinctively I wanted to call Angelina so that I could hear her say everything was going to be all right. I looked at the picture of her that I kept on the desk and picked up the phone. Maybe I could ask her to come with me. She'd always liked my mother. My father had always liked her. But then I realized I was really reaching. She was not going to allow me to manipulate her with my parents. She'd see right through that. The same way she saw through it with Katrice. My once trusting wife was now suspicious of everything I did. I had been a fool, but foolish though I was, I was no quitter. I was not a man who gave up. If Angelina was feeling as sad as I was, she was vulnerable. I might be able to weaken her resolve—get her to fall into my arms, and then our bed. I'd been successful before. I decided I had nothing to lose by finding out.

Chapter 6

Angelina

"I can't believe this year." I picked up the water goblet, put it to my lips, and took a sip that was long overdue. Although concerned that it was a bit unorthodox to be meeting with my good-looking, single, black male attorney over dinner, I was thirsty and hungry, so I was glad he had asked.

"Sometimes it's like that." Bernard Hightower raised his own glass, took a sip, and returned it to the table. "I've heard many a client say those exact same words. The tough parts of life seem to come in patches, you know."

I nodded.

"My mother used to say, the devil circles when he thinks we're down. Only someone who's afraid they won't win kicks a man when he's down. You'll come out of this year a stronger, wiser woman."

Bernard, as he'd insisted I call him, was staring straight into my eyes. I felt myself blush from the heat of his stare. I cleared my throat. "I know about tests making us stronger, but if you had asked me what my test was going to be this year, I would never have thought the end of my marriage and a criminal investigation." I laughed a little. I knew I was trying to push the pain back down. I was fighting tears that wanted to erupt. "Oh," I threw up an index finger, "let's not forget I sold my dream home."

"It'll work out, Angelina." He reached across the table and gave my hand a pat. "You don't mind if I call you by your first name, do you?" He moved his hand back and opened his menu. I had not extended the same courtesy to him when he'd extended it to me.

"Of course," I said, thinking, *Mavis calls me by my first name.*

We discussed my legal problems over dinner. Bernard tried to hide his true feelings under the mask of empathy, but I could tell he was excited about my case. He loved fighting the government, especially the Internal Revenue Service, and he boasted a 95 percent win rate in trial.

"You mentioned trial earlier, but didn't go into detail." I frowned. I couldn't believe it could come to that.

"Don't worry. The IRS doesn't like trials, and they definitely don't want to go with me again." He smirked, his confidence coming through in a way that eased my nerves. "Besides, they're likely looking for your accountant."

"Don." I wanted to strangle him. "How can I find him? Should I hire a detective?"

"I have someone on it. It's a part of your fee."

And what a fee it was—a ten thousand-dollar retainer just to take my case.

"I trust things are going well with your divorce settlement. I know Mavis is the best."

I nodded. "Actually, my divorce looks like it'll be uncontested, and my husband is being very generous."

"I'm surprised, a man letting you go without a fight." He smiled, and I thought he was flirting with me, so I said nothing. I was not up for flirting.

We talked more, ate, and when we got to the parking garage, my car wouldn't start. It was late, and I was tired, so when Bernard offered to take me home I accepted. I could get a rental in the morning and let my roadside service deal with it, but once I arrived home, I immediately regretted letting him drop me off. Greg's SUV was in the driveway. "Thank you for everything, Bernard," I said. "I'll talk to you soon." I opened the door to climb out, but being the gentleman that he was, so did Bernard.

"Are you sure I can't see you to the—?" Bernard rose from the vehicle, but his words died when he saw Greg.

"I'm sure," I said. "Really, we'll talk tomorrow. Thank you for dinner, and thank you for listening." Bernard hesitated like he was considering whether he should leave. After a moment, he slid into his car and pulled away. I turned to a stone-faced Greg.

"Who in the devil is that?" he asked, pointing at the back of Bernard's car. I thought I smelled liquor on his breath.

"That was my attorney, Greg."

"That's not Mavis."

I rolled my eyes. "My criminal attorney, and please tell me what you're doing here. Why am I answering your questions?"

Greg pushed the door closed to his car. "I need to talk to you. Can we go inside?"

"It's late."

"Come on, Lena. It's eight o'clock. It wasn't too late for old boy there. I just want to talk."

I allowed him to follow me into the house. We stopped just inside the foyer, and I watched as Greg took in my new surroundings. This house was a third of the size of the 4,500 square foot home we'd shared, but it was also a third of the expense and less to clean for a single mother who could no longer afford a weekly maid service.

"I didn't tell you where I lived. How did you find me?" I asked.

"The address is on the divorce papers," he replied like that made it okay for him to pop over. "This is nice. Cozy. Reminds me of the house we owned when I was in my surgical residency."

I thought back to that house. He was right. Maybe that's why I'd fallen in love with this one when I saw it. I'd chosen that house too. The memory of those early years made me sad; looking at Greg did the same. "What do you want, Greg? Why are you here?"

He took a few steps toward the stairwell and asked, "Where's Katrice?" In the hollow of the narrow space his voice echoed.

"Shhh . . . You might wake her." I walked and he followed me past my small galley kitchen and into a sunken family room where my babysitter was buried in a mountainous heap of books.

"Oh, Mrs. Preston, I didn't hear you come in." The young woman removed a single earphone. I wondered briefly how she would hear Katrice, but surmised that she only had one ear closed and Greg and I had been quiet. She gathered up her books, shoved them into a backpack, and stood.

"Chelsea, this is . . ." I realized I didn't know how to introduce him, so I just figured his name would do. "Dr. Preston. Greg, this is my neighbor, Chelsea. Chelsea was also involved in a youth training camp I funded last year."

"Nice to meet you, sir," Chelsea said.

Greg smiled curtly. He didn't even try to mask his desire to see her leave.

"How was Katrice?" I removed my wrap and lay it across a nearby chair.

"She was wonderful. I put her to bed at seven-thirty. I checked on her ten minutes ago, and she was asleep."

I reached into my purse and handed Chelsea money. "I appreciate you coming at the last minute."

The girl looked at the bills in her hand and smiled. "No problem. I need to get every penny I can, so please don't hesitate to call me to sit with her." She shuffled past us, and I followed her to the door where I watched the girl cross the street and enter her own home. When I pushed the door closed, then turned back to the interior of the foyer, I almost bumped into Greg. He reached up and caressed my cheek. With his other hand he pulled me to him.

"Honey, I miss you." His lips were on mine before I could say another word.

I entered the bedroom and was greeted by the gentle sound of Greg's even breaths. They were too light to be considered a snore and too heavy not to be. He didn't often sleep this hard when we were together, but then again, Greg rarely drank like he must have before he pulled in my driveway.

I set a coffee mug on the nightstand, crouched to my knees next to the bed, and stared at him. The fine baby-like hairs that framed the top half of his head seemed to be sprinkled with more gray than had been a few months ago.

I looked at my watch. It was almost 6:00 A.M. I had no idea if he had an early surgery, so I reasoned that I had to wake him, but in truth, I wanted to just keep staring at his manly perfection. I was completely honest with myself. I wanted to wake him, but not for surgery. I dropped my head. *God help me. Help me get over this man.*

Greg's cell phone alarm beeped at a decibel of seven, and his eyes popped open. I reached for the noisy contraption and silenced it. He closed his eyes for a second, and then reopened them. A hint of surprise registered when he saw me, but then his eyes searched mine like he'd been looking for me all his life.

"Lena," he whispered my name. His voice had a deep intonation that I could not attribute to grogginess. It was a painful, longing sound. He rolled from his side to his back, closed his eyes again, and raised his hand to wash his face. "If I'm imagining you, please give me more of whatever I drank last night."

I stood and reached for the mug. "I can't do that, but I do have coffee." Greg rolled back toward me. He swung his long legs over the side of the bed and sat upright. I handed him the mug, and he took a few long sips that nearly drained the cup.

"It's coming back to me now with startling clarity." He did a quick stretch. "I must really be losing my touch. Not only did I wake up alone, but you and I did not—"

I raised a hand to cut him off. "You haven't lost anything, Greg. I've just made up my mind that I'm not going to be that woman that creeps with her ex-husband. It's not right."

"First of all, I'm not your ex-husband. Not yet." He emptied his coffee mug and stared at me intently. "And second, please tell me you're not seeing that Bernard guy."

"No, I told you he's my lawyer, besides, I just met him."

Greg shrugged. "I'm not trying to accuse you of anything, but I'm just saying, the man dropped you off pretty late for business."

I pursed my lips. "We had a dinner meeting because that was all he had available, and then my car wouldn't start."

"That's all he had available for the gorgeous new client." Greg smirked. "And how convenient for him to have you break down. I'll have to get you a new car so that doesn't happen again." He gave me a suspicious look. "Anyway, I'm glad to know you're not dating. The thought of losing you to another man is too much."

"You lost me to a man. You lost me to you, Greg."

"I messed up, but I'm not out yet." He stood and put his hand on my face. Moved his thumb across my cheek and touched my lip. "Divorce is a formality. We can fix that anytime you want."

I moved his hand, retrieved the mug, and crossed the room. "Katrice will be awake soon. You have to leave. There's a toothbrush in the guest bath." I exited the room.

Five minutes later, Greg walked into the kitchen.

"More coffee?" I offered. He nodded, and I refilled his cup. "Toast?"

He shook his head and sat down on one of the stools at the counter. "I don't want to trouble you, and I respect the fact that you need me to leave." He took the mug from my hand. "I could use an aspirin. I've got a slight hangover."

I had known that was coming. Greg always had a headache when he drank. I slid a napkin with three pills across the bar.

"We have to get back together," he said. "No one else knows me like you do."

I crossed my hands over my chest. I didn't know how to respond to the fact that he'd made me think about some other woman getting to know him as well as I did. That had my heart thudding.

Greg swallowed the pills and took the glass of water I slid to him as well. Our eyes caught, danced for a few seconds, and I broke contact by turning my back to busy myself with nothing in the sink. His eyes were hypnotic. They'd been doing a number on me for almost twenty years if I included the time we dated.

"My uncle Simon died."

I turned around. "I'm sorry to hear that."

"And my father is misbehaving."

"What's he doing?"

"Same things he always does. Too much liquor and fine food for an old diabetic." He paused like he was considering his own words, like he was still trying to digest the weight of what he'd said. "I'm flying to New Orleans in the morning."

I nodded.

"Would you come with me? It's just for a few days. The funeral is the day after tomorrow."

I shook my head.

"Katrice, I bet she's never been on a plane, and you could use a trip away from all the stupid business with your company."

I shook my head again. "I can't."

He nodded understanding. "I haven't been home without you in fifteen years. My father would instantly recover if he saw your face, and he'd stop drinking."

"We lead separate lives."

He shook his head and put the mug down. "This is too much. I swear I can't do this."

"You have to." My voice was firm. I'd been suppressing my annoyance about his showing up last night like we didn't lead separate lives and the fact that he'd nearly weakened my resolve on the "No making love to the ex policy." I'd tossed and turned all night as I thought about him lying in the next bedroom. "Don't do what you did last night. You have no right to come here trying to seduce me."

"I was desperate." He stood. "I've got to go, but this conversation isn't finished. I'm not done with you, Angelina. I don't care what those papers say. You will always be my wife."

The toilet flushed at the top of the stairs.

"Go," I whispered. Greg walked around the counter. I could tell he was going to touch me, so I raised my hand to block him. "Give your parents my love."

"I'd rather have it." He gently took my hand, and then surrendered by letting it go. "I'm not giving up." I watched his back as he left the kitchen. In the distance I heard the door open and close when he left the house. I found myself wishing I could get him to leave my heart as easily.

Chapter 7

Greg

Home left a bad taste in my mouth. It was like old coffee or the unwelcomed aftertaste of a night of drinking. The funny thing about it was that I wasn't really sure why. I couldn't put a finger on why New Orleans was like that for me.

The city itself was breathtaking. I loved the magnolia trees and the misty, swampy waterways that made up the bayou. The food remained my favorite, and I took every opportunity to seek out the red beans and rice and sausage and shrimp-laden dishes in various restaurants in Atlanta. I was a fan of the cityscape—the bungalow-style houses and Creole townhouses with their large courtyards and intricate iron balconies. And then, of course, there were the large antebellum homes flanked by hundred-year-old oak trees like the one I was looking at.

"G!" I heard the voice before I saw her. "Is that you?"

I looked up and smiled. It was Miss Annie, the housekeeper who'd been with my parents since before I was even born. I understood she hadn't been out of her teens when my mother hired her so many years ago. I was forty-four, so on the low end, Miss Annie had to be sixty. She'd spent her entire life caring for and catering to the needs of Levitt and Renatta Preston, and she was the only person in the world who had ever given me a nickname. My father detested them, so "G" was our secret. I stepped out of the car.

"Lord Jesus, Ms. Catherine told me you were coming." Miss Annie reached up, and I hunkered down so she could wrap her arms around my neck. "Boy, you just get more handsome with age." She let me go, stepped back, and looked at me. "You're just a taller version of your daddy."

The juice in my smile lost some of its zeal.

"I'm sorry about your uncle. He was keeping to hisself even before he got sick, so I can't say as though I've seen him for years."

"Me either."

"Well, we know you haven't seen him, not unless you using Skype."

I chuckled. "Miss Annie, what do you know about Skype?"

"My grandson Skypes me. He's still in Afghanistan." Her eyes became sad.

"When's he coming home?"

The joy in her eyes turned to concern. "I'm not sure, G, but I do know they appreciate all the packages your office sent to their unit. They're still drinking the coffee, and, of course, they love all the movies and books. That was so kind of you."

"I'm good when I can be."

"You always been good. You just want to be a devil."

"Gregory." The voice of my mother came from above us. I looked up and saw her standing on the second-floor balcony. It was an image I had etched in my memory as I had seen it my entire childhood; my mother on the balcony, looking down, calling me and my sisters for dinner or chores or bedtime. Her balcony was what I'd always thought of as her refuge. It was a little place in the world that belonged only to her, and Lord knows she needed it. She needed a space of her own, even if she had to come outside to get it.

"I'll be down in a minute." She disappeared through the glass doors.

"I made you some cinnamon lemonade," Miss Annie said. "Come on in the house."

I popped the trunk for my bag and after retrieving it, followed Miss Annie into Prieto Palace, our family home.

If Catherine hadn't called me about my father, I would have thought my mother was the one who was sick. She didn't look well. I released her from my embrace, which was tighter than it should have been. Guilt beat from my heart like blood. I didn't come home often enough.

My mother raised a hand to her throat, then tilted her head to take me in. I scanned her as well. Her long, auburn hair was curly, not straight as it had always been from my earliest memory. Hair dye was losing the fight to keep the gray away, but it was not unattractive. On the contrary, it made her look more regal than she already did. She was also slimmer than she'd been, but true to her fashion, she was impeccably dressed in a linen dress, shoes, and jewelry like she was ready to step out for an early afternoon social event. "You look well considering all you're going through," she said.

Miss Annie interrupted us with a tray of lemonade and cookies. "Where would you like it, ma'am?"

My mother nodded her head in the direction of the library, grabbed my hand, and we walked into the room where she always received guests when I was growing up. Not a thing had been changed. It was a room out of a nineteenth-century-French renaissance chateau. Knotty walnut wood panels covered the walls. Large bookcases lined those walls from floor to ceiling on two sides; heavily draped windows showcased light because the floor-length velvet drapes were tied back. The furniture was red. My mother had been through three or four sets of red furniture over the years, but all were the same square, straight-legged, floral uphol-stery that fit the elegant tone of the room.

I sat on the sofa, and she took a seat next to me. Miss Annie put down the tray, poured our glasses, and left the room.

"How is Angelina?"

I picked up a glass, drained it, and returned it to the table before I spoke. "She's disappointed, hurt . . . free of me." I shrugged. "I don't know, Mother. I'm trying to get her back." My mother patted my leg. I couldn't tell if she was encouraging me or she pitied me. I wasn't ready to ask. "Where's Dad?"

"Golfing."

"A man after my own heart," I said.

"If I remember it correctly, he taught you the game." My mother laughed.

I nodded. "I guess you're right. I've been playing so long I forget I wasn't born with a club in my hand." I smiled at the vision of that, and then thought more se-riously about my father. "How is he?"

My mother didn't meet my eyes when she responded. "Did Catherine call you?"

"She did."

Mother shook her head. "I wish she hadn't. There's nothing you can say to your father that's going to change his behavior."

I was perplexed. Of course, my mother knew my fa-ther better than anyone. If he truly wasn't concerned about his health, she would know, but she wasn't a quitter. The sound in her voice carried the tone of surrender. "I can try," I said. "Besides, Catherine had to tell me about Uncle Simon."

My mother stood. "You don't come to funerals, Greg. Catherine knows that. You didn't come to your aunt Helen's funeral." My mother spoke of Uncle Simon's wife, my father's sister. She'd passed a few years ago. Her eyes chastised me briefly for that, but then she let out a breath and her disapproval disappeared with it. A lock of her hair came loose from its bun. My mother took care to retuck it. "But I suppose your father is still in the land of the living, and you are his son. Perhaps you're right about trying." She walked to one of the windows on the opposite side of the room. "It's good you're home. Not much family here to make a proper showing."

"Can we expect Tiffany?" I asked, referring to my younger sister.

My mother sighed and turned away from the window to face me. "You know better than that. She's worse about these things than you are."

I heard heels pounding on the tile in the foyer and knew Catherine was coming. Even as a child, her steps were heavy and quick. She entered the room and brought the weight of her miserable disposition with her. I stood, took a few steps, and hugged her.

"Thank you for coming." She sat down and reached for an empty glass and poured herself lemonade. She held the pitcher over my half-empty glass, and I nodded. She refilled it.

"You don't have to thank me."

Catherine shrugged. "Sometimes it seems I should."

I didn't respond to the dig. I had been summarily chastised by both of them for my long absence. They were quick to forgive, and we slipped into easy conversation. My mother and sister caught me up on family business and a little bit of New Orleans gossip.

An alarm beeped on Catherine's cell phone. She turned it off, put a hand on mother's shoulder, and said, "It's time for your nap."

"Nap?" I asked. "I just got here."

"And she rests at this time every day, Greg. I don't think your arrival should change that," Catherine snapped.

My mother cleared her throat and offered me an explanation. "I don't sleep well at night, so I've taken to resting midday." She came closer to me and touched my hand. "I'll see you at dinner, son." She exited the room.

"What in the world?" I shook my head. I knew what in the world—control. My sister always had to have it.

Catherine reached for a cookie. "Don't question me or dare come here and try to switch anything up."

I threw my hands up. I'd spent less than twenty minutes in the house, and she was frustrating me. "Catherine, if you didn't want change, why did you call me?"

"I called you for Daddy."

"But what's wrong with my mother?"

"She's old. Do you think you're the only one aging? That time is standing still here?" Catherine clenched her fist on her lap. "I don't mean to be nasty, but mother's tired. Her blood pressure has been higher than it should be, and she has an ulcer."

The blood pressure concerned me. There were many medical implications with that, especially for the elderly. "How long has her pressure been high?"

Catherine didn't attempt to mask her aggravation. "Years. It's usually controlled with medication, but it's been going up for a few weeks."

I sat down, let out a wind of frustration. I wasn't going to fight with Catherine. I could talk to my mother's doctor tomorrow, so there was no point pushing her for specifics.

"So, what's going on with Angelina? I heard she left you."

The change of subject shocked me, and the lemonade I had in my mouth went down uncomfortably. "We've had some problems." I coughed through the statement.

Catherine guffawed like the news gave her pleasure. "Problems? I can just guess."

"What does that mean?"

"Ah, Mr. Handsome, don't think I don't know the acorn didn't fall far from the tree."

I rolled my eyes upward. "What are you talking about?"

She shoved a cookie in her mouth, ate it whole, and then washed it down with lemonade. "You cheated, didn't you?"

I didn't answer her. I hated being predictable.

She took another sip and wrinkled her nose like it was too tart. She was silent for a beat. "I never told you what happened with Richard." Catherine referred to her ex-husband. She'd been divorced for almost thirteen years, longer than she'd been married. "I told everyone we just grew apart, but the truth is he was having an affair and he wasn't going to stop." She paused. "He told me I was the perfect wife. He wanted me to be the woman who stood next to him when he ran for senator, but his girlfriend was someone he needed too. You know the type of woman who tries to rise from her poor upbringing on the arm of someone else's man. They acquire skills that decent women don't have time to master."

Catherine was ranting to herself, but when she was done, she looked me in the eye. "Anyway, Richard actually expected me to agree to his having a mistress. Like I would do that. I left him right after he announced his campaign for senator. He's never forgiven me for losing the election and all the money it cost."

"I didn't know," I said, but my mind had drifted to Samaria.

Catherine shrugged. "I know you didn't know. That's why I'm telling you. You need to know that unfaithfulness hurts, and the things you saw growing up are wrong." Catherine sighed heavily. "I loved Richard, but I was not going to live my life like mother."

"What do you mean like mother?"

"Don't act like you don't know what I'm talking about. I'd think knowing how much Daddy hurt mother would make you sensitive to that." Catherine's eyes were narrow slits of disappointment.

"I'm not sure I know what you're talking about." I was confused, but curious.

Catherine stood. "All those Saturday afternoon car rides you took with Dad. You weren't fishing." She smoothed the front of her dress. "I'm going to check on Mother." She left the room.

That was a whirlwind of a conversation. *Jesus.* I reached for a cookie and sat back in my seat. I wanted to dissect what Catherine had said, but I really didn't know what was going on between my parents. My memories of my childhood were sketchy. Everything that happened in this house happened a long time ago, but I knew no one was beaten or otherwise abused.

Miss Annie entered the room. "I have lunch for you, G, and I'm making your favorite dishes for dinner."

"All of them?" I asked, feeling like a kid who was about to get some candy.

"Every one," she said. "You lookin' a little thin."

"Now *that's* a homecoming." I stood, looped my arm through hers, and followed her into the kitchen.

The viewing for my uncle Simon's body was well attended. We didn't have much family, but Uncle Simon had been a judge for more than thirty years. His wife, my father's sister, Helen, preceded him in death a few years ago. She had been involved in every meaningful charity in the city. They had been one of the most important couples in New Orleans society, black or white, so people honored him with their presence.

I avoided questions about Angelina by saying she was working. I didn't want the word about my pending divorce all over New Orleans. I knew the Preston family would take it to the grave, so rumors were not milling.

My father, whom I had not seen before now, arrived in a limousine of his own. Although he hadn't been home to climb into the family car, he was dressed appropriately. I wondered how that happened since he was supposed to be playing golf. I stood on the veranda of the funeral home and watched him meander up the walkway. Several people stopped him for handshakes and cordial hugs.

Levitt Preston, or Preito as had been his Cuban birth name that he'd changed to Preston when he came to the U.S. in 1956, made an unsteady approach across the red brick walkway.

A hearty and authentic smile conveyed his joy at seeing me. "One of New Orleans finest," he said when he got close enough for me to hear. He'd been slightly bent over, but he stood up straighter and looked in my face. His color had an ashen gray pallor, and I could tell he was struggling to breathe. His health was declining. It was all over his face. "Catherine must have lied and told you I died."

"How are you, Dad?" I shook his hand and pulled him into a quick shoulder pat.

"Feeling my mortality." My father gazed out at the sea of automobiles that were parked in neat lines in front of us. "Glad to see you, though. Always a pleasure to see my son." He turned and walked into the funeral home, and I followed.

Chapter 8

Greg

"You really messed up with your wife. I'm disappointed." My father's words assured me I was not going to enjoy my breakfast as much as I imagined I would when the scent of pancakes and sausage accosted me. I supposed I had this lecture coming. I decided to take it like a man, so I reached for the syrup anyway.

I looked in Miss Annie's direction. She was busy flipping more pancakes. Not that she wasn't listening. She knew everything about our family, but still, I was a little more than embarrassed that I hadn't been able to hold on to my wife. I met my father's eyes. "I know. I don't know what I was thinking."

"You were using the wrong head, for sure. Got yourself entangled with the wrong woman."

I choked on my coffee. I didn't think my father knew the specifics about Samaria seeking out Angelina. I couldn't imagine that Angelina would tell my mother those details, so I wasn't sure what he was talking about. "What kind?" I asked.

"You have to be selective. You don't get caught cheating on your wife. Getting caught is irresponsible and disrespectful."

I took a sip of coffee. Maybe it would help me to process this bizarre marital advice. "I thought you were going to advise me about keeping my vows, Dad."

My father let his fork clank down on the table. "You're a grown man, more than grown, Gregory. All that talk of vows and such is for the wedding. It's for the church house. No man lives by that, and no woman, no real woman, expects him to. But even still, Angelina was wrong to ask you to leave. These young women don't know how to keep a man. They don't understand that men are different from women."

My sister entered the kitchen, and I could tell she had been listening to our conversation. She'd sneaked up on us, because I hadn't heard her heels pound on the tile outside the kitchen.

But even in her presence, my father continued. "The complexities of appetite, the desire to conquer something new—women don't understand that. They want you sissified." My father wagged a finger. "They want you to be their best friends. You're not their girlfriend. You're a husband, provider. If more women understood that, they might be able to keep a husband."

Catherine took a seat. Her eyes met mine, and I felt horribly for her. I wondered if Dad knew about what happened with Richard. He likely did. The New Orleans social circle was small. He was preaching to both of us, telling me to be a dog and Catherine to put up with one. *Jeez.*

Miss Annie placed a plate of pancakes in front of my sister. Catherine closed her eyes, said grace, and then picked up her fork. I could tell she had gone from being hurt to angry in sixty seconds, but she said nothing in response to my father's statements.

"That gal ought to appreciate you. The lifestyle you've given her. She's ungrateful, and you're probably better off without her."

"Dad, when did Angelina become a gal?"

"When she left my son or put you out. I can't believe you actually moved out of your own house. Craziness. Now that I think about it, how did that even happen?"

"Dad."

"Don't Dad me. You know what I'm talking about."

"I love my wife, and I'm sorry I hurt her."

My father sat back in his seat. One corner of his mouth was turned up. His facial expression had changed from disapproving to sympathetic. "Well, if you love her, then get her back. I always say, you just have to find the right piece of jewelry." He stood. "I have an appointment with my doctor. I'm going to get ready. I don't trust a thing he says. I swear I have suits that are older."

"What happened to Dr. Ward?"

"He retired a few years ago, and this young fella took over his practice. He won't give me my sugar pills without an appointment. You'll come with me? Translate doctor talk?"

I glanced at Catherine. Her lips locked tight. I knew that she had been handling such matters. It was probably a smack in the face for him to ask me, but she met my eyes and nodded approval.

"Of course," I replied.

"Good. We're not putting Simon in the ground until afternoon. We have plenty of time." My father took one last sip from his coffee mug, pushed his chair in, excused himself, and left the kitchen.

"It's good timing you going to the doctor. He hates Dr. Jones, and anytime I agree with him, it makes me the enemy." Catherine's words were coming out so fast I suspected she was talking away hurt. Between my father's ravings about the rules of infidelity and his disregard of her dutiful servitude, she was likely fuming. "His real problem is the drinking, and he won't stop eating sweets. Miss Annie has sugar-free syrup, but he won't try it. He stops at a bakery every day and eats beignets. The man at Holson's Bakery stopped selling them to him, so now he goes to a different one. He's gone back to all his old habits."

We ate in silence for a few more minutes before she spoke. "And then there's church." Catherine wasn't looking at me. She stared into her coffee cup. "He hasn't been to church since Danielle died. Said he's angry with God for taking his only grandchild."

I swallowed as I thought about my own position on all things godly.

"He's too old to be cross with God, don't you think?" Catherine looked at me now, and I had a feeling my sister was trying to tell me something as well. I didn't think she knew that I was boycotting church. She and Angelina weren't close, so I can't imagine it's a conversation they'd have, but Angelina might have told my mother, and my mother then shared it with Catherine.

"I'm concerned about after he passes. If he's going to bury himself, he needs to at least plan for his eternal soul. We all should." Her eyes told me that that message was for me also. Catherine stood and picked up our dirty dishes. "I don't mean to be doomy and gloomy, but with Uncle Simon and Aunt Helen's passing, we have to consider that our parents are right behind them in age."

I didn't say anything. I knew she was right, but I'd be a hypocrite to tell my father to go to church.

Catherine placed the dishes in the sink and walked to the entrance of the kitchen. She stood there for a few moments. Neither of us spoke. My sister was forty-one, but she looked much older. She looked tired. I wanted to say something before she left, something to refute our father's hurtful statements. The atmosphere in the room was so heavy, so somber, so pain filled that I couldn't find my voice. Tiffany and I had left all this, the burden of our parents, on Catherine with no regard for what it had done to her. I felt terrible about it.

"Good luck with Daddy at the doctor's office," she said.

"I'll make sure to get him back in time to ride in the family car," I replied.

Catherine shook her head. "You see if you can manage that. I don't believe he'll step in that church, not even for Uncle Simon." She turned on her heels to leave, and then looked back over her shoulder at me. "By the way, I don't think a piece of jewelry will work for Angelina. You'll likely have to redeem yourself through your actions. She's not shallow." Then she walked out of the kitchen.

My father swore he would do better. By the time I finished explaining to him how his body was going to start breaking down from the diabetes, I think he was scared to death. I wasn't sure if he would actually change his habits, but I had been a good son; I'd tried. I also knew now that I needed to visit more often and at a minimum take the time to call and remind him, first of what he should do, and second, that I love him.

We were returning to the house for lunch when my dad said, "Turn left up there. I need to make a stop."

I figured he'd decided not to take my advice. I was sure to find out the location of the mysterious bakery he frequented for his beignets, but I found we were moving away from the city, heading toward New Orleans East. I drove for ten more minutes; then my father instructed me to turn into the driveway of a stately home that sat way back from the road. The front of it was hidden by a thicket of trees; oak, orange, and crepe myrtle, covered with Spanish moss.

"Pull over there." He pointed to a place in the grass off the driveway. I followed his instructions and parked the car under a large magnolia tree. "I'll be back in a few minutes."

I watched him walk to the house, push the door open, and go right in. I thought it strange that he didn't knock on the door.

I took out my cell phone and checked my voice mail for messages. Then I logged on to the Web site for the airline and confirmed that my flight was still good for tomorrow. I was tempted to call Angelina. I wanted to hear her voice, but what would I say? My sister's words came back to me. She'd told me I had to redeem myself through my actions. I didn't know how to begin to do such a thing. I was so used to knowing I'd always have her. I didn't know how she'd see my actions when she wouldn't really see me.

I called the office to check on things there. My office manager, Marsha, answered the line and assured me things were fine. We talked a few minutes about scheduling issues and some other business. I asked her to order some flowers for Angelina. "Something really extravagant and have them sent to her home address. It's in my Outlook address book."

"The card?" Marsha asked.

I gave it some thought and chuckled a little. "I apologize for the other night, but I'm not sorry about the other night." That was the truth. I wasn't sorry about jack. I didn't care what Angelina said; her lawyer didn't give her a ride home to just be nice. I wasn't stupid; my wife was too fine for that. If I wasn't there, he might have gotten in for coffee and more conversation. I could see now that I was going to have to work at keeping myself in Angelina's thoughts. Competition was everywhere.

Marsha and I ended the call. I looked at my watch and realized I'd been waiting for more than twenty-five minutes. What was my father doing? I had a mind to knock on the door and find out, but instead, I just put the convertible top down and sank lower into the seat. I was looking straight-ahead when something familiar caught my eye. It was a gazebo to the far left of the house near the backyard. I couldn't see the dark color clearly, but I knew that many years ago it had been painted purple. I sat up and really looked at the house. The porch was dark, but when I squinted, I realized behind the screen that the front door was also purple. I knew this house. I'd been here before, and now I remembered.

"Son, you sit here. I'll be back in a few minutes."

I shook my head. But the image of my father walking to the porch and opening that door without knocking would not leave me.

I was bored. I hadn't brought my books or my slingshot or anything to keep me entertained. I also needed to use the restroom. Not "Number One" as Miss Annie had always called it when I just had to pee. I needed to do "Number Two," and I couldn't do that at the side of the car. I got out of the car and walked to the house. As I climbed the steps, I could hear music in the distance. It was loud, old-time jazz music that I often heard being played in the quarter when I went shopping with Mother on Saturday mornings. I knew I should have knocked, but I didn't think anyone would hear me over the music. I knew there was a restroom off the main parlor in houses like this, because this was the same style house my friend Timmy lived in. I could probably go in and use it and get back to the car before my father even knew I had come in. He always said he'd be a few minutes, but in reality, it was a long, long time. Maybe an hour.

I tugged at the screen door and for a moment I stared at the heavy wooden door beyond it. It was purple. I'd never seen a house with a purple door in this part of New Orleans. Color was common in the French Quarter, but not out here in the country. I knew then that the person behind this door was a different kind of person, not someone who Mother and Father approved of because even though we weren't an old-line family that had deep roots in New Orleans history, they had money, education, position, and class. People of distinction copied the ways of the old-line families. They didn't paint doors purple, so why was my father here?

I entered the house without making a sound, although I realized I hadn't had to be so careful, because the music was very loud. It was coming from upstairs. I went to the room I thought should be the restroom, but when I turned the handle to the knob it was locked. I began to perspire. My stomach was bubbling. I had to go bad. Again, I figured there was a restroom at the top of the stairs, but I didn't want to get in trouble for going too far into the house, so I called out. "Dad, Dad, I need the restroom." Nothing returned to me except the familiar sound of guitar, saxophone, and clarinet music.

I climbed the stairs. The restroom was exactly where I thought it should be. I went in, did my business, and came out. Then I heard it, sounds above the music. A creaking bed and noises like the kind my mother made at night sometimes. It was coming from behind the door across the hallway. I walked toward it. The door was cracked, so I didn't have to open it. I looked in and saw my father on the bed. He wasn't wearing any clothes. Neither was the woman who was under him. They were both moving and moaning

and doing what me and my friends in school called
"the nasty." The bed creaked, the woman's face dis-
torted like a monster as she moaned and yelped like a
hurt puppy. I jumped back, bumped into a small table,
and knocked over a vase that landed with a crash.

The noises stopped. "What was that?" I heard the
woman ask.

I made a dash for the stairs, ran down them and out
of the house, past the tacky purple door that belonged
to the noisy woman who got naked with my father.
I didn't go back to the car. I kept running down the
road until I couldn't run anymore, and then I walked.
About fifteen minutes into my escape, my father
pulled alongside of me and ordered me into the car.
He didn't say anything. Didn't offer an explanation.
He just took out a cigar and began to smoke like he
always did when he came out of that house.

The car door opened. I had been so caught up in my
memory that I hadn't seen him approach. My father
climbed in. "Sorry it took me so long."

I looked at the time on the car radio. I'd been here for
thirty minutes. "I remember this house."

My father pulled on his seat belt. "What do you
mean, remember?"

"I remember coming here as a kid and sitting under
this tree waiting an hour for you to come out. I remember going inside and breaking a vase. You never
brought me back after that." I spoke with an accusatory
tone, but my father's response was flat and emotionless.

"If you remember all that, you have a good memory,"
he said.

"Dad, you've been coming to this house for thirty-
five years?"

He reached into his pocket and pulled out a cigar. "My memory isn't as sharp as yours, but I think I've been coming longer than that."

"Is she a mistress or a prostitute?"

My father looked at me like I was crazy. "A gentleman does not spend his time with prostitutes."

This was more bizarre than the conversation at breakfast. "You've had a mistress since I was nine?"

"On and off. She got married some years back, was with him for fifteen. Then he died. I managed to find a suitable replacement during that time." He pulled out his lighter and lit the cigar.

I was incensed. Why would he have been unfaithful like this for all those years? "Does Mother know about her?"

"Of course not. Your mother doesn't know anything about my women. That's what I was talking to you about earlier. Your lack of discretion."

I shook my head and started the car.

"What?" The cigar smoke caused him to have a coughing fit. When he recovered he said, "Don't you judge me. The only reason you sitting in that apartment is because you got yourself caught. Would you have stopped seeing your woman if your wife hadn't found out?"

I didn't respond to that. I wasn't going to give him the satisfaction of knowing he was right when he was so wrong about everything else on this subject.

"You could stand to take a lesson from your old man about how not to get caught. Keep everybody happy."

I swallowed my disgust, backed up, and pulled back through the trees onto the driveway. So, this was what Catherine was talking about. How had I blocked this out? How had I forgotten my trips to this house and my father's disappearing acts over the years? And the house with the purple door, how had I forgotten it?

We drove in silence for a few minutes before I spoke. "Dad, you've been married for over forty-five years, and you've had a mistress for more than thirty-five of them. I don't get that."

My father didn't answer. He continued to puff his cigar like he didn't have a care in the world.

"Do you love my mother?"

He removed his cigar and looked at me like I was stupid. "Of course, I love your mother. She's my wife."

"So . . ."

"I care about Ramona too. But Ramona would not have made a suitable wife and mother for my children, so I had to choose."

"Choose?" I shook my head. He hadn't chosen at all.

"I chose a wife and mother, and I've never regretted that, but Ramona is important to me as well."

We drove to my parents' home in silence. I was caught up in my thoughts around my own infidelity. Over the last couple of months I'd asked myself a thousand times why—why had I taken up with Samaria? Why had I made a decision to get into a long-term relationship with someone other than my wife?

Angelina was everything I ever wanted in a woman. I loved her. I wasn't bored with the sex. I wasn't missing something at home. I couldn't even really come up with a reason why I had stepped out there. But now as I drove from my father's kept woman's home, I wondered if hunting and fishing and a Southern gentleman's manners weren't the only things my father had taught me.

Chapter 9

Greg

My father did not go to the service at the church. When we arrived at the cemetery for the interment, I found him sitting in his car, sleeping with a bottle of Cuban rum on his chest. I'd never known my father to drink Cuban rum or eat Cuban food, or do anything that would remind anyone that he was actually from Cuba except speak a few words in Spanish, and he only did that when he was angry. He passed for African American, and many attributed his light eyes and wavy hair to a Creole lineage, but my father had come to the United States in a boat at the age of sixteen.

His first order of business was to hide his true lineage by changing his name. He decided on Preston. It was the name of a wealthy attorney from New York who was staying at the hotel where my father worked in the restaurant. It was perfect because it was close to Preito. It made him feel as if he hadn't completely abandoned his surname. He worked three jobs, finished his secondary education, and applied to Tulane University where he completed an English degree, and then went on to law school. He'd met my mother in undergrad, married her, and disappeared into the upper-crust of New Orleans society into the social circle that was my mother's.

"Dad." I moved the bottle of rum and placed it on the backseat of his convertible Mercedes coupe. I shoved his shoulder a bit, and he roused.

"Is it time?" He pulled a pocket watch out of his jacket and checked it. "Simon in the ground yet?"

"Not yet. I'm waking you for the burial."

My father shook his head. "I'll sit here and wait it out. Simon was a good brother-in-law. He married my sister, even though she didn't have the right background. I'll always appreciate him for that."

"Mother did the same with you."

My father blinked a few times like he couldn't see clearly. "What's your mother got to do with this? Why are you bringing up your mother? Are you still salty about earlier?"

I shrugged. "I'm just saying."

"You're trying to make me feel bad about your mother. I'm good to your mother."

"You'll embarrass her by sitting in this car drunk."

"I'll embarrass her more if I come over there drunk." My father burst out laughing. He laughed so hard he began to gag. "I'm best . . . left here where no one can see me cry about Simon. I don't want to watch them throw dirt on him. I'm tired of watching them throw dirt on my family and friends." His words slurred. *"La muerte es triste."* I recognized the words death and sadness in his mumbling. He was asleep within seconds. I decided to leave him there and join my family, so I made way to the area where people clamored under the tent around the casket.

I'd been sitting on the front row shaking hands and nodding at others who chose to pass by me when I realized how much I hated graveside interments. It was for the same reason my father did—the throwing of dirt.

The last funeral I had attended had been for my daughter. I hadn't really thought about that until just now. I try very hard not to remember that time in my life. It makes me so sad that I want to die myself. Once I was done being sad, I become angry, unbearably so.

"Gregory Preston."

I looked up into the face of one of the finest women I'd ever seen. She was smiling and leaning over so far that her creamy brown breasts were in my face. My heart started pounding a million seconds a minute. "Yes," I replied.

"Abigail Dumas. We went to high school together. I was a few grades behind you. Simon was my uncle."

Abigail Dumas—Abigail Dumas. I didn't remember her.

"Is this seat taken?" Abigail asked.

Catherine appeared from nowhere and slipped in the chair Abigail had been trying to claim. "Hi, Abby."

Abigail stood upright. Her beautiful mouth was a thin line. I was almost relieved I didn't have to look at her chest anymore. "Catherine, how are you?"

"I'm blessed," Catherine replied.

Abigail grunted. "It was good to see you, Greg. Perhaps we can catch up at the repast."

I nodded. "Sure." Abigail turned and walked away and the view in the back was almost as good as the view in the front. I looked at Catherine, whose face was twisted by obvious disapproval. "Should I know her?" I asked.

"No, not really," she replied. "Not unless you're looking for trouble."

My mother sat down next to me, and the psalmist began to sing.

The service at the church had been one long eulogy wherein everyone in New Orleans society came out to say a few words about Uncle Simon. We viewed the body and were dismissed here where a minister stood behind a lectern with a Bible. He was going to preach. I thought I'd escaped that because it hadn't happened at the church. I thought that's where the preaching part was supposed to be done. He directed us to turn in the program to the page where the scripture was noted in the NIV Bible. Deuteronomy 30:19. I read it.

"This day I call the heavens and the earth as witnesses against you that I have set before you life and death, blessings and curses. Now choose life, so that you and your children may live."

The minister proceeded to preach about choices and highlighted all the good ones Uncle Simon made by being involved in the church and community. I was in awe of my uncle by the time he was done with his résumé. He didn't forget to put a dig in at us sinners—the standard end of the funeral reminder that we needed to get right with God or face spending an eternity in hell. No wonder my father was in the car. I wished I was with him.

I made an earnest attempt to appear interested in catching up with friends and family at the repast, but in truth, the soliloquy about Uncle Simon's full life only reminded me of how empty mine had become. In between drinks, appetizers, handshakes, and glances at pictures in wallets, I found myself reflecting on how unbelievably unhappy I was. The reverend's words "choose life" had not gone in one ear and out the other. They stuck with me because I realized money and success had not given me all that I thought they should. In trying to get the best life had to offer, had I not chosen life? I found myself pondering this question, but as sure as I tried to keep my mind focused on the right thing, the devil will come along. I wasn't looking for trouble, but trouble was looking for me.

Abigail Dumas said she'd see me at the repast, and she found me. The chatter was innocent enough. We caught up on old stories about our days at Saint Patrick Preparatory Academy. We laughed about various pranks and other events from our high school years. She reminded me of my stats during my senior football season. She remembered more about me than I did; then the conversation switched to the personal. "So, where's your wife?"

I sipped the last of my wine. I tried to escape the implications of what I was about to say to this woman who was looking for an opportunity to give me something I wanted, but should not, would not, take. "She's in Atlanta."

"I can't believe she lets you go anywhere alone." Abigail did a sweep of the immediate vicinity. It was one of those is-anyone-in-earshot-type inspections. "I wouldn't let you out of my sight."

I tried to turn my eyes away from her chest, but it was an impossible task with her breasts jiggling every time she moved. "What about you? Do you have a family?" I asked.

"I was married to Simon's nephew, Cecil Dumas." She raised her wine flute and used her tongue to play with the lip of the glass. "You and I aren't blood cousins." She laughed. "You remember, Cecil?"

I didn't really, but I nodded that I did.

"He and I have been divorced for three years."

"I'm sorry to hear that."

"Don't be. I got most of his money and our children. He got his mistress. Everyone was happy." She paused and took a drink. "So, when are you leaving, Gregory?" She stepped closer.

I could feel the heat from her body. I looked down, and those twin globes of flesh appeared to be swelling. "In the morning."

"What are you doing tonight?" She tilted her head; her long auburn hair fell in ringlets around her throat. She smiled seductively.

She had a beautiful neck. I lowered my eyes. She had a beautiful body. "Spending some time with my mother."

Abigail looked around the room. I followed her eyes to spot where my mother had taken up residence for the last hour with some women from the church. "Mrs. Preston looks like she retires early." She reached into her purse, pulled out a card, and stuck it in my pocket. "You call me if you decide you want to do something after your mother goes to bed." She emptied her glass and put it down on a nearby table. "I'll make sure you're not disappointed." She raised a finger, stroked my hand from the wrist to the tip of my index finger, and walked away.

My skin was sizzling. I threw my head back and gave it a good shake. I hadn't had sex in months. I hadn't gone this long without sex since the eighth grade. That very distant cousin by marriage sashaying her behind out the door was fine. Tap that and worry about the consequences later.

What was I supposed to be doing, really? I mean, I had signed divorce papers, my wife wouldn't give me any because she insists she's through with me. But I still felt like a married man, even if I hadn't behaved like one when I was with my wife, so getting naked with my ex-cousin-in-law seemed like a bad idea.

Bad though it was, hours later, I still had not shaken the thought of being with Abigail from my mind. I'd driven my father home. Catherine and my mother rode in the family car. My father had still been drunk, so I'd taken him upstairs and put him to bed. Miss Annie made my favorite fudge pecan brownies, and she'd picked up some other scrumptious pastries from a bakery in the French Quarter. No doubt I had a box of goodies to fit in my suitcase. I'd have to spend a month at the gym to work it all off, starting with the huge brownie I had in my hand.

Miss Annie served my mother and me on the veranda. The night air was slightly cool for this time of year, but it was a pleasant temperature, one that awakened my senses and reminded me that I was still alive.

"I hate that your visit is so short," my mother said. "I feel like I've scarcely talked to you."

"I'll plan a longer trip, soon. This was last minute, and I had to reschedule my patients."

She interrupted me with a pat on my hand. "You don't have to explain, son. I know you're working. I appreciate that you came to pay respects to your uncle."

We sat in silence for a moment before I spoke. "Mother, have you had a happy life?" The moon was high so I could make out the expression on her face. She was perplexed. "I'm just curious. I've never heard you complain, not one time. I have to wonder if that's because you're happy or you're good at hiding things."

She didn't answer for a long time. "No, son, I'm not happy. I've been happy, but there are things that happen that just have the ability to suck the happiness out of your spirit, like burying a grandchild and a brother after a pointless war. I think death is a thing that can change you forever. You never really get over losing people and thinking about them every day makes it difficult to feel happiness."

I sucked in a long breath of air and let it out. That was exactly how I felt about Danielle, like I had been changed forever. "It gets easier with time, but you never get over it." We sat in the quiet some more, listening to crickets chirp and an owl hoot. "What about your marriage? Have you been happy with Dad?"

My mother laughed. Loud. Louder than I think I'd ever heard her laugh. "Why in heaven's name are you asking about your father and me?"

"I don't know. I guess I want to either do what he did right that kept his wife for forty-five years, or avoid what he did wrong if you just stayed with him because it was expected," I said. "I want Angelina back. I want to love her and make her happy."

"You want to connect with her. You used to before you had the baby. What did you do back then? How did you keep the love in your marriage?"

I sighed. "I don't even remember. I don't know that I did. I think she just put up with me." I picked up a cup of tea and took a sip. "She's done putting up with me, so now I need to either cut my losses and move on with someone else, or figure out how to make the woman I love happy."

"Gregory, are you really ready for what I have to say? Do you *really* want to hear my answer to your problem?"

I sat back and let out a breath. "I respect you, Mom, in more ways than you can imagine and for more reasons than you know, so, yes, I want to hear what you have to say."

She reached for my hand. "You have to love her the way she wants to be loved. But you can only do that through Jesus."

I frowned. "What does that even mean?"

"It means that you develop a relationship with God, and He'll take over your heart and show you how to love your wife."

I shifted in my seat.

"I know that's not what you want to hear. You want to believe it's about money and things and trips and jewelry. Well, I've had all those things, and the only reason I didn't leave your father a long time ago was because it just wasn't done. Angelina is from a different time. Even as a Christian, there's only so much she's going to put up with. She wants you to change, son. This separation isn't about your mistress. In some ways it is, but it's more about the root cause for the mistress."

I nodded and swallowed. "How did you know I had someone else?"

My mother laughed. "You are your father's son. If you don't have Jesus, what other model are you going to have for handling problems except the one you learned in this house?" She stood.

"I don't mean any disrespect, Mom, but you love God. Why aren't you happier?"

She smiled. "Because God is not a genie, and happiness is fleeting. I have joy. That's a state of being, not an emotion." She kissed me on the forehead. "Find your way back to Christ and you'll come to understand."

"I'll think about it," I said.

"Don't think long. God has a way of getting you on your knees, one way or another." She walked into the house.

I sat there for a while staring at the stars, and then out at the landscape of my family's property. It was beautiful. Pure splendor. Had God really made all this? I'd always believed He had, but then my scientist mind turned on and told me that there were other ways for nature to have evolved. My scientist mind was further encouraged by my broken heart. God was wonderful and loving, but I'd buried my only child, so in my mind's eyes, wonderful and loving didn't exist in the realm of Him.

My phone vibrated. I reached into my pocket and pulled it out along with Abigail Dumas's card. Visions of her came to me. The tilt of her neck, the bend of her back, and the curve of her calves . . . her breasts, her lips . . . the promise that I would not be disappointed . . . the reminder that no one would know.

My phone vibrated again. It was a text message confirming the flowers I had sent Angelina had been delivered. Visions of Abigail went away. They were replaced with memories of Angelina . . . her mouth, her breasts, her neck, and her thighs. I had to work at it, but eventually my wife replaced the thoughts of my temptress. I realized months ago that fighting this demon was a mental game. I was determined to win, because if there was one thing the events of the last few months had taught me was that a few hours of pleasure could definitely result in a lifetime of pain.

Chapter 10

Angelina

I clutched the edge of the toilet and wretched for the second time this morning. I was glad I had a doctor's appointment later this week, because I needed something for nausea. I knew it was stress. I'd been sick like this in the past, but now I just didn't have time for it. I was a working single mother. I had to be able to get out of bed in the morning and get Katrice to her Pre-K3 program. I also had to deal with the disaster at work. Especially the money problems, because they couldn't wait.

I washed my mouth out and climbed back into the bed. I had fifteen minutes before I had to get up and get moving. I needed to spend them resting. As soon as I sank into the soft, deepness of my pillow, a text message came through. It was likely from Felesia because she was the only one who woke me up with a text these days. Sure enough, it was her asking me to call her if I was up.

"I didn't wake you, did I, *chica?*" I could hear the hum of the road behind her, and I knew she was already on her way to her job.

"No, I'm up. I was just hugging the toilet bowl again."

"You need to go see a doctor. You've been sick for weeks. I know you're stressed out, but you can't assume that's all it is."

"I know. I'm going on Friday."

"Promise?"

"I promise. So what's on your agenda today?"

"I'm headed to the Dominican Republic tomorrow."

"Again? You just got back."

"I know, but we're having some manufacturing problems. Our people down there are idiots. I need to work through the cultural stuff. I'm leaving at noon, but in the meantime, Nordstrom is having a secret sale and I need a warm weather wardrobe. Want to meet me for some shopping?"

I thought about the closets full of clothing that Felesia owned and laughed. "You have a warm weather wardrobe."

"Okay, so I need a warmer weather wardrobe. It's hotter than Hades down there right now."

"Well, I guess it's a good thing you're not going to Hades. As for the shopping, I'd love to. I need to get some things for Katrice for church."

"Church? Good. We'll be glad to have you back."

I paused a second before delivering my news. "Fee, I'm not going back to Greater Christian."

Felesia was silent, so I went on to explain the question in the air. "I live too far now. I've been attending a new church. The pastor is a great teacher; it's a nice small congregation which is what I want right now; and it's less than five minutes away, and . . . I need a change."

Felesia sighed. "This isn't about that woman, is it?"

"No, Greater Christian is a thirty-minute drive. It's bad enough I have to commute up that way for work every day. It's too far with these gas prices and an antsy three year old in the back. Plus, I'd never do weekday activities at that distance. This is a good change."

"Okay, just as long as you're not letting Samaria's drama run you out of your church," Felesia said. "I admit I was getting a little worried about you."

"You know I'd never let anything separate me from the church."

"I know, I know," Felesia said, "but sometimes when people are hurt at the church they stop going, and before you know it, a year has gone by, then two."

"Not happening," I promised.

We agreed on a time and place to meet at the store and ended the call. I rested against my pillow and picked up the remote control to check the weather forecast on the news station. Rain today. Lots of it. *Great.* I grabbed the remote to turn off the television, but before I could turn it off, Samaria was on the screen. She and Mekhi were exiting a building downtown, wearing formal attire. I turned up the volume.

"Music producer Mekhi Johnson spoke at the annual fundraiser for the Boys and Girls Club of Metro Atlanta. He was accompanied by his fiancée Samaria Jacobs and R&B pop star, Benxi. Benxi's third album will be released in June. Johnson's long-time girlfriend and future wife is out on bail, pending drug charges."

I turned off the television. Long-time girlfriend? Right. If she'd been his long-time girlfriend, she wouldn't have been in bed with my husband, or would she? Maybe the woman was just a tramp. I shook my head. I didn't like to label people, but I wanted so badly to categorize her, to villianize her more than I'd already done.

How had someone I'd known for such a short period of time disrupted my life so? My marriage, my community, and now my church were changing. I knew it wasn't all her fault, but it just seemed like her presence was the catalyst for change. I sighed. I was not going to think about Samaria.

I whipped the comforter off my body and got up to start the day. Quickly I rushed into the bathroom, hit my knees, and hugged the toilet again. I'd start the day right after I threw up.

I spent a few hours in the office looking at bills. Rent, utilities, invoices for services my agency had been providing to families that I could no longer continue to support. Something Extra was not going to last long without donations. It had only been a few weeks since the IRS investigation started, but the halt on incoming funds had me in the red. I realized I was really running this place on a wing and a prayer. I had some cash, but I had to save it for the upcoming summer retreat I'd planned. I'd still have it, assuming the Atlanta Sparks were still on board. I sighed.

The alarm beeped on my BlackBerry. It was time for me to head over to Lenox to meet with Felesia. I grabbed my purse and went out to the reception area. Portia was reading a paperback novel, which she closed when I approached her desk.

"You're going out?" she asked. "It's a torrential downpour out there."

I'd heard rain beating down on the roof. I could see through the miniblind slats that it was indeed pouring. "I have to. My best friend is going out of the country tomorrow, and I promised I'd have lunch and do some shopping with her. I'm going to be gone for the day, so why don't you lock up and go home? Not like there's much going on."

Portia's excitement bubbled out of her.

I raised my umbrella, exited the building, and made a run for my car.

Traffic was heavy. I decided to take the Peachtree Industrial Exit to Lenox Mall, but I was going to be late. I reached into my purse for my phone and pushed the speed dial button for Felesia's number. A humongous semitruck passed me on the left and splashed a wave of water onto my windshield. I had zero visibility for a few seconds. When I could see, an SUV jumped in my lane. Its red brake lights came on. Panic filled me. *No time to stop.* I braked, hydroplaned, and slid into the back of the truck.

I opened my eyes to a bright light over my head. "You're a lucky lady."

My tongue felt like it was glued to the top of my mouth. I looked at the woman who had proclaimed my good fortune, and then my surroundings. This was a hospital.

I unlocked my lips. "What happened?"

"You were in an eight-car pileup." The nurse put a blood pressure cuff on my arm and pushed a button to inflate the sleeve. "A tractor trailer and seven vehicles. You were number three in the group."

"Did the truck hit me?"

"I don't know the details."

"I feel like the truck hit me." I winced from the sharp pain that shot through my head.

"Well, you have a concussion and some bruising, but your baby seems to be just fine."

Baby? Katrice! "Where's my daughter?"

The nurse had been charting some information. "You had a child in the car?"

"You said my baby was okay, my three year old." I was confused. I was on the way to meet with Felesia, wasn't I? Katrice was at school.

"I didn't know you were admitted with a child. I can check on her." She walked out of the room.

I struggled to get my breath and to speak loud enough and fast enough to stop her, but my head was hurting. I needed my phone.

Another woman walked into the room and I recognized her as a physician. "Hello, Mrs. Preston. Dr. Isley, the on-call physician." She stuck out her hand for me to shake, and I weakly did so. "We're going to keep you overnight. You were unconscious for a little while after the accident, so we want to monitor your head injury." She leaned closer to me and pulled a penlight out of her pocket. "May I?"

I nodded, and my head felt like it would split.

She shined the light in my eyes and did some other cursory pokes and pushes on my body.

"I need my cell phone. I have to make arrangements for my daughter. What time is it?" I asked.

"Three P.M., and I do believe your friend that was here earlier, a Ms. Sosa, said something about picking up your daughter. You'll want to call her first."

Relief washed over me. Felesia was my girl. I could always count on her.

"The nurse will bring you some Tylenol. The phone on the table works, but I'll have someone get your personal belongings so you can place your call." She smiled and walked out.

After a few minutes, the nurse who had been with me when I woke up returned. "Mrs. Preston, I checked the admission log. You were the only person in your vehicle."

I tried to think clearly. I was going to the mall. "My daughter, I think she's at pre-school."

"You mentioned your baby being in the car."

"Because you said my baby was okay and I was trying to remember if she was with me."

The nurse looked confused. "Mrs. Preston, I wasn't talking about a three year old. I was talking about your baby. You are aware that you're pregnant, aren't you?"

Chapter 11

Angelina

Pregnant. I closed my eyes for a second, opened them, and shook my head in disbelief. The shaking of the head was a bad idea. It felt like someone pushed a knife into my temple. I raised a hand to the bandage that was across the front and around the left side of my head. After the pain subsided, I reached for the cup of ice water that the nurse had poured for me. "Are you sure?" I asked. "That I'm pregnant, I mean."

"Well, we're about 100 percent sure. We did a pregnancy test when you came in. We had to know whether you were pregnant."

I took in a breath and closed my eyes again. "I, I can't believe it. After all this time."

"Have you been trying?" the nurse asked.

"Sort of." I heard my own voice trail off. Not lately, I was thinking.

The door to my room opened, and Felesia walked in. "Hey, Mami. You got those eyes open?"

I moved a little, then pushed the button to raise the bed. "Barely. How is Katrice?"

"She's good. I gave the sitter pizza money, and she said she'd get her to preschool tomorrow and pick her up for you."

"Wonderful. I am so in love with having a neighbor who's good with kids and money hungry."

"That you are." Felesia approached the bed. "I feel horrible. You would have been in your office if I wasn't a shop-a-holic."

"Are you kidding? Girl, you know this is not your fault."

Felesia sighed. "I still feel bad." She scratched her head. "I was thinking about calling Greg."

"Why?"

"You're still his wife. Just seems like he should know."

"Maybe," I said. Then I dismissed the thought. "Look, forget Greg for a moment. I have something to tell you."

"What?"

"You're not going to believe this."

Felesia put her hand on her hip. *"Vamos!* Spit it out already, *chica.*"

I paused, shocked that I was about to say these words. "I'm pregnant."

"What?" Felesia's mouth hung open.

"One of the nurses told me."

"No way. How could you . . . I mean, you're pretty far along, aren't you? You guys have been separated for a while—" Felesia smiled knowingly. "Well, maybe not as far along as the separation," she laughed.

I blushed from embarrassment, and then smirked at her. She was smiling too brightly.

"Anyway, how could you not know you were pregnant? When's the last time you saw Aunt Flo?"

I shrugged. "I can't remember."

"Girl, what the heck you mean you can't remember? You 'round there throwing up, missing Flo, and it didn't occur to you that you might be pregnant?"

I felt stupid, because it hadn't. "I've been so busy with work and Katrice and lawyers I just didn't think about it." I shifted in the bed. My ankle stung. "Plus, I was taking that fertility pill. When you stop, your periods can be irregular for a few months."

"Well, God answers prayers. I'm going to be an auntie, Tia Fee-Fee!"

I laughed. "Well, I'm glad you're excited about your auntship. I'm going to be the single mother of two kids. Crazy, isn't it?"

"Angelina, you don't have to be a single mother."

"There you go again. Please do not take the joy out of this moment by lobbying for Greg yet again."

"I'm not lobbying for him, but you can't possibly be thinking about going ahead with the divorce now that you know you're pregnant."

"Are you kidding? I'm divorcing him because he's unfaithful. How is my being pregnant going to change that?"

"Angelina, I think you owe it to your baby to try to make your marriage work."

"I've been trying to make my marriage work." I was getting heated. "Look, this pregnancy doesn't change things. I don't believe in leaving somebody for one reason and going back for another. The reason I left is still there. He's still not faithful."

"He'll go to counseling."

"Fee, I'm not judging Greg, but counseling alone isn't going to fix the problem. Greg is not spiritually where I want him to be. I don't want to live the rest of my life with an unsaved husband. No matter how much counseling he receives, he'll still be unsaved."

"So, he's got to be perfect."

"I'm not looking for perfection, but I'm tired of living with someone who's not on the same page as I am," I said. "He's lost his way, and he doesn't seem to want to find it."

Felesia crossed her arms in front of her chest. Her expression told me she was still not hearing my argument.

"Fee, if it was just about Danielle's death I might be more sympathetic, but Greg was backslidden before she died. When we got married we were both committed to the Lord, but he has decided that's no longer for him, so where does that leave me?"

Felesia sighed and dropped her arms. "I don't have all the answers. I just know being by yourself with two children isn't going to be easy." Felesia reach for my hand and squeezed it. "Call the lawyer. Have her put things on hold and give yourself some time to think about it."

"I'll think about it," I said, but I wasn't convinced I would. A luminous smile came over my best friend's face, and I honestly felt betrayed by her satisfaction. "My goodness, you're on Greg's side. You're as bad as my mother."

"I'm on the side of your marriage like any good friend is going to be." Felesia squeezed my hand again and let it go. "So the baby was okay with being bumped around."

I lowered my hand to my belly and rubbed. "Yes, the little precious is fine."

"How's your head?"

"Hurting. But I don't think I can take anything other than Tylenol."

"For good reason." Felesia cooed. "Look, I have to go back to the office for a few, and then I have to pack, but I'll be here in the morning. If they release you, I should be able to zip you home and head for the airport."

"I appreciate you, girl," I smiled.

"I hate to leave you all banged up," Felesia replied. I could see the wheels turning behind her eyes. She reached into her purse for her phone. "I can put it off for a day or two—"

I reached for her phone and stopped her from dialing. "I'll be fine, and I'm not that banged up." Felesia squinted like she wasn't sure she should go, so I continued. "I'm blessed. Eight-car pileup. I could be dead."

"Don't even say it." Felesia shook her head. "If you're sure?"

I gave her the best smile I could manage without moving the muscles in my face that would cause my head to ache. "I'll be fine."

She leaned over the bed rail and kissed me on the head. "Call me if you need me. Otherwise, I'll see you in the morning."

After she left, I reached for my cell phone and called my house. Chelsea answered and assured me that she and Katrice were fine. I spoke to Katrice, apologized for not being home with her, and told her I'd see her tomorrow. After I hung up, I pushed the button on the remote to darken the room. I needed to rest my pounding head. I wasn't sure if it was hurting because of the injury, the news I'd received about the baby, or the memory of the last time I was intimate with my husband.

Greg had let himself in with his key, came up the stairs, and climbed into bed with me. When he first touched me I nearly leapt out of my skin. I'd been sleeping hard.

"What are you doing here?" I'd asked. He didn't answer with words. He put his lips on mine, on my face, neck, chest, arms. I remember my mind was saying "No, stop. Get out of here." But my body was saying the opposite and Greg knew it, so no matter how hard I tried to put up a fight, in the end, he'd won. We'd made love. The next day I told him I was getting the locks changed, and I did. I was determined not to let my physical needs get me into emotional trouble with Greg. I wasn't stupid. That was a dangerous place to be when you loved someone.

So, now I was pregnant, almost twelve weeks if memory served me correctly. I'd almost gone through the first trimester. Who does that? At least I knew why I was exhausted and nauseated.

There was a light knock on the door, and then Greg stuck his head into my room. I'd been expecting him. He'd called a few hours ago. He held a small gift bag and a bunch of balloons. He put both down on my bedside table, examined my bandage, and took a quick peek at the medications hooked up to my IV. "They taking good care of you?" he asked.

"I have no complaints," I replied.

Greg took one of my hands in his and massaged it. "Honey, you scared me to death." He looked at me longingly, and all I could think was he was hoping this accident would serve as an opening for him to get back in my life. I pressed my lips together and pulled my hand free of his. Sadness filled his eyes for a moment, but he recovered. "The story about the pileup is on the news," he said.

"So, I'm news again." I raised the bed. "Is that how you found out?"

He shook his head. "No. The reporters didn't say names. Just talked about how it backed up traffic."

"Did Felesia call you?" I was suspicious of my girl.

Greg shook his head again. "No, but she should have. I'll have to have a talk with her." He wagged a finger like he would surely straighten her out. His tone had been light, but then it became somber. "I'm on your next of kin record for this hospital. Remember, you've been here before."

This was the hospital where I'd delivered Danielle. Sadness came with that thought, and I could tell Greg felt it too. I assessed him. He was thinner, which made him look even taller than his six foot two inches of height. He'd gotten a tan in New Orleans, and it gave his skin a bronzy tone. He also had a five o'clock shadow, which I'd always found attractive on him.

A beat of silence passed, and I decided to occupy my thoughts with something besides Greg's good looks, so I asked, "How was your trip?"

"Interesting."

"An interesting funeral?"

"No, some other things. I'll talk to you about it all when you're better. I'm still processing it."

I nodded, but I was also very curious. "How's your dad?"

"Drinking, hating his doctor—" Greg waved his hand, as if to dismiss the entire conversation. "On from that . . . I checked on your car. The guy at the auto shop where they towed it said it's in bad shape."

"Really? Are they going to total it?"

"Not likely, it's cheaper to fix, because it's still worth a considerable amount." He reached for the bag he'd placed on the table. "I think this should help." He handed it to me, and I pulled out a key ring.

"What's this?"

"I took the liberty of getting you a new car. It's at your house." He smiled. "But it's not in stone. It's a loaner. You can go to the dealer and get anything on the lot when you're better."

"Greg, you didn't have to—"

He threw his hands up and came closer to me. He leaned in so that his face was inches away from mine. "You were due a new car, and this one is much better on gas." He took my hand. "I always want to take care of you. Don't you know that?"

I pulled my hand from his and subconsciously moved it to my belly. He would really want to take care of me if he knew I was pregnant, but I didn't dare mention it. I'd never get rid of him. I'd never have time to think.

"My heart froze when the hospital called me. I swear I couldn't breathe until they told me you were okay." He shook his head. "But, I didn't come here to make you feel bad about not calling me. I just wanted to check on you."

There was a knock on the door, and the nurse entered. "I need to get your vitals."

I sat up a little in my bed. Thought about how this nurse might make some more assumptions and blurt out something about my pregnancy. "Greg, do you mind stepping out?" I asked.

He looked confused. "Step out because . . ."

I cleared my throat. "I'd like some privacy."

"Privacy for your vitals?" He said the word like it gutted him. "There's not something I don't know about this accident, is there?"

"No." I was firm. "I would just like some privacy."

An uncomfortable beat passed between us before he said, "Why don't I just leave? I have an early procedure in the morning anyway."

I avoided his eyes. "That's fine. I'm tired."

"I should be done by ten. If they release you, I can take you home."

"Felesia was going to come and get me. She's leaving for the Dominican tomorrow, so . . ."

He shook his head like he understood. "I'll stop by when I'm done with my day, if that's okay. I'd like to help."

"You helped enough by getting the car."

He closed his eyes. My rejection was hurting him. I knew it, but I didn't know how to stop his hurt, because the only thing that was going to end it was me giving in to what he wanted. He raised my hand to his lips and kissed my fingers. "Don't hesitate to call me."

"I won't."

He left the room.

The nurse had been waiting. "That is a very good-looking man." She smiled. "One of the coworkers told me Dr. Preston is a neurosurgeon."

"That's right." I stretched my arm out for the blood pressure cuff she was untangling from the pole she pulled from the corner.

"Well, I'll assume he's not your brother. It don't take no brain surgeon to see he's in love." The nurse slid the blood pressure cuff on my arm and proceeded to take my pressure. She finished that and my temperature and did a quick exam of my extremities. "You get some sleep, but let know if you need to get out of bed. We don't want you falling."

I nodded I would, and she left.

I realized the keys to the new car were still on my lap. I smiled. *Pretty expensive get well card,* but Greg had always been good to me that way. Money . . . He made lots of it, had lots of it. His spending money had never been a problem. Spending money had absolutely nothing to do with love and commitment. It was easy to throw money at problems when you had a lot of it. It was easy for Greg to buy me something when he wanted to get out of the doghouse. What I wanted was for the love he claimed to have for me to match his actions. I wanted to be bigger than his libido and his ego. I wanted to be bigger than his pride. I wanted to be first. Until I was sure he could give me what I wanted, no gift or pregnancy was going to change the course our marriage was on. It was time for me to get what I needed.

Chapter 12

Greg

At first, sleep had come easy. I lost an hour coming back from New Orleans, and I was exhausted from the heavy double patient load I'd had when I got back. But now it was after midnight, and I was staring at the ceiling over my bed. I had to be at the hospital by eight in the morning, but thoughts of my wife and snippets of conversations I had with my family traded places in my mind.

My father's advice was easy to dismiss, because it was egotistical ranting from a man who betrayed my mother with another woman for over thirty-five years. I wanted to be angry with him about it, but what would be the point? He was seventy-one years old. My anger would only serve to hurt me, as was usually the case with grudges. I didn't think I was like my father. Even after I fussed at him in the car about his mistress I felt like I was better than him, more faithful, but was it really true? Had the acorn not fallen far from the tree? I had been keeping Samaria. I was paying her bills in excess of $1,000 a month, and I was prepared to do more and keep doing it. The only reason I'd stopped was because I'd gotten caught. How was I any different from my dad? I wasn't.

I swung my legs over the side of the bed, stood, and walked to the windows. Atlanta was quiet at night. The silence made me feel even more dejected and lonely, but I wasn't likely to feel good no matter where I was. I sat back on my bed and pulled open my nightstand for a novel I'd throw in there. What I found was the Bible Angelina had given me in college. She'd packed it for me when she put me out, and I made sure to put it in exactly the same place it had been in our house for all those years, tucked away and unread in my nightstand.

The Bible, God's book of stories, rules, and regulations. Was it even the truth? I was raised in church and attended private Christian schools. I had, no doubt, been taught almost everything in these pages, but the last few years, I just didn't know anymore. What was God?

He was supposed to be an omnipresent, omnipotent being that controlled things, but I didn't see that. I didn't see anyone controlling anything. I removed the book from the drawer, opened it, and decided to read the very first scripture my eyes fell on. It was Psalm 14:1 in the NIV. *The fool says in his heart, "There is no God."*

I closed it and chuckled. "So what, God? Was that a personal warning?" What were the chances I would open the Bible to that scripture when I was questioning the very existence of God? I didn't want to be foolish, but where did serving God get you? My wife was a good person. She'd lost a child and presumably her marriage was ending. She had spent more time at church than anybody I knew. And like Angelina, there was my mother, a faithful, good, upright woman who also loved the Lord. What was their reward for loyalty to Him? I didn't get it. But the Word said, "The fool says there is no God." I wasn't going to be a fool and question it.

I lay back down and tried to fall asleep again. Angelina returned to my thoughts, specifically her asking me to leave her room for her vitals. I thought that was bizarre, but was it just me thinking it was crazy? Was I in denial? Had my wife already gotten over me and moved on, and I couldn't see it because I was trying to hold on? I shook my head. I wasn't ready to accept that. I knew my wife. I knew that look in her eyes. She still loved me. But if it wasn't about how she felt about me, then what was she hiding?

Part II
Samaria and Mekhi

"The way of a fool is right in his own eyes: but he that hearkeneth unto counsel is wise."
~ Proverbs 12:15

Chapter 13

Samaria

Bling! The rock on my finger caught the light and reflected off the glass door to Airamas Records. With an up-and-coming music producer for a future husband, I'd soon be living the good life that this ring promised. And to think, six months ago I had my sights set on a surgeon. Surgeons made money, but not music-industry cash.

I passed through the lobby, and as I made my approach, the security guard opened the studio door. This place was like Fort Knox inside and out because a superstar was in residence. That added to the excitement and heightened the intensity of what was happening for Mekhi and me. He was going to be rich, and I was going to be a rich man's wife.

I entered the cavern of speakers and silver sliders that comprised the producer's cockpit. Benxi bellowed a slow ballad. Although the soulful sound of her voice could be heard through the room, Mekhi was wearing a headset, nodding and instructing Jay, his engineer, as the man moved the sliding knobs on the mixing console.

Benxi hit a high note just as I came to stand directly behind Mekhi. He turned when he felt my presence, and I placed a hand on his shoulder. Benxi's note went sour. The music stopped.

"Sorry," she said. She reached for a bottle of water on the stool next to her, took a long sip, and attempted to return the bottle to its place when it dropped. She bent over to pick it up, and I swear I could see all her goodies in those tiny booty shorts she was wearing. I felt heat rise to my face. Why was she dressed like that in a studio where there was nothing but men?

"Hey." Mekhi stood, kissed me on the lips, and took one of my hands in his. "Surprised to see you."

I knew from that statement that he'd forgotten we had a meeting about the wedding ceremony at the church this afternoon, but there was no point reminding him of that. I understood he was busy. I cleared my throat and pulled my eyes away from the half-naked woman in the booth. "I thought I'd stop in and see if you were almost done. I'd like to take you to dinner."

Mekhi smiled, let go of my hand, and gave Jay some instructions. "Have a seat, babe," he said to me.

Jay spoke into the microphone. "Just go back to 'When I found you.'" He'd marked the place in the song that I recognized before Benxi messed up and showed us all her behind.

Benxi nodded. The music started again, and she began to sing. I stepped back and sat down on a chair behind Mekhi. He was lost. Lost in his music and lost to the woman who had made it possible for him to live his dream. A woman who was looking my man right in the eye as she sang the words to a love song. At least now I knew what man she was wearing the shorts for.

My phone rang. I pulled it from bag and answered it. Mekhi and Jay turned, and that was my cue to take my call out of the studio. It was my wedding planner, Tanisha. I realized I'd forgotten her. I stepped through the studio door to take the call.

"Samaria, did we have a mix-up?"

Tanisha came highly recommended as the best choice in Atlanta to pull together a celebrity wedding on the quick, so I knew she was good at what she did, but she was like Mary Poppins about my schedule—be here for that, be there for this, make a decision about A, B, and C. She was getting on my nerves, and we had just gotten started. "I'm sorry, I had a rough morning and I forgot," I said. I was as bad as Mekhi about this wedding, and I wasn't even that busy.

"Well, where are you? Is it possible for you to get here in the next thirty minutes? I'll wait."

I looked back through the studio doors. Benxi had finished singing, and she was exiting the booth. Her booty shorts were riding hide on the top of her thighs. There was no way I was leaving her alone with my man. "I can't. I'm too far away. Let's reschedule."

"Can we choose a day and time now, please? Showings are not easy to fit in at the last minute." I could just see her businesslike manner through the phone. She was pulling out her iPad and pulling up her calendar as she spoke. Who did this chick think she was dealing with? I was paying her. It wasn't the other way around.

"Look, Tanisha, I appreciate you wanting to get me another showing, but I don't have access to my calendar right now. I'll e-mail you later with some dates, and we'll reset it."

She grumbled a reply, and we ended our conversation. I slid back through the door and found Benxi standing next to Mekhi. One of her hands held an earphone, and she had her free hand on her hips. She was smiling and nodding as she and Mekhi listened to the song she'd just recorded. Jay had joined the other engineers and one of the freelance song writers in the adjacent space Mekhi called the beat room.

Benxi put her earpiece down and threw her arms around Mekhi's neck. "That was hot!" She held on a little too long for my taste and even after she turned him loose, one of her hands remained pressed flat against his chest. "I love it. This is going to be my best album yet."

"Yeah, it's on point." Mekhi looked at me, and I raised an eyebrow. He took Benxi's hand, removed it, moved closer to the beat room door, and opened it. "That's on y'all. Go ahead and start working on the sequences for the hook."

Jay waved him in, and Mekhi turned to Benxi and me. "Just a second, ladies." Then he disappeared into the room.

It was then that Benxi looked at me. "I'm sorry, Samantha. I didn't know you were here."

Samantha? I kept it in the forefront of my mind that this woman was a cash cow and didn't give her the satisfaction of acknowledging she'd said my name wrong. "I just arrived."

"So, what did you think of the track?"

"It's great. It should go straight to number one." Like I could say anything else?

Benxi smiled, but it didn't reach her eyes. "Mekhi is the man. I knew it from the first time I met him."

I nodded and looked through the glass at him. "He's special. He knows his music."

"Oh yeah," Benxi said, looking through the glass into the next room where Mekhi and his crew were working. "He has lots of talent."

I swallowed and counted to ten. What was this heifer trying to say? I was so glad Cole, one of the kids who also wrote lyrics, came through the door behind me at that moment.

"Benxi." He handed her a SD card. "This is the cut I was telling you about."

She took it, and they discussed it for a few seconds. I left the room, went back out to the lobby where Jay's woman, a girl who was barely out of high school, was watching old episodes of *The Game* on the television. She was laughing out loud at the antics of Tasha Mack like it was the first time she was seeing it. I was sure it was not.

Glad to have the weight of my baby off my feet, I sat and removed one of my shoes. I might have to stop wearing four inch heels. I couldn't take it anymore. I hoped Mekhi was going to be home early. I needed a foot massage, badly. Heck, I needed a full body massage. I'd never been this stressed before, and as if I didn't have enough drama, Bonita Jones, aka Benxi, the hottest, sexiest recording artist in the world wanted my man. I couldn't help but wonder by the familiar way she pressed a hand against his chest if she'd already had him. I let out a long breath and whispered a *Good Times*, James done died round of "dayums."

My cussing pulled Jay's girl out of her television-induced comma. "You a'ight?"

I didn't even try to fake a smile. "Tired."

I couldn't remember Jay's girl's name. I knew she made herself handy by answering the phone, serving up drinks, and running out for food and such. She was dutifully on the job when she asked, "Can I get you something?"

I nodded. "Juice, cranberry if you have it." I knew they had it. It was Mekhi's drink of choice when he wasn't guzzling PowerAde.

Jay's girl popped out of her seat and returned within seconds with a bottle of juice. Mekhi walked out of the studio with Benxi at his side.

"You sure you guys don't need me to stay?" Benxi asked him, but she looked at me.

"No, we can use the auto-tuner to do what we need to do," Mekhi responded, referring to the voice recording device usually used to correct pitch issues. In Benxi's case it was used to keep from wearing out her voice while they worked through the sequence. "You go rest that voice of yours, and I'll see you first thing in the morning."

"Okay, if you say so." She was clearly disappointed. Didn't she have something else to do, like go get her nails done or weave tightened? "Samantha, good to see you," she said, and then she walked toward the door. She tapped Jay's girl on the shoulder. "You be good, Inga."

She was swaying way too much of her half-naked behind. I could tell Mekhi had to fight the urge to look. I didn't hold it against him. I was looking myself, and I wasn't even a man.

Inga gushed visibly and actually raised her hand to rest it where Benxi had touched her. "She is so the truth."

The truth? *Ha,* I thought. She remembered the name of the engineer's girlfriend, but she couldn't remember mine. No, that chick was not the truth.

I finished my drink and bent to retrieve my shoe. Mekhi picked it up and set on the table in front of me. Like a gift from God, he began to massage my foot. He removed the other shoe and massaged that foot too. He seemed to sense that I was tense, and I knew he knew it was because of Benxi. He was trying to reassure me with his hands that I was the woman he wanted. Mekhi was good with his hands, and he was doing a convincing job.

"I thought you were looking at dresses this afternoon." He made his way to my calves and squeezed and kneaded the tight muscles with his palm.

I shrugged. "I forgot."

"Forgot?" he asked as if he couldn't believe her answer.

"I know. I had a rough morning. I wanted to see you, and that's all I had on my mind."

He nodded as if he understood.

"But you can't do dinner?"

He shook his head. "Not out. I mean, we can grab something across the street, but I have got to get this track done."

I nodded. Mekhi had explained that there was a lot of money going out and not near as much coming in. They had released two singles from Benxi's album, and they were selling like crazy. The videos were hot too, but downloads on iTunes weren't as big a deal as people thought they were. The real money would come when the CD dropped, hit platinum status, or in Benxi's case, double-platinum, and Benxi went on tour. Japan was first on the roster, and it was a virtual goldmine for her.

Airamas was not exclusively Mekhi's. He was president of the label and chief creative operator. On paper he owned a 55 percent interest in it, but Airamas was part of larger machine, United Music Corp. UMC was the money behind the business, which Mekhi had told me was not in endless supply. UMC wanted a blistering hot album, and they wanted it fast or Mekhi would be out and Benxi, tied to Airamas/UMC, would belong to them until Mekhi earned out the initial debt to the company. Mekhi believed UMC was behind him, but the business was cutthroat, and they'd turn him out on the streets faster than a drug addict could blow through ten dollars if he didn't deliver a selling album.

"Forget work." A broad smile played across his lips, and he put my foot down and extended a hand to my abdomen. "How is my baby today?"

I looked down at the small bulge in my belly. "The baby must be a little heavier because my heels are killing me."

Mekhi chuckled. "Heavy?" He placed his hand on my belly. "He's so small. When's he gonna pop out?"

"I'm only sixteen weeks, but still, I guess I'm going to carry small." I smiled with Mekhi. "What's with all the references to he?"

"That's what my moms talkin' 'bout. She had a dream or something." Mekhi smiled again. "When will we know for sure?"

I paused for a moment. "We could know when I have the ultrasound, but I was thinking, let's wait to find out."

Mekhi's brow wrinkled. "What do you mean, like until you deliver it?"

"Yes, why not do it the old-fashioned way, you know, before all this technology. Let him or her tell us."

Mekhi chuckled. "Are you serious?"

I nodded again, swallowed, and tried to keep my eyes with his. But I kept seeing Greg's green, sometimes yellow, hazel eyes. A chill came over me. "Why not?"

"Because that's not like you. Not like you to not want to be sure and not like you to not want to shop."

"I'll still be shopping. I just won't buy blue or pink."

"Baby, there's only so much green and yellow I can stomach, especially if it's Mekhi Jr."

I leaned forward and kissed him. "I want to wait." I added finality to my tone. "Now, help me up and let's go eat. I'll take the thirty minutes I can get. I want to talk to you about something."

***

We crossed the street, but I felt like I'd left my mind back in the studio, back in that moment when I saw Benxi touch Mekhi in the familiar. As if I didn't have enough crap to worry about. I at least thought I had Mekhi on lock.

I decided I wasn't going to ask him about her. Although we had the truth pack, he'd feel compelled to lie, and I didn't want to put him in that situation, not yet anyway. Besides, Mekhi could have his secrets. I had mine. He was marrying me and no booty shorts were going to stop that, especially not now that I knew what I was dealing with. I'm not going to say the idea of Benxi being with him didn't make me want to stomp a hole in both of them, but I wasn't in the position to start no mess. I needed him.

Mekhi waived the waiter over, and when he arrived he said, "We need to order. We're in a hurry."

"Yes, Mr. Johnson." The waiter was more than happy to rush it. He wrote our menu items on a pad, left, and returned in a flash with our drinks. They knew Mekhi Johnson, knew him as Benxi's producer, and that knowledge had them skittering to make sure we were properly served. Those were perks that came with money and status.

Mekhi raised his glass and took a long sip. "So spill. What'd you want to talk to me about?"

I perked up and went into my *sell him something* mode. "I was reading an article in a magazine that talked all about building your business through branding, and I was thinking Mekhi Johnson and Airamas Records need a brand."

Mekhi nodded. He was definitely interested in anything that could help his business.

"You have to establish yourself as an entity separate and apart from Benxi. I mean, no doubt, she's hot and she's your star, but does everyone know that you're the one on this next album? Are the blogs buzzing about the songs you produced for her? No. All they're doing is chatting up her talent like she does it all herself, and you do have other artists you want to bring up. You're the next Russell Simmons and Jay-Z, boo."

Mekhi raised his hand to his chin and began rubbing like I had laid out scientific data he needed to decipher. "Okay, I hear you, but how do I do that?"

"Online. Everything is done through the Internet now."

The waiter interrupted with our meals and broke my stride, but I got back on it as soon as he left. "Baby, you start with what's free. You need a stronger presence online. An active fan page on Facebook, you need to be twittering and doing stuff on all the social media sites. You need a blog and a Web site."

"Yeah, so I've heard, but when would I have time for that? I'm working sixteen-hour days as it is."

He sat back and let out a deep breath. I became aware of how tired my man was. I'd been so into myself and my problems that I didn't realize how much he had on him. "I could help with that. I could set up all your accounts and keep them current for you. Put Facebook statuses up and get on Twitter and tweet."

Mekhi reached across the table for my hand. "You're busy with the wedding and decorating the house. I don't want you stressing while you cooking up my first-born."

"Khi, I'm bored. I need something to do. It would be good for me to do something else, because no matter how things turn out, I won't be able to practice as a nurse anymore."

"You don't know that."

"Oh yeah, I do. Stealing medication at the hospital will definitely end your nursing career."

"Well, you don't need to worry about nursing anyway. I'm blowing up, and my woman doesn't have to work at nothing but being fine and raising our child."

"I know you're blowing up." I raised my hands in quotation marks for effect and chuckled. "But I worked hard for that degree. The thought of not having the license really kicks rocks."

Mekhi reached across the table and took my hand. "I know you worked hard, but like the words from the new single Benxi just recorded say—Life is in chapters. Let the past stay in the past and open a new chapter for the present. You just be wifey and mommy. I got the rest. I promised you a long time ago that I was going to take care of you."

Uneasiness settled over me. Trust, promises . . . difficult words to take in. I had a flashback of those promises he'd made. We lay on the rooftop of his building in the housing project where we grew up, listening to music, sharing our dreams, and making love. Mekhi had promised he'd take care of me, that he'd get me away from the rat- and crack-infested neighborhood. He hadn't kept that promise. I'd gotten myself away, but he'd dang sure put the taking care of me part in the scenario when he bought the 6,000 square foot mini-mansion we now lived in. Still, I didn't know if I could trust him. Could men ever be trusted?

"Sammie?" He was staring like he was trying to use X-ray vision. "What's on your mind?"

I shook my head. "Nothing."

"You get that same faraway *nothing* look every time I try to assure you that I'm your man."

"I know you're my man."

"Nah." Mekhi shook his head. Disappointment replaced the joy. "But I'ma work with you on forgiving me." He squeezed my hand.

I squeezed his hand back; then he released mine and grabbed his fork.

"Back to your brand. I want to do it. It's the least I can do for you. You're doing everything for us, and I feel like all I'm doing is costing money. I've even thought up a job title. 'Social media specialist.'"

Mekhi laughed and all thirty-two of his gorgeous white teeth were showing. "Okay, my social media specialist. Do I have to pay you?"

I sat back in my seat and pursed my lips. "I'ma let you slide until Benxi goes triple platinum. In the meantime, you can pay in foot rubs."

Mekhi chuckled. "Triple platinum, huh, from your lips to God's ears."

"I'll help you get there," I said. I raised my fork to eat my meal. I had just inserted myself into Airamas Records. Aside from the fact that everything I said about his brand was true, I now had a reason for coming and going to the studio. Benxi could diss me by calling me Samantha all she wanted, but I was going to keep that booty-shaking hoochie off my man.

Chapter 14

Samaria

After my dinner with Mekhi, I headed over to the church for my meeting about the wedding ceremony. I'd gotten saved in a tiny little storefront church on the southwest side of Atlanta a few months ago. It was not my style, but the people seemed nice and genuine and really wanted me to be a part of the congregation. Mekhi's publicist, Omar Devlin, an employee of UMC, whom I was starting to think was "the devil," had insisted I attend a church for Atlanta's elite. He strongly suggested the famed Grace Tabernacle, otherwise known as *Bling* Temple, and I joined. I faithfully attended Sunday services every week. The only problem was I wasn't learning anything.

The minister, Chatman was his name, had been assigned to be my spiritual counselor. I had met with him once when I first joined Grace, but then had to cancel our subsequent meetings because things always came up. He stuck his head out of his office and invited me in. The receptionist who had been at the desk in the waiting area joined us.

"Sister Jacobs, I know that your time is precious, so I'll get right to the point of why I asked you for this meeting."

I nodded. I was thinking the "your time is precious" comment was a dig at me for cancelling our new member counseling sessions. If so, this was not going to be good.

"I regret to inform you that pastor won't be able to officiate a wedding for you here at Grace Tabernacle."

I didn't think I heard him correctly. "But I already confirmed the date was available. If it's about me missing our sessions, I can make those up before the wedding."

He shook his head. "It's not that."

I glanced at the receptionist who turned her eyes away from mine, and then looked back at Minister Chatman. "Then what is it?"

He slid off his reading glasses and cleared his throat. "Sister Jacobs, while we appreciate the fact that you want to be married at Grace, there are rules."

I was still foggy on the rules. They had a million of them. Which rule did he need me to learn to get married? "I don't understand."

"You listed your address and your fiancé's address as being one and the same on this application. We do not allow couples who are cohabiting to be married in the church."

My jaw dropped. Was he kidding? "But we're getting married. Won't that fix it?"

"Sister Jacobs, I realize that you are planning to get married, but fornication is still fornication."

I didn't even know what he was talking about. "Refresh my memory again. What's fornication?"

"Sexual relations before marriage," Minister Chatman said.

He had to be kidding. But he didn't look like he was kidding. He looked 100 percent serious. "But nobody goes by those old rules in the Bible anymore. I mean, who does that stuff?"

"Christians, Sister Jacobs."

"I know a lot of Christians who have sex and aren't married."

"People who are committed to following Christ follow His Word, and the Word is very clear about fornication."

I was about to speak, but he raised a finger to stop me. "And, you've also indicated that your fiancé is not a believer. We do not marry believers to nonbelievers."

Now I was getting pissed. This was too much. "Why not? I'm teaching him things about the Bible all the time. Isn't that good? Isn't that evangelism?"

"It's more likely pillow talk."

No, he didn't. I looked at the receptionist. I was expecting to see a smirk on her face, but she looked embarrassed for me. I cleared my throat. "I think you're being a little judgmental. Doesn't the Bible say judge not unless you'll be judged or something like that? The way I teach my fiancé about the Bible shouldn't be judged."

"Sister Jacobs, you cannot pull someone out of sin when you're living in sin yourself."

I swallowed. *Sin? He was calling me a sinner.* I thought I'd left that behind when I got saved, but apparently not.

"The Word is very clear about whom we should marry. Allow me to share a scripture with you." Minister Chatman opened the Bible. I could see it was the Second Book of Corinthians. "Be ye not unequally yoked together with unbelievers; for what fellowship hath righteousness . . ."

I shut him out. I knew that scripture. I knew what the word *yoke* meant. I thought back to the lunch I'd had with Angelina so many months ago. It seemed like just yesterday when I'd sat at a picnic lunch with her and let her teach me about the Bible. Unfortunately for both of us, I was sleeping with her husband. When she found out about my duplicity, she'd told me to go to the devil. Angelina was a good Christian woman. Angelina was a teacher and a friend. I'd ruined that relationship, a relationship that I needed so badly now that I wasn't learning jack at Grace except how to give money. I put my head in my hands and shook it.

"Sister Jacobs."

I raised my head. My eyes were wet with tears I had not shed.

"Do you have any questions?"

I pulled a tissue from the holder on his desk and wiped the corners of my eyes. "No, I understand," I said, and I did, because Angelina had explained it perfectly. I'd just forgotten.

We said our good-byes, and I escaped his office and all the rules inside of it. I let the massive door to the church close and made rapid steps to my car. *Humiliated.* That's how I felt. If I had known the paperwork was a setup, I'd have used a different address, but no matter. It was too late now. I pulled out my cell phone and called Tanisha to let her know she needed a judge or somebody to preside over the wedding. As I pulled away from the church I wondered if not having the Lord's blessing would curse my marriage to Mekhi. I sucked my teeth. I probably should have given a bigger offering last Sunday.

I entered the house, and my first order of business was to set up Facebook and Twitter accounts for Mekhi Johnson and Airamas Records. I went to the pages of Def Jam and Hidden Beach looking for inspiration on how to design Mekhi's pages. I used Benxi's face. Uploaded her two new singles to music players and posted videos. I wrote the first Facebook status—

What up, e'rybody? This is Mekhi Johnson, the CEO of Airamas Records. Have you heard Benxi's new single yet? Hit me up with what you think.

Then Twitter—

Mekhi Johnson, Airamas Records. Just finished working out Benxi's new single. Make room on your player for it. It's hot.

Then I started the tedious process of finding people to follow on Twitter and friending folks on Facebook. I worked and worked at this until my fingers were tired and I heard the chime from the alarm system ding that Mekhi was home.

He entered the office and put down his attaché case. He had one hand behind his back. That meant I had a surprise coming. I stood and rotated my neck to work out the kinks, walked over to him, and gave him a kiss. He pulled a bouquet of yellow roses from behind him. I took the bunch from his hand and kissed him again.

"What you doing over there?" Mekhi stepped back and peeled off his jacket.

"Being your social media specialist."

"Is that right?" he asked, loosening his tie.

I nodded. He looked good. Especially since the realization sank in that Airamas Records was no itty-bitty deal as I visited Def Jam and UMG and VEVO's Web sites today. I mean, I knew that, but the potential for Mekhi to blow up way beyond Benxi was there. He just had to push up some more artists.

"Are you hungry?"

He shook his head. "Not for food."

I stepped back and began to undo the button on my top. "We have the appointment with my lawyer tomorrow." I let it hit the floor, and then stepped out of my skirt. I might have had a small pregnant belly, but it was not that noticeable in the magenta silk teddy I wore.

Mekhi's eyes traveled the length of my body, getting bigger and bigger as they beamed in on my flesh. "Don't mess up the mood in here talking about your lawyer." He followed my lead by removing his shirt and stepping out of his pants. I let the thought that this was premarital sex exit my mind, especially since the church had already called me a sinner. I extended a hand to the nearby stereo and pushed the power button, which invited the mellow crooning of the late great Luther Vandross to fill the room. Mekhi closed the distance between us, picked me up at the back of my thighs until my legs wrapped around his waist, carried me to the sofa, and wordlessly told me how hungry he was.

Chapter 15

Mekhi

"The intent to distribute charge has being dropped," Bernard Hightower said.

I let out my breath. Samaria squeezed my hand, and I saw every muscle in her body relax.

Hightower was the best criminal defense attorney in the city. He almost always won, even if it was a deal cut with the district attorney to avoid a trial. The man was also said to have a gift for choosing juries.

"They didn't have anything to prove intent to distribute. So we're left with the felony theft, grand larceny, illegal possession of controlled substance, and theft by possession charges."

Samaria squeezed my hand again. "How much time?" she asked.

"I'm still trying to negotiate with the DA. I'm thinking I can get the grand larceny down to petty larceny if we just deal with the value of the drugs that were in your possession at the time you were arrested. I might be able to get rid of the larceny altogether. The drugs technically belonged to your employer, and they're not likely to want to press charges."

"Why not?" I asked. Samaria looked at me like I'd betrayed her with the question. So, I cleared up my reason for asking. "I'm just curious."

"Hospitals don't want this kind of publicity. It brings their ability to care for their patients into question. They will, however, want some type of financial restitution."

I nodded. Samaria repeated her question. "How much time?"

"The DA will want five years. If you're convicted, you'll likely get three to five and you'll do a year to two of the time."

I swallowed and felt my chest get tight. Samaria gasped and let out a series of short breaths. I watched her move her free hand to her abdomen. She was worried about the baby. This situation was messed up. "What are the chances she'll be convicted?"

Hightower put down the pen he'd been holding. "The Georgia Bureau of Investigation has video of her taking the drugs. She was arrested in possession. She doesn't have a drug problem, so the underlying suspicion is that she was stealing with the intent to sell. We can make that go away if your mother is willing to testify that she was the recipient of the drugs."

"That's no problem," I said.

"You're sure?" Hightower asked, raising an eyebrow. "Drug addicts can be very unreliable witnesses, even mothers."

I thought about the Oxy that Wang was delivering to my future mother-in-law on a daily basis and knew she'd do anything to keep that supply coming. "She won't be a problem."

Samaria's big brown eyes found mine, and she squeezed my hand again. "It's going to be okay," I said to her. I looked at Hightower. I'd pay him double the money I'd already given him if I could get that look out of her eyes.

Hightower schooled us on a couple of other things he was working on, and then we stood. I shook his hand, and so did Samaria. He escorted us out of his office and into the waiting room.

Samaria stopped walking, and I bumped into the back of her. I heard her gasp, but not from the weight of my body. I followed her stunned eyes across the room and noted a woman sitting in one of the chairs. The woman stood, and I thought she looked vaguely familiar.

"Angelina." Samaria said the woman's name like she was a long lost relative. Angelina did not look pleased to see my baby. On the contrary, she looked pretty annoyed.

I could tell she had to force herself to speak. "Samaria."

Samaria stepped forward, slowly at first, but then more quickly. She looked like she wanted to hug the woman, but a blind man could see that Angelina did not want a hug. "I'm so sorry about the IRS thing. I couldn't believe what they're saying on the news. I wanted to call you, but—" Samaria went on and on. She didn't notice that Angelina wasn't interested in any of it.

Angelina cleared her throat and looked at me. "Mr. Johnson." The greeting surprised me. "We met a few months back, when Samaria's mother was in the hospital."

Then I remembered that's where I'd seen her. I stretched a hand out to her, and she took it. She smiled. She was much warmer to me than she was to Samaria. What was up with that?

"Angelina, please come in," Hightower said. His perky receptionist popped to her feet and handed him a folder. Angelina walked past Samaria and me and extended a hand to Hightower.

"Thank you for seeing me on such short notice," Angelina said.

"Please, let's go into my office." Hightower swayed a palm in the direction we'd just come from.

Angelina turned back to Samaria and me. "Have a good afternoon," she said, and then she disappeared into Hightower's suite. He waved at us one final time and closed the door.

Samaria's eyes were wet with unshed tears. She gave me a weak smile and said, "Let's go."

Chapter 16

Samaria

"So, you were sexing her husband." Mekhi's condemning statement was a translation of the story I'd just told him. It sounded a little uglier coming out of his mouth. We were in the car, and even though he wasn't facing me, I could tell he thought it was foul.

"Yes," I replied, knowing it was foul.

"Where did you know her from? I mean, what was the deal that you know her and not just him?"

I leaned back on the headrest. I was starting to get a headache. Between Hightower's three to five years and Angelina's diss, it had already been a bad day. Now Mekhi wanted me to air my dirty laundry. He wanted me to share the details about my slutty ways. "I don't want to talk about it, Khi."

I could see him tighten his grip on the steering wheel. "It's pretty obvious that seeing her shook you up. You were trippin' more about seein' her than you were about what Hightower said."

I rolled my eyes. "What Hightower said was an improvement over the ten years that had been hanging over my head."

"All right, but we're not talking about the jail thing now. We're talking about Angelina. I want to know what was up." Mekhi wasn't fooling anyone. He didn't want to know about Angelina. He wanted to know about Greg.

I looked out the window and thought about the first time I'd seen Angelina Preston. I'd been sitting in the back of her church Bible Study class waiting for her, the teacher, to appear. My interest in her was cold and calculated. I wanted her husband, and I thought knowing more about her was one way to get him. I'd gotten lucky that night. She'd felt sorry for me and taken me under her wing through the church's mentoring program, but what I didn't expect was for so much to come out of the mentoring relationship. I didn't expect her to be kind and good to me. She taught me about Christ and the Bible. She loved me like a sister-in-Christ. I didn't expect to meet someone who I respected, someone who respected me, nor did I expect to make my very first female friend. I sighed. The weight of all that I'd lost in that relationship weighed heavy on my soul. If I could take it all back . . . I clenched my fist.

"Sammie, what's up?" Mekhi cut into my thoughts.

"Baby, I really don't want to go there. I'm trying to be a different person, a better person, but I can't do that if I keep having to explain my past."

"I'm just trying to—"

"Stop it, Khi!" I rolled my eyes. "Dang, what's with you? It's bad enough everyone else is questioning who I am, Hightower, the DA . . . I gotta go there with you?"

Mekhi shook his head. "You don't cry, Sam. You looked like you wanted to cry when she walked away. I just want to know what's hurting you." I didn't answer, but he wasn't going to let this go. "I always want to know what's hurting you, but you won't open up to me."

I rolled my eyes again.

"You must have known her first. She was a friend, and you got involved with her man?"

"Khi, it wasn't like that. Just know I knew her after I started seeing him."

Silence filled the car. I considered this might be a good time to spill the beans. I would tell Mekhi all about the mess I'd made of their marriage and my relationship with her, and tell him that Angelina's husband might be the father of the baby. But it was just too ugly. Something in the back of my mind made me think he'd never look at me the same again. He might stop loving the baby. He might stop touching my belly like it was the most precious thing in the world. I could lose him completely.

Mekhi almost ran a red light. He had to put on the brakes a little more sharply than he should have. I eyed his profile. He was angry. He turned to me. "I remember when I met her, she thought your name was Rae Burns."

"Yes, I told her my name was Rae." I'd used an alias at the church. I had to make sure Greg didn't find out his jump-off was snooping around his wife.

"Give me the details. I want to know," Mekhi continued.

Through my peripheral vision, I caught sight of a limo passing through the intersection. Mekhi followed my eyes and saw the fuchsia pink Hummer also. Benxi. We were minutes away from the studio, and she was on her way there as well.

Mekhi's chest rose and fell, and then he turned his head toward me. Our eyes locked. I was the first to look away.

"I'm not asking you about your past," I said. He knew what I meant, or if he didn't, his guilt had him twisted. I heard him swallow. This conversation was closed. The light changed, and he pushed through the intersection, following the trail of the tacky pink Hummer with the woman in it that held one of his secrets. I was glad I didn't have to worry about him pressing the subject of Angelina and Greg anymore, but I was not glad to know that based on the way he'd backed off of the discussion that my suspicions were probably right. He and Benxi had a past that had nothing to do with music. Now my questions were, how much of a past and was it over for her.

Chapter 17

Mekhi

The receptionist poked her head in my office and said, "Mr. Johnson, Omar Devlin is here to see you."

Omar Devlin made his way past her and dropped his six feet, 260-pound frame into a chair that I hoped wouldn't hit the ground. "Mr. Johnson," he teased. "We're getting fancy."

"Samaria hired her. She thought I needed to class up the place a bit."

"She was right," Omar said. "But dude, I go out for surgery for a minute, come back, and you're engaged. What's up with that?"

"My lady said yes."

"I'm sure she did. Why not?" Omar smiled, but his eyes were clouded with insincerity. "So let me ask you this . . . You sure you ready to go that way? I mean, brother, you're not even thirty years old. You just coming into your own with your business."

"Well, this is the time to build it all right. Personal and business life."

Omar shook his head. "Naw, why turn in your player card before you really get to live it up? You gonna have honeys throwing behind left and right, and you gonna put yourself on lockdown."

I chuckled, but wondered why he cared and what this had to do with his job. "Omar, look, I hear you, but, um, you know this is my girl. She's been the only woman for me since I was like eight, so . . ."

"I know, but y'all just hooked back up. I understand about her being your childhood wifey, I'm just saying."

I let out a deep let's-cut-the-crap breath. "O, tell me what you trying to say. You pushing this a bit."

"Okay, let me just go all the way and put my publicist hat on. It wasn't that long ago you was dealing with Benxi. I don't know if you noticed, but she's not quite over you."

I stood and moved near the window. "Benx and I talked."

"And she what . . . said it was okay?" Omar chuckled. "Come on, Mekhi. She's got her pride. What else was she gonna say?"

A wordless beat passed.

"Look, Mekhi. You got a lot of good talent on this label. You got a good ear, and you know how to make music, but let's not get it twisted. Until one of those talents blow up, Benxi *is* Airamas Productions."

More beats of time.

"She's feeling you. Really feeling you, and you don't need no mad woman holding the keys to your future."

"I hear you, but . . . I talked to Benxi. It's cool. We're cool, and Samaria . . . it's time. She's pregnant, so this marriage needs to happen."

"If your mind's made up, try to get it done before the album. It could be good PR," Omar said.

I nodded and stood.

We shook hands, and he said, "Just watch that Benxi situation, and next time, don't make me find out your good news on Bossip.com. Let me spin it for you. That's what UMC pays me for." He let himself out of my office.

I heard him exchange some words with Benxi right before she came in. "I was wondering where you disappeared to." She was breathless with excitement. "You gotta come hear the new track. I wrote the words myself."

I walked around my desk. Benxi grabbed my hand like we were high school kids and led me out the door. I managed to disengage our palms by the time we got to the studio. I could see my guys all in the beat room, grooving and nodding to the sounds they were mixing.

"Here." Benxi handed me a headset. Her makeup-free twenty-two-year-old skin glowed like an expectant mother. "It's just the hook, but it's hot," she said. I listened.

She doesn't matter to me. I know our destiny. I know where we will be.

Get her out of our lives and let's do this thing, baby!

You are for me. Today and forever. I won't set you free.

You are for me. I know what's in my heart. You are my destiny.

You are for me. I've seen the future, and I know where we'll be.

She doesn't matter. No, she doesn't matter to me.

The song had some real potential. It was soulful, and Benxi hit so many high notes that I knew I was listening to our first Grammy for Best Vocal of the Year. I removed the headset.

"You wrote that?"

She nodded, and the smile on her face was bright enough to light up the Statue of Liberty.

"Jay hooked up the arrangement for me," she said just as Jay exited the beat room.

"Hotness, right!" Jay's face was busting with pride. "Hooked that right on up."

I raised my hands and clapped a few times as if applauding to let them know I was pleased. "Yeah, you did, so, now I'm trippin'. Whatcha'll need me for?"

They laughed.

"That's one song." Benxi shook her hair, and her strawberry blond ringlets jiggled like Shirley Temple. "I've been writing songs since I was ten and never came up with something like that. We need you for the other fourteen tracks on the CD."

I nodded. "That's real good work, Benx." I looked at Jay, and we fist bumped. "Genius, my man."

"I thought you'd like." Jay spun around and went back through the door of the beat room.

Benxi grabbed my hand and pulled it to her chest. I mean, slammed between her breasts. "I told you we would make beautiful music together."

I looked in her eyes, peeped the affection that I saw in them; then I thought about the words to the song, and for the first time since we'd been working together, I realized that Omar was right. I might have a serious problem with Benxi.

Chapter 18

Samaria

"Do you like any of them?" Tanisha tapped on her iPad. When I didn't answer she raised her head. "Samaria?"

I looked up on the stage in front of me at the six women in gorgeous designer wedding gowns ranging from optic white to butter-cream ivory. The stick-thin models had fake pregnancy pillows stuffed at their bellies. It was supposed to give me an idea of what I would look like in the gown when I was further along in my pregnancy. I thought the prop was silly. It only made me self-conscious about walking down the aisle knocked up. And whose idea was the white? For a pregnant bride? I wouldn't be talked about at my own wedding. At least not for that.

"I like them all." I threw my hands up in resignation. "They're all perfect."

Tanisha's smile was tight. She was losing patience with my indecisiveness. "You like them all, but you can only wear one."

I nodded and just decided to choose. I was so not into this. I was depressed. *Three to five years*. I looked at model number three, and then model number five. Three was a better option in my world right now. "Number three," I said and an off-white, sleeveless, backless, empire waist Vera Wang original was mine.

The seamstress took my measurements, I paid, and Tanisha and I exited the bridal shop. "Make sure to get the preliminary total of guests to me. It's okay to overshoot it, but not by more than fifty or so people. Otherwise, venue could be an issue."

I nodded. Mekhi and I didn't know fifty people, not well. As much as I liked to spend money, I didn't like the idea of us spending $50,000 to entertain people who weren't family, especially when it was possible we didn't have it.

"And please let me know who your bridesmaids and Mekhi's attendants are going to be. We need to get them fitted. Once we do that, we can really dig in on the guest list, focus on your theme, and finalize the menu."

Tanisha was good. Real good. She would most assuredly have everything under control. She didn't have her reputation for nothing, but I didn't want her to think she was managing some big huge wedding party.

"I only have one girl," I said. "My cousin is going to be my matron of honor, and Mekhi's younger brother will be his best man."

Tanisha frowned. "One?"

"One," I repeated.

Her frown deepened. "Why?"

I started to make up a story about how both of my besties were out of the country. One was serving in Afghanistan and the other was an agent with the CIA and she was in South America, but I was facing three to five. My time was precious. I wasn't going to spend it lying to a stuck-up, pretentious wedding planner, especially one who had signed a privacy contract. She couldn't tell the world I was unpopular. "I don't have any friends."

"But I thought you grew up here."

"I never had much use for women," I said. Tanisha blinked rapidly, like she got it. I wanted to make a teeth-chattering sound like Hannibal Lecter. Yeah, I was *that* girl. *I'll take your man.* Snap, snap, and a circle.

Tanisha pressed her iPad against her chest. "I've never had such a small wedding party."

"Well, then, you have a chance to paint your masterpiece. Think about how pretty you can make the front of the ceremony with just one girl in the way."

"I suppose," was all she said. Then she pasted on that phony smile I was getting sick of and patted my shoulder. "I have to go, but we'll talk tomorrow."

She took purposeful strides to her car, and I walked to mine. As I climbed in, my phone chirped, and I knew it was a Facebook comment. I looked at it.

So what's up with M.J.'s future wifey being a future jailbird?

I smirked and answered.

Rumors and speculation—You can't believe everything you hear about M.J. unless it's from your speakers. Then you know it's the truth.

I pushed the button to update the post. Within seconds, there were over forty people clicking they liked my response.

Rumors of my death were in the air. There had been a few of those over the last few weeks, but not many. Most people wanted to know things about Benxi and the album and the tour. I'd gotten supercreative by posting video footage of her recording and fifteen-second clips of the music. I even interviewed the heifer about the release of the album and made it viral on all the networks and Airamas's new YouTube channel. He already had 30,000 likes on his Facebook page and 40,000-plus people following him on Twitter. I'd managed that quickly. At the rate I was going, Mekhi Johnson would be trending and everyone would know he was the master behind the music of their beloved Benxi.

I entered the studio and was greeted by the temp I'd hired for the reception area. I was glad to see her instead of Inga. Inga was still around, but she took up residence in the lounge instead of the lobby. Although Mekhi didn't have a lot of visitors, the media and paparazzi were always hanging around. Legitimate magazines and newspapers would call to set up interviews and didn't always go through Omar Devlin; for those reasons, Airamas needed to look like a professional shop.

I walked into the production studio. Benxi was in the cockpit talking on her cell phone, and Mekhi and Jay were at the control panel chatting it up about something. I took out my phone and took a picture of Benxi and a picture of Mekhi and Jay. This would make a good Facebook upload. Especially the picture of Benxi on a break during recording. She had a bottle of water in one hand and a magazine in the other. She was dressed in jeans and a cutoff midriff tee shirt. Her supercasual attire gave the picture a nice, natural quality. I found that our followers loved those everyday shots.

I also took a few picture of Mekhi. I was trying to brand him as a superstar producer, so pictures of him working were essential. His attire was the complete opposite of Benxi's and everyone else's in the studio. He was all business in his dress shirt, tie, and slacks. If one could dress their way to success, my man was already there.

"Hey, baby." He touched my arm and spoke into his wireless headpiece and told Benxi they were ready.

Benxi came out of the cockpit. She greeted me, and then told Mekhi she needed two more minutes on her call and a restroom run. The men in the room relaxed, and Mekhi took my arm and motioned me out the door.

"Omar told me you're doing a great job with the social media stuff," Mekhi said. "He says he wants to hire you to work a few of his clients."

I smiled, glad I was helping. "Are you making our six o'clock for the tuxedo fitting?"

Mekhi shook his head. "No. We're going to finish this song today. I can't do anything but get this single ready. Then I need to work in a few of my other artists later this week." He continued. "I'm sorry, but I'm mad busy for the next couple of months."

I sighed. "You sure you have time to marry me?"

"About that—"

My heart froze.

"I was wondering if you might be willing to do it in Puerto Rico."

My heart started beating again. "Puerto Rico? Yeah, but why the change?"

"We need to shoot a video in the Caribbean, and I thought we could just do it while we're down there. It would get you out of Atlanta for a minute. We can stay a few extra days and have a honeymoon. I'm not going to be able to take a second off after the album drops. Pretty soon you won't be able to travel." Mekhi rubbed my belly. He hesitated before saying, "Because of the pregnancy, so we should do this."

"I like it, and I could definitely use a trip. Might be my last one for a really long time."

Mekhi shook his head. "It won't be."

"Mekhi, we don't talk about it . . . my going to prison, but I think we should discuss some things."

"We'll talk if we need to. But I don't expect we'll need to. You're not going to prison, Sam. It's going to be okay."

Benxi came out of the nearby restroom and breezed by us. She went back into the production room.

Mekhi said, "I'm not letting you leave me, so don't worry about it."

I knew my man wanted to protect me. I knew he wanted to save me. I knew he wanted to make up for the way he'd left me flat years ago after I was arrested for helping him steal. I needed his help. He'd disappeared without even trying to get an attorney for me. It took us eight years to find our way back to each other. But I'd made a hard bed, and I was lying in it. It wasn't likely that he could make this right. "What are you going to do? Bribe a judge?"

Mekhi raised his head. "If I have to." His eyes were serious.

"You can't bribe a judge. We can't both go to jail."

"Sam, don't be so negative. You're the one that goes to church every week. I'm just trying to have some faith."

I was taken aback by that word. *Faith.* He was right about my lack of it. But how could I have faith when I was guilty and believed it was possible I was going to pay, maybe not for this crime, but another one I'd committed and thought I'd gotten away with?

"Okay," I said. "You go work, and I'll go find some faith."

Mekhi pulled me into a kiss, a passionate one with all tongue. It was one of those I-got-something-to-prove kisses. I pulled back and stole a peek through the door at Benxi. Mekhi released me and went into the room. I wondered if the kiss was for her benefit or mine.

***

I opened my eyes. It was almost midnight. I looked at the empty space next to me. Mekhi wasn't home. I heard the garage door closing and realized that the opening was probably the noise that woke me. *Why is he so late?* I'd left the studio at six, and he'd said they only had a couple hours of work left. Had he been with Benxi?

I stood, went into the master bath, and freshened up. As I came out, Mekhi entered the bedroom. He looked exhausted and disheveled, like he'd been in a fight.

"Baby, where have you been?"

He began to shrug himself out of his clothes. "Wang and I had a problem." His teeth were grit tight. He was angry.

"What kind of problem?" I asked. My cell phone rang.

"That problem." Mekhi pointed at my phone and disappeared into the bathroom.

I rushed to my side of the bed and picked up my cell. My mother. Oh God! What had she done?

I pushed a button to talk. "Mama?" Before I could get another word out, a string of explicates came through to my end of the phone.

"You can tell Mekhi to keep his . . . I don't need . . . Wang . . . They ain't God over me. I'm grown . . . police . . . They don't come 'round here treating me like a child."

"Mama, what are you talking about? What has Mekhi done to you except try to help you?"

Mekhi came out of the bathroom. I could tell he was angrier than he'd been when he went in. "Hang up!"

I didn't think I'd heard him correctly. I moved the phone away from my ear. "What?"

"Hang it up!" Mekhi yelled with such force the walls shook, or at least it felt like they had.

I pushed the END button in the middle of my mother's rant.

Mekhi sat down. He was so heated that his eyes were wet from the steam of frustration that was boiling underneath the surface.

I sat next to him, but stayed silent until he wanted to talk. It took a few minutes, and then I wished he hadn't . . . "I pulled your mother out of a crack house tonight."

I snatched my head back. "What?"

"Wang has been looking for her for a couple of days to give her her stuff. He finally got your stupid cousin—" Mekhi paused and shook his head, "he finally got June Bug to tell him where she was." There was another pause while I watched his temper begin to boil. "She's started smoking crack."

"Crack?"

"And that ain't the worst of the story." He shook his head like he couldn't believe what he was about to say. "I went to get her out. I was dragging her, because she was screaming like a lunatic." He chuckled, but I knew it was not humor. "The house got raided. I got put in a police car." He kicked his shoes off. "You want to know what for? Assault. She told the cops I was taking her against her will." He pounded a fist against the bed, stood, and walked into his closet. He came out with his pajamas. "I knew one of the cops, so I talked my way out of it, but reporters were there taking pictures and . . . I was recognized. So tomorrow the front page of the paper is going to say I'm a crackhead because I was in a police car during a raid at a known crack house."

I was stunned. I couldn't even speak. *Oh, God, oh, God . . . How could she?*

"Do you know what UMC is going to say about this? Mekhi Johnson, the producer, a crackhead. It's bad enough I have the stuff with—" He stopped himself.

The stuff. The rest of it hung in the air. The stuff was *my* stuff. "I know, baby." I heard my own voice trembling so hard I barely recognized it. "I'm sorry. I'm so sorry. I'll talk to her."

"No!" Mekhi yelled. "Just stay away. You can't be seen with her and that mess."

I blinked back tears that were brimming in my eyes. "But, Mekhi, she's my mother."

"No, Sammie." He shook his head. "She's a problem for you, and she's a problem for me. Wang is going to watch her. He'll keep her out of the spot."

My fingernails dug into the mattress. He was telling me to stay away from my own mother.

Mekhi nodded like he'd read my mind. "Don't go over there. She's just going to suck you into her mess with all that guilt trippin' she does. Let us handle it."

It was hard for me not to be sad about the crack, but I also felt guilty about Mekhi's role in keeping her in line. "How, Mekhi?" I was scared of the answer. "How are you going to handle it?"

"The same way we've been handling her."

I was confused at first, but then realization came to me. "You're going to give her crack?"

"Yeah, that's what she wants. We gonna give it to her."

"Mekhi, you can't."

"Yes, I can." He wouldn't look at me.

"Would you give it to your mother?"

This time he did look at me. "Sam, don't go there. Your mother ain't like my mother. Your mother can't be reasoned with. If your mother can't testify for you . . ."

"I can't just let her be on crack, Khi. I have to try to talk her into rehab."

"You been trying to talk to her. She won't go. Just let her be. We'll deal with rehab later. Right now, we can control her. If I give her what she wants, we can get her into court."

"Khi."

"Sam!" His voice rose an octave I've never heard used with my name. "Let me handle this." He walked into the bathroom and slammed the door so hard it almost came off its hinges.

I raced downstairs and booted up my laptop. My first stop was the blog BlackGossip.com, and there was a picture of Mekhi in the back of a police car. "Mekhi Johnson On Crack!" *Oh God. Oh God, how could this happen?* All the work I'd done to get Mekhi's name and brand out there, and it was all undone in a single night by my mother. I picked up the phone and dialed Omar Devlin. It didn't matter that it was the middle of the night. He was going to need to do some serious damage control.

Devlin was not happy to have his sleep disrupted, but he became furious when he found out it was my mother Mekhi was tussling with. "I don't have the right to say this on a personal level, but I do on a business level. You are a problem for Mekhi and for this label."

I swallowed. I wasn't expecting him to say what he was thinking.

"You've been a problem. The people at UMC are not happy about all this bad PR. This isn't the days when bad boys could run the music business. We need him to be liked and respected."

Mekhi entered the room. With his eyes, he questioned who I was on the phone with.

"Where is Mekhi?" Omar asked.

"Here," I managed to get out past the knot in my throat. I handed the phone to Mekhi and went over to the sofa and sat down.

Mekhi walked around the desk. I could hear Omar screaming. Mekhi said a few things, tried to counter Omar's rant, but largely he took his whuppin' like a man.

Omar was probably right. I was a problem. I don't think Mekhi anticipated who he had to be before he invited me into his world. And they didn't know that this wasn't all of it. There was the baby . . . If it wasn't his, if we had to endure a DNA scandal, Mekhi would most definitely be done with me. Who wouldn't?

I needed a Plan B. I had to have one for my baby if I went to jail. There was only one other place I could get help. I had to tell Greg about the pregnancy.

Chapter 19

Samaria

I stepped into Greg's office and waited for the office manager to leave and close the door behind her.

Greg was seated behind his desk. His brow furrowed over his light hazel eyes. His fair cinnamon skin a reminder that everything about him was distinct from the texture of his multiracial hair to his prestigious height.

"I'm humoring you." He stood like the gentleman he was raised to be and pointed to one of the wing chairs in front of his desk.

I took a seat and clutched my purse close to my body before speaking. "I'm pregnant."

A flash of irritation moved across his face. "And what does that have to do with me?"

"I'm seventeen weeks."

Greg knotted his fingers together in front of him on his desk. "I repeat, what does that have to do with me?"

I rolled my eyes. Was he seriously going to sit there and pretend we hadn't been intimate a little more than four months? "Greg, the last time we were together was about that time, and I know I'm not the only one who remembers that the condom broke."

Greg sat back. He seemed thoughtful; looked like he was trying to remember. "I thought you were dating that music producer. The one I've seen you on television with."

"I am. But that didn't begin until after I got out of jail."

"So what? Doesn't he have enough money for you? You have to come here trying to shank me even harder than you already have?"

"I'm not trying to shank you."

Greg chuckled bitterly. "Samaria, I'm not giving you a dime. In fact, you're still under the protective order to stay away from my family."

Nausea engulfed me, and I felt like I was going to be sick from my fear. "This is not about money!" I stood. "I don't want your money. I'm telling you I wish to God that I knew for sure it was Mekhi's baby, but I don't."

Greg stood too. "So, do what you do." He stuck his hands in his pockets and pushed out his chest. "Lie."

I rolled my eyes. "I have lied, but DNA won't. If this baby is born with hazel eyes and wavy hair, I'm done."

"Pin it on your mother. I've seen a picture of her. You got yellow roots in the family tree."

"He'll want a DNA test!"

Greg came from around the desk and grabbed my arm. "Keep your voice down. These walls are thin." He let go of my arm and ran his hand over his hair. "I can't believe you have the nerve." He paused and then continued, "You have ruined my life, and now you want to come in here and try to pin a baby on me too. Is it never enough with you?"

"I didn't ruin your life, Greg. Angelina wasn't my wife."

He stepped back. A heavy sigh escaped his lungs, and he shook his head like he'd gone over that very point a million times. "You made what I did more personal. You made it worse. Hanging around the church and—" He shook his head again. "What kind of person does that?"

I swallowed and bit my lip. He was right. What kind of person does what I did?

"Even after you got to know her, you still kept on with your scheme. What did you think I was going to do? Leave Angelina for *you?*" He laughed. Laughed at my personhood and my womanhood. "You were nothing more than a lay. So coming in here with this baby story . . ." He paused. "Just trust me. I am *not* the father of your baby." He took more steps backward away from me until he reached his side of the desk. "Now, please, get out of here."

"I'm trying to talk to you." I didn't realize I was trembling until I raised a hand to my throat.

He shook his head. "If he and I were the only men you slept with during that time, you've got no worries. Well, except prison, which is probably where you belong."

Tears began to stream down my face. "I have to know. If it's not Mekhi's child and a DNA test proves it's yours and I'm locked up, will you take the baby?"

"It's not my kid."

"Greg, I need to know."

The intercom buzzed on his phone. "Doctor, your next appointment is in room two."

Greg pushed a button on the phone and replied. "Thank you. Please come and see Ms. Jacobs out of my office." He picked up his stethoscope, hung it around his neck, and walked to the door. "It's not my baby, Samaria. Get out and never, ever come back here or the next time, I'll call the police." He left. Cold-blooded dog. What had I expected? After all, I, of all people, knew how he treated his wife.

I moved toward his desk and pulled a tissue from the holder just as his office manager entered the room. "Ms. Jacobs." I kept my back to her, wiped my tears, and squared my shoulders before I turned.

"No need for an escort," I replied, looking at the confused woman. I reached across Greg's desk, picked up a pen and a sheet of memo paper, and scribbled my phone number and some words. "Please give this to Dr. Preston," I said, folding the note before handing it to her. "I can see myself out." *I remember how I got into this mess.* I passed by her and left his office.

Part III
Angelina and Greg, Samaria and Mekhi

"A wise man feareth, and departeth from evil: but the fool rageth, and is confident."
~ Proverbs 14:16

Chapter 20

Greg

I held Samaria's nasty little note in my hand. *I'm not the only one who's exactly where they belong,* she'd written. I shook my head. I'd been shaking my head about the note for almost a week, torturing myself daily with the reminder that she was not completely out of the picture. I wasn't going to spend a lot of time trying to figure out her next move, but she was certain to contact me again about her supposed pregnancy.

I was sure I didn't have to worry about her baby being mine. If I could have gotten someone pregnant, it sure as heck wasn't going to happen during some isolated condom break when I'd been trying to get my own wife pregnant for over a year. No, this was not my problem. Samaria just didn't know it, because I'd never shared with her that I had a fertility problem. She really must have thought she found herself a big payday bedding a music producer and a surgeon, but this baby drama was all his. Poor guy. He'd hit the wrong note when he'd slapped a ring on that gold digger's finger, but he would have to learn that one on his own.

The intercom buzzed, and I pushed the speaker button. It was Marsha. "Dr. Preston, I'm sorry to disturb you. Someone from the insurance company is on the phone. She says it concerns your wife's recent visit to the hospital."

I instructed Marsha to put the call through and picked up the line. "Dr. Preston, we're trying to reach Angelina Preston to set up a telephone meeting. The telephone number in our system is disconnected."

"Yes, we moved," I said. I was thinking, not together. "What can I help you with?"

"A contact number for Mrs. Preston, sir."

I pulled the phone back from my ear. Was she trying to be a smart aleck? "My wife is still recovering from her injuries. I can answer any question you need answered."

"Due to privacy laws, we're not able to disclose the nature of the call," the woman said. "Do you have a contact number for Mrs. Preston?"

"Look, I know all about HIPAA," I said. "I'm a surgeon, and my company pays for the insurance as you can well see. If it's something for the insurance claim I can answer your question."

"Sir, I would need to speak with your wife." She sounded like a broken record.

I hated HIPAA. No reason why a husband shouldn't be able to find out what was going on with his wife. "I'll tell you what. I'll call Mrs. Preston and have her contact you." I ended the call, but not my curiosity. What in the world could the insurance company want to talk to her about that they wouldn't talk to me about? HIPAA was about medical information, not billing stuff.

I buzzed Marsha, and like always, she came into my office right away. I was going to ask her to do something pretty illegal, but she was an eager-to-please type of employee. "Do me a favor. Call this number back. Pretend to be Angelina and find out what these people want."

Marsha's eyes opened pretty wide, but then she took the number and left my office. It was only a little illegal.

Angelina was my wife. Ten minutes later she reentered and said, "They want to set up a care coordination interview."

"Care coordination?"

"Yes, make sure she sets up her doctor's appointment and answer any questions she has. And tell her about the services they provide on their Web site."

I shook my head. "Appointments and services for what?"

"Prenatal. Your wife is pregnant."

Marsha left my office. I sat there in complete shock for a long time, so long that I lost track of time. It could have been ten minutes or ten hours. I reasoned it was the same day because the sun hadn't gone down. No one had popped their head into my office and said, "Good night, Dr. Preston," nor had the evening cleaning crew come and swept up around me. In the time that I sat, I tried to process the fact that Angelina was pregnant. The shock overwhelmed me.

I remembered the last time I made love to her. It was the night I let myself into the old house. At first she wasn't happy to see me, but then I managed to get her in a better mood. I thought her letting me into her bed would get me back into my house, but it didn't work out that way. Not only did she not let me come home, she had the locks changed so I couldn't creep back in again. She was so stubborn. But what was she being stubborn about now? Why hadn't she told me she was pregnant? It had to be mine. Didn't it?

I remembered the lawyer guy bringing my wife home and shut down that thought immediately. Angelina was not the kind of woman who slept around. She barely knew that guy. She'd never do something like that. Plus we were still married. She wasn't going to commit adultery. It was definitely my baby.

I stood. Went to the windows and looked out. I tried to come up with a reason why she wouldn't tell me, but I couldn't so I picked up the phone and figured I'd get the answer from her, but I got her voice mail each time I called.

The intercom buzzed on my desk. "Dr. Preston, your two o'clock appointment is in room three." I put down my cell phone. I was glad Angelina hadn't answered. Things like this were better handled in person anyway.

I picked up my stethoscope and put on my white coat. It was going to take a move of God for me to concentrate for the rest of the afternoon. "Angelina is pregnant," I said the words out loud. I laughed and let my heart fill with joy. I was going to be a father again. I was going to get my wife back. I'd gotten the miracle I was hoping for.

I closed the file on the desk and put it in the pile for Marsha to take back to medical records. I spotted Samaria's note that had been buried underneath the file. Angelina pregnant. Samaria claiming to be pregnant. I had refuted Samaria's claims because I assumed I hadn't been able to get my wife pregnant, but now I wondered if I had gotten Angelina pregnant, had I gotten Samaria pregnant as well? I'd wanted the miracle of another child, but the thought that I could have gotten myself caught with Samaria would not be a miracle; it would be a curse.

Chapter 21

Samaria

Sometimes you need a Plan C. Angelina Preston opened her front door and stared at me for what felt like an eternity before she asked, "What are you doing here?"

"I need to talk to you." I was glad she hadn't slammed it closed in my face.

"About what? I still have a restraining order. How dare you show up at my door like this. What is wrong with you? And how did you even find me?"

I let out a breath and chuckled nervously. "Can I have the list of questions again? I forgot the first one."

It took a moment for Angelina to stop the steam from coming out of her ears. "Let's start in reverse. How did you know where I live?" She crossed her hands over her chest and tapped her foot.

"I have a friend who's kinda good at finding people." I knew it wasn't the best response, but it was the truth.

She twisted her neck sista style. "So, you're still breaking the law?" She uncrossed her arms and grabbed the doorknob.

"Wait!" I yelled. "Don't close the door. My answers get better. Let's go through the rest of the list." My smile was all teeth and nerves.

"I have a better idea. Get off my property before I call the police." Angelina pushed the door, and I pushed back. I wasn't going to let her close it. Not yet.

"Please, I know I have no right to be here, but I'm appealing to you on behalf of a child that may go into foster care. I need help."

The expression on her face told me she was weighing whether she should entertain my scenario, so I pushed on the crack I'd made. "Can I come in? I just need a few minutes."

She didn't move at first. I could tell by the way she was looking from me to her watch that she was getting closer to a yes. She pulled the door open and showed me into a small living room to the right of the foyer.

Thank you, Jesus. I almost said it out loud. One thing I'd learned about good people, you could pretty much always count on them to be "good," so the fact that Angelina was willing to listen to a story about a helpless child didn't surprise me. I took a seat on the sofa. My feet were killing me.

She followed suit and said, "Make yourself comfortable." Her tone was sarcastic.

"I'm sorry. My shoes are not made for walking, and I've been walking all day."

"Can I get you something? Water, juice?"

"I'd love some water."

She disappeared and moments later she returned with a bottle and handed it to me. She watched me open it and take a long sip. The expression on her face was anything but open. She was tolerating me, just like her husband had.

"So?" She sat. "What is it you need to know that you couldn't find out from calling your local Family and Youth Services office?"

"How do they find homes for kids?"

Angelina popped up from her seat. "Samaria, you can Google that information."

I shook my head. "No, that's not what I mean. What if there was a child who needed special attention for a short period of time . . . a year or so? Could you, if you had an interest in the child's case, find the right home for it?"

Angelina looked confused. "I don't understand what you're asking for."

"I'm asking for favoritism. I'm pregnant."

"Pregnant?" The word fell from her lips like a hunk of rock from a cliff. Angelina examined me more closely, but I knew the empire waist sundress I was wearing was a good cover for my condition. "You're pregnant?"

"Yes, but I might be going to prison, so I'm trying to find out the options for my baby." Angelina seemed perplexed, so I kept talking. "I think Mekhi will keep the baby, but I don't know."

"What do you mean you don't know?"

"I don't know if he'll want to keep a baby."

A shadow of concern fell over her face, and she raised a hand to her lips. "I saw the news story. Is he on drugs?"

"Oh, no!" I waved my hand. "Mekhi is as clean as a whistle. There's a long story behind those pictures."

Angelina shook her head. "So if he's not on drugs, what's your issue? You're marrying him in a few months, aren't you? Why would you marry him if you don't trust him?" Then she smirked. "Oh, wait, we're talking about you, aren't we?" She rolled her eyes.

"I'm not marrying him for his money if that's what you're thinking. I told you I'm pregnant. That's the reason we're getting married."

Angelina gave me a side eye before asking, "And when did you decide to practice morals?"

"Honestly, since you told me who I was."

She squinted like she didn't know what I was talking about.

"The Samaritan woman story, remember, when you and I had lunch and you introduced me to the different stories in the Bible? One of them was about the Samaritan woman."

I could tell she knew what day I was talking about. It was one of many days when she'd shared her faith with me, when I, her husband's mistress, was fishing for inside information about her marriage so I could ruin it. I swallowed against my disgust at myself. "That story has stayed with me. I couldn't shake it. I couldn't forget that my name was actually in the Bible. I kept reading and reading about her, and then one day I decided I wanted what she had—what you have. I wanted to be saved. I joined a church and gave my confession."

Angelina raised her hand and pushed her hair behind her ear. "That's great news, Samaria. Really good news."

Angelina's eyes softened. Just like I'd thought earlier, good people were predictable. "My whole life has changed. I—I mean, I'm still me, but with a conscience or something."

"The Holy Spirit."

"Yes, the Holy Spirit." I hadn't been sure I had that yet. "Anyway, I'm trying to live right, like Christians do, and I'm pregnant, so I'm getting married."

Angelina was curiously quiet on that statement.

"Isn't that what I'm supposed to do?"

"You get married because you're in love and you want to build a life with someone. Someone that shares your faith, your values, and you both have the same goals."

"Mekhi and I have all that."

"So then, why are you here telling me that you don't trust him? Questioning whether he'll keep his child? He may have to hire some help, but it's his baby too."

"I don't know. I—he's let me down before."

"But he wouldn't, not if you were in jail."

"You don't know our history. I never did get a chance to tell you what happened . . . why just months ago I couldn't stomach the sight of him."

Angelina took her seat again. Even she enjoyed a juicy story.

"Years ago, eight to be exact, Mekhi and I got in some trouble. Legal trouble, and he was supposed to help me, but instead of getting me a lawyer and bailing me out of jail, he disappeared on me."

"Legal trouble." She raised an eyebrow. "This isn't the first time you've been in jail?"

I wrung my hands. "No, but it's worse this time." I paused. "Anyway, he didn't do what he was supposed to do. He ran like a punk and hid out in Florida."

"But weren't the two of you barely out of your teens?"

"Yes, but I wonder, do people really change?"

"You just said you were trying to change."

"Touché." I bit my lip, pondered that thought, but then realized this wasn't really about Mekhi's character. It was about mine. He would take care of *his* baby. He just might not take care of somebody else's. "I don't know, Angelina. Men and babies. What if I get a long sentence like five years? What if they convict me for intent to distribute?"

Angelina asked, "Were you selling drugs?"

"No." She was waiting for me to say more. "My mother is addicted to OX. I was stealing for her."

Angelina looked really sympathetic now. I know in her line of work she knew about drug-addicted mothers.

"Nothing about that situation has changed in the last few months. She's still using. As a matter of fact, it's worse. That's how Mekhi got caught in front of that crack house. He was trying to save my mother." I dropped my head back. Tension filled every muscle in my upper body. "I'm not trying to make you feel sorry for me. I just want you to know, I'm not a drug dealer. I'm not using drugs. I'm just stupid. I should have never been stealing for my mother. I shouldn't have been doing a lot of things that I was doing."

Angelina frowned. "Back to the baby. We don't have a lot of issues with placing infants who are healthy, so I don't think that would be a problem, but honestly, Samaria, Mekhi is not going to let his child go into the foster-care system." Angelina paused for a few moments. Her face took on an entirely different countenance. She looked down at my belly, looked like she'd figured me out. "That is, unless it's not his."

Chapter 22

Angelina

"It's Mekhi's baby," Samaria answered quickly. She made an exaggerated "Are you kidding expression?" for good measure, like I had to be joking, but I wasn't sure she was telling the truth. She was a skilled liar, a manipulator, and, for all I knew, she was sitting in my house pregnant by my husband. I felt my lungs tighten.

"I'm going to ask you again. Are you sure there's no chance that this is Greg's baby?"

Again, she didn't hesitate. She didn't even blink. "It's Mekhi's baby. He's the only man I've been with. I had a sonogram, so I know how far along I am."

I felt relief wash over me. The thought of him having a baby with someone else was sickening.

Samaria's eyes roamed the room. "You've moved, and this isn't exactly surgeon money. Are you and Greg getting divorced?"

I couldn't believe she went there. "That's pretty inappropriate for you to ask, don't you think?"

She shrugged. "I know it might seem that way, but I care about you. Greg doesn't care about me." She paused like she'd flashed a bad memory. "He made sure to let me know that when he found out about the Rae thing."

I lowered my head. I had some bad memories of my own, like the night Greg came home and told me he was having an affair, when he'd told me Rae was Samaria.

"She's not who I thought she was," Greg shook his head.

"They never are." I put as much venom on that statement as I could.

Greg met my eyes. He was grieved when he said, "She's not who you thought she was either."

And then I knew . . . I had a Judas in my court. A Judas my husband had carelessly let in. "I'm not so sure that he cared about either one of us."

"No." Samaria shook her head. "He loves you."

I bit my lip. I hated to ask my husband's mistress this question, but she was here, and I was curious. "Did you love him?"

She chuckled, like the thought was absurd. "I was just trying to get in his pockets." She wrinkled her nose. "Even if Greg and I hooked up, we wouldn't have been compatible. I honestly didn't give that much thought."

I believed her, and what a crime it was that I'd had to pay so dearly for her greed. My experience working with young mothers through DYFS taught me that self-esteem, or the lack of it, created a slippery slope that would take a young woman down into a rabbit's hole where their reality was totally different from what they wanted it to be. Samaria was no different. But this woman had slept with my husband, and she reminded me of that by bringing him up. "It's time for you to leave."

"Why, because I asked about Greg?"

"You've overstayed your welcome. It's incredible enough to me that you have the nerve to ask for my help, but then you want to ask about my husband."

"Angelina, I've messed up. I admit that. I'm trying to be a better person, but how am I supposed to do that if my past keeps slapping me in the face? Tell me, how do I become new with the old smeared all over me like I've been mud wrestling in it?"

I raised a hand to stop her questions. "Becoming a better person is a process. You can't expect people you hurt to automatically trust you just because you're saved."

"Why not? God isn't using our mistakes to define us." She paused, her eyes got misty. "I'd give anything to erase my past, but I hear you. The saints have to watch and wait. I just wish I didn't feel like people were waiting to see me fall." Samaria dropped her head in her hands for a few seconds. Then she stood and handed me the empty water bottle. "Thanks for your time." She turned and walked to the door.

I followed and pulled it open for her. "If it's true that you're really trying to change your life, things will work out for the best."

Samaria stepped out and turned back to me. "I hope so, because doubling up on my tide check at church didn't help." She smiled. "I appreciate you talking to me. I sure miss those church sister hugs."

I pressed my lips together. After a few seconds, she took the hint that she was not getting a hug, so she turned on her heels and went down the walkway to her car. I closed the door and fell back against it. "Did she just say *tide* check?" I don't know why, but I was feeling conviction big time. I reasoned that I didn't owe Samaria anything, and I most definitely didn't owe her a hug.

I pushed my body off the door and almost lost my footing. I felt dizzy and light-headed, so dizzy that, before I fell on the floor, I had to return to the love seat where I had been sitting. I sat for a full ten minutes before I felt better. This was the second time I'd almost passed out. *Stress.*

As if I didn't have enough on my mind, now I had to deal with a Samaria pregnancy . . . as pregnant as I was. I'd kept my cool while she was here, but my mind was filled with all kinds of questions. The first and foremost—was it Greg's? She wasn't showing, so maybe she was telling the truth. It had been a little over four months since Greg and I broke up, so if it was his, she'd be at least that far along, maybe more. I'd be able to see, wouldn't I? I knew the answer to that question; no, not really.

Then there was the thought, the ultimate in disgusting thoughts . . . that my husband could have two women pregnant at the same time. Who does that? That's for television and movies, Maury Povich "Who's the Daddy?" episodes and bad reality television shows.

Jesus. I raised my hand to my head. This was not my life. I was not going to share the season of my child's birth with Greg's mistress. Was I?

Chapter 23

Greg

I'd waited a week. I wasn't going to wait anymore. Angelina hadn't called me to tell me about the pregnancy. I blew my horn and startled the woman in the minivan in front of me. I wasn't usually this impatient, but I had had enough of this game my wife was playing with our future. My nerves weren't going to hold out much longer, so she and I were going to talk tonight.

I pulled onto her street, and from where I was I could see her car was not in the driveway. I slammed a fist on the steering wheel. It was almost seven o'clock. Where was she? Didn't she have to put Katrice to bed?

I came to a stop in front of the house. Out of the corner of my eye I thought I saw an SUV like the one I'd gotten for her turn the corner at the end of the block. I pulled out, gunned the gas a little, and followed. Once I turned the corner, I could see her and the little gold sticker from the car dealer on the temporary tag. It was her. I reached for my phone and pressed the speed dial for her number, but she didn't pick up. She never even moved her head side to side the way people do when they hear a phone ring or decide to check it. I could see that her hands were also on the steering wheel, so she wasn't fumbling for it. Angelina was famous for forgetting to take her phone off of vibrate.

I followed her for a few more miles on a pretty busy four-lane road. Was I stalking? Where was she going? What if she had a date or something? I was tripping. I sped up until my car was alongside of hers. I could see Katrice strapped in the back playing with her dolls. We came to a red light, and I tapped my horn. She looked over. She was surprised at first, and then she frowned. I put my window down and told her to do the same.

"Greg, what are you doing?"

"Following you," I replied.

She guffawed. "Really now?"

"No, not really. I saw you pull off from the house. I was trying to catch you."

"I have church. It's Bible Study night."

I infused desperation into my voice. "I need to talk to you."

Angelina bit down on her lip like she was reflecting on something and said, "I need to talk to you too, but I'm not missing church."

"Okay, can I come after?"

She hesitated for a moment, and then frowned. "I suppose. Nine should be okay if it's that urgent."

"It is. I'll meet you at nine." I had to fight to keep from pumping my fist.

She put her window up and pulled off. I could see her turn into a small church about a half mile down the street.

I decided to kill time by having dinner. I looked around for an eatery, but really didn't know where I was. I pulled out my phone and sought out a diner or Waffle House, but neither was particularly close. This area was residential, but I decided to take a ride anyway to see if I ran into anything. I passed the church. It was a small white building with a great looking, old-fashioned steeple. In fact, I noted the name, Steeple of Love Christian

Church. Unbelievably different from Greater Christian, the church where Angelina last attended with its 3,000 or so plus members. She was changing everything in her life. That was a scary thought. *I could be a part of some early midlife crisis movement. Jesus.*

I kept driving. The street became a single-lane road. I turned left, and then right, and then ran into a dead end. No restaurants. I took another winding ten-minute ride to nowhere and decided to give up. It was getting dark, and I wasn't really that hungry. I set my GPS using Angelina's address and hoped it would take me back there without incident. As soon as I saw the church again, I felt confident I wasn't going to end up in South Carolina. I looked at the time on the dash. It was only seven-forty. I'd be sitting outside Angelina's for over an hour. I turned the car around and pulled into the church parking lot. Why not? Angelina couldn't be angry that I came to church. I might even earn some brownie points with her. I parked next to her vehicle, climbed out of my car, and went inside.

I stepped into a large vestibule with carpeted stairs on either side that led down. One sign read "Children's Church" and the other read "Fellowship Hall." The restrooms for Men and Women were on my right and left. The sanctuary doors were in front of me. I got closer, looked in through the beveled glass, and saw Angelina sitting alone on a pew about five rows back. I pushed the door and stepped in. The minister stopped talking, and everyone looked back at me. Most of the thirty or so occupants were women, and they all smiled except the one who I sat behind. My wife.

"Welcome, sir. I'm Reverend Hines, senior pastor. There should be a Bible in front of you. Please join us in Deuteronomy chapter thirty."

Angelina turned. "What are you doing here?" She scowled. I thought that was illegal in church, but apparently it wasn't. Talking, however, I knew was, so I raised a finger to my lips and shushed her. She smirked and turned back around.

"As you can see, the lesson is about choices. The Word is telling us to choose life. Abundant life," Reverend Hines said.

My ears perked up. I thought the Deuteronomy thirty part was familiar. This was the same scripture the minister referenced at Uncle Simon's funeral. I pulled the Bible from its holder and opened it to the text. Quickly I skimmed the words as I listened to the lesson.

"You ask, how do we live an abundant life? We live by choosing this day, every day, that we are in Christ. What will be our mission for the day? How will we interact in our relationships? How will we carry out our duties? How will we respond to the circumstances and challenges that come before us? We're constantly choosing, but we shouldn't do so in a passive way. Jesus was not passive. Jesus was a man of action. He told the disciples to step out, cast their nets, go up, go out, go to the other side."

Reverend Hines walked back and forth across the small space in the front of the church. He was an older man, near sixty I'd guess, and he had a booming voice that bounced off the walls of the sanctuary and penetrated my consciousness. He had paused, but now continued. "Read the ministry of Christ from a visual perspective. Note that Jesus is always moving—always making choices. Sometimes we let life happen to us. We blame people for who we are and our shortcomings. We live out generational curses that our daddies passed down or our mothers passed down, accepting it as the only way. You know how we do that. 'That's just the way my family is.' 'Everybody's divorced,' or 'Everybody has children out of wedlock,' or 'Everybody is overweight.' 'Nobody ever goes to college.' That's the choice of death to accept failure. The choice of life is to exercise your faith, through action and with courage, to seek to transform who you are and to make sure it lines up with God's will."

I sat back against the pew. Amazed that the message so many others had been trying to get to me had been broken down so simply. This stuff that he was saying was really common sense. Any motivational speaker on any given day would say the same thing, except the part about God's will. God's will—how did you know what that was?

I met the reverend after the lesson. I took the liberty of introducing myself as Angelina's husband, which pissed her completely off. What was I supposed to say—I'm the fool she's divorcing?

I trailed her back to the house. She hustled Katrice up the stairs to put her to bed. Starving at this point, I helped myself to a few apples from the fruit bowl and flipped through the channels on the television until I heard her on the landing.

Angelina entered the room. I could see now that she was a little heavier than she had been. Her face a little rounder. She had that glow that pregnant women get, and I couldn't believe I hadn't noticed it before. She looked exactly as she had when she was pregnant with Danielle. I stood.

"When were you going to tell me?" I asked.

Angelina claimed a wing chair and lay her head back against it like she was exhausted. "Tell you what?"

I got down on my knees in front of her. "That you're pregnant."

She didn't make eye contact with me. Her forehead wrinkled a little, and annoyance raised her eyebrows. Her eyes settled on mine. "I just found out. After the car accident. They told me in the hospital."

I remembered her strange behavior. "So, that's why you wanted me out of the room when the nurse was around? You didn't want me to hear anything?"

Angelina nodded.

"But still, Lena, that was weeks ago."

"I've been trying to . . . I don't know, give it time to sink in."

I stood. "Sink in? We've been trying to get pregnant for over a year, and you don't tell me?"

"Trying?" She raised an eyebrow. "I don't remember you trying very hard." Her tone was indignant.

"Just because we didn't go see a fertility doctor doesn't mean I wasn't trying," I said. I knew the chances were pretty slim with me having a low sperm count, but I usually had sex on command when she was ovulating. "I was hoping things would happen naturally."

Angelina rolled her eyes. "Don't give yourself so much credit. I can remember you leaving our house some nights to go for a drive." She paused. "Isn't that what you told me? But in fact, you were out spreading your sperm around with your girlfriend."

She'd shoved my claims about how dutiful I'd been about trying to get her pregnant right down my throat.

"You have a selective memory, but I don't!" Her voice was louder than she intended because I saw her look toward the stairs like she remembered we weren't alone. She dropped her head in her hands and shook it a few times before she returned them to her lap and found my eyes again. "Look, I'm happy. I'm just sad at the same time. I didn't expect it to happen this way."

I got back on my knees. Begging was in order. "I know things are messed up. I know I messed them up, but tell me what you want from me. How can I fix this? I'll do anything." I leaned into her body, pressed my head into her belly, and closed my eyes.

Angelina placed her hand on my head. The heat of her touch—I wanted to take her in my arms and kiss her a thousand times. I wanted to make love to her so badly I thought I would explode. I loved her. I'd always loved her. I raised my head, anticipated I would see hope in her eyes, but that would have been too easy, too perfect. My wife was crying. She shoved me a little. Just enough to let me know she wanted me to move away from her, and my heart dropped. I didn't know what to say, so I didn't say anything. I watched her cry. I absorbed her pain like a sponge and wished I could wring myself out and end the agony.

Angelina reached for a tissue and wiped her eyes before she spoke. "I decided I wasn't going to take you back, and then I found out I was pregnant." She paused. "I considered the future of my child and thought I had to take you back. I had to try."

Relief washed over me. I wanted to pump my fist, but instead, I raised my free hand and wiped her tears. "Good. We can work it out. I'll go to counseling, you know, whatever."

"Wait." Angelina raised a finger. Her tone told me I should not feel relieved. "I said I *thought* I should reconsider, but I don't think I can do it."

I squinted. Had I just heard my pregnant wife correctly?

"Samaria." The name stung like venom from a snake bite. "You asked me how long I've known I was pregnant. How long have you known she was pregnant?"

Chapter 24

Angelina

Greg fell back on the floor on his butt. He clenched his fist open and closed for a long time before he said anything. "Not long. How did you—?"

Oh God, I thought. *If Samaria went to see Greg, if he knew . . . It was possible that it was his; otherwise, why? Why would she go see him?* I felt like I was going to be sick.

"Angelina?"

I swallowed. "She came to see me."

Greg's coloring went from a caramel brown to red in an instant. "Came to see you," he stuttered. "Why?"

"She's looking for help with putting her baby into foster care if it turns out Mekhi won't keep it. I put two and two together. It doesn't take a rocket scientist or a brain surgeon to figure out that she's not sure if it's his."

"She didn't tell you it was mine, did she? It's not." He made the statement with certainty that I wasn't sure he was feeling.

"Greg, are you sure?"

"I'm . . ." he paused, "reasonably sure." Our eyes caught. I know he saw disgust in mine. "We used condoms, Lena. We just . . . had an accident once."

"Oh, yeah." I bit my lip, and then guffawed. "I know how passionate you can be. Imagine, what I thought was reserved for me was just technique."

I heard Greg swallow. He wasn't even going to try to excuse that one. Not that he could. There was no excuse for a married man getting a mistress pregnant, because a married man should be trying to protect his wife. "Do I need an HIV test?"

"No," he said. "We always used condoms."

"But you're only *reasonably sure* that she's not pregnant by you?" My words were bubbling over with sarcasm.

Greg managed to ignore my tone. "I don't know if I'm even on the short list of possible men. I mean, who's to say she wasn't sleeping around with lots of guys, and I'm just the one who makes the most money, or that she's not running around telling all of us that she's pregnant to see who she can get money out of?"

"That's cruel. Don't start talking about her like she's some kind of low-life piece of trash."

"She is."

"Really?" I stood and chuckled. It hurt coming out. "And what does that make you?"

Greg got up off the floor and took two steps toward me. "A fool."

I moved out of his reach. He followed, and I raised a hand to halt him. How could he do this? How could a pregnancy be possible? "Do not try to touch me."

Greg hesitated for a moment. He raised his hands to cover his face for a moment, groaned, and dropped his arms. "Lena, we're having a baby. We can be a family. Tell me what I can do to put this behind us."

"There's nothing you can do."

He shook his head like he hadn't heard me clearly. "What?"

"She's pregnant. We have no idea how far along. She claims it was after the arrest, so I'm thinking almost five months or something like that. But whatever it is, you have to wait until she has the baby." I turned away and closed my eyes tight to cut off the pain. When I opened them, I found myself staring at my attaché case. I'd rested it on the table in the hall when I'd come home. It was filled with files I had to go through to make decisions about the services I was going to cut due to my financial situation. I hated that Something Extra was going under, because I loved children. However, now, my own husband was making me reject one. He had brought out the worst in me.

I heard Greg mumbling more about how it wasn't his baby, but I wasn't hearing any of it. My mind was made up, and nothing he could say was going to change it. I turned back to face him. "Samaria's child has to have a DNA test. If that baby is yours, our marriage is over."

Greg left, disappointed and distraught, but he was no sicker than I was. I hadn't asked for any of this drama to land in my life. He had created all of it—from the affair to a potential pregnancy. I was the casualty of his and Samaria's crap, and I was tired of feeling like a victim.

I climbed into my bed and tried to find a comfortable spot to rest my aching head so I could fall asleep, but each time I closed my eyes, the memories from the last few months came to me. Samaria's first visit to the church; her introducing herself as Rae Burns and inviting me to coffee. Working with me on the health fair. All lies and deceit. And then there was Greg—refusing to talk to me about Danielle. Refusing to make love to me sometimes when I was ovulating. An affair for six months. All those late nights and early mornings, the times he came in with perfume and lipstick on his clothes. He even had a key to her apartment. He laid in her bed, made love to her, and what else? Conversation, gifts, promises? What had he taken from me that he'd given to her? I banged a fist on the pillow.

I hated him.

I hated her.

I hated them.

Tears began to leak from my eyes. Heartache. It kept finding me, and I had no control over it. Even if we got lucky and it wasn't his baby, could Greg really be trusted not to do this exact same thing to me again? Lie and cheat like the liar and cheat he is?

"No," I cried. I was not going down that road with him again. I had to end this. I was the one who had to stop the pain. Reverend Hines had told us to choose life. I had to choose the life I wanted. But was it really that simple? Was it ever simple when children were involved? When the heart was involved? I still loved Greg. For the life of me, I could not put my finger on exactly why, but I did. His behavior for the last two years had not completely erased the memory of our thirteen years of marriage, when he'd been a better husband and a better man. But now there might be an outside baby. How could I endure that? How did anyone? It's the worst kind of betrayal. Everybody knew how not to get pregnant.

I curled into a fetal position, placed my hand on my own belly, and rubbed it. I couldn't let him and Samaria upset me like this. I had a life to bring into this world. I didn't want my baby feeling my stress. This kind of stuff affected unborn children. My baby deserved better than this drama.

"God, please help me," I whispered.

I repositioned my head. Finally, I'd found that sweet spot where the aching stopped. As was my habit, I said the Twenty-third Psalm. When I was done, I went back to "the Lord is my shepherd, I shall not want." I repeated those words over and over again until I was too sleepy to say them any longer, and then I asked my shepherd to save my husband and please not let Samaria's baby keep my family apart.

Chapter 25

Samaria

Everything was working my nerves. I listened to Omar go on for a few more minutes. When he was done, I hung up the phone. First there was Greg, and now there was Omar making me feel like trash they wanted to sweep away.

Omar continued to give me heat for the media fiasco around Mekhi's current public image issues. He might have just been doing his job, but I felt Omar took every opportunity he could to insert a nasty dig. Then he had very specific instructions on how I was to approach Mekhi's fans and followers on the Internet. I had been doing an amazing job up until now, and I felt like I knew the people better, but he was the spin doctor. He was on UMC's payroll, so I listened like a good little unpaid employee and did what he said.

I spent most of the afternoon on Twitter and Facebook trying to renew the interest in Benxi's album by using material Omar e-mailed to me. There were pictures from the recent video shoot for one of the songs. Most of them were juiced about having the opportunity to see Benxi in makeup and on the costume set and at lunch. *For heaven's sake*, I thought. Groupies. Some people were still making comments and asking questions about Mekhi being in a crack house, but it was quickly becoming yesterday's news.

As if the *Coincidence God* were standing over my shoulder, my phone rang, and it was my mother. I started to ignore it, follow the command I'd gotten from Mekhi, but she was my mother. I couldn't not take any of her calls.

"It's a good thing you answered this time. I was about to get a ride up to that fancy house and snatch you out," my mother said.

I sighed hard and heavy. "Really, Ma, and what reason would you have to snatch me? It seems if anybody needs to have themselves snatched and straightened out, it would be you."

"I'm the parent. You the child."

I rolled my eyes. I'd been hearing that my entire life. It did not justify her behavior. "I'm not always sure," I replied.

"Look, I was just trying to check on my grandbaby and find out about the wedding. Ebony told me y'all moved it up, and you not getting married in America."

"I'm getting married in Puerto Rico in three weeks. Mekhi has to go there to shoot a music video, and I'm going with him."

"I thought you had to stay in the country."

"Puerto Rico is a U.S. territory. I can go there."

"I thought pregnant women didn't get on airplanes."

"Pregnant women fly all the time. As long as my doctor okays it, I'm going," I said. "It's a short flight."

"Well, as long as you don't mess around and have a foreign baby," she said. "This the best country. Why you think all them Mexicans come over the border?"

I had no words. "I'll make sure not to cut it too close." That was the best I could do.

My mother got quiet, which meant she wanted something. I knew it could not possibly be money. I wasn't going to ask, but I figured I'd cut her off at the pass by letting her know how much I disapproved of her new habit. "Mama, you really need to go to rehab. Crack is nothing to play with."

"No, so why ya man giving it to me?"

I swallowed.

"What's Mekhi up to?" she asked.

"He's trying to keep you off the streets so you don't get arrested or kill yourself."

"Well, he gonna have to give me some more to do that."

I dropped my head back. *God, please give me strength.*

"Wang being stingy."

"It's crack. Do you expect them to just give you a bunch of it?" I felt tears welling up in my eyes. This wasn't right. "Mama, please, don't you want some help? I'm having a baby. You're going to be a grandmother. You don't want your grandbaby to have a crackhead—"

I heard the dial tone.

Let me handle it, Mekhi had insisted. Was this what he called handling it? My mother was sick. She needed help not drugs. I was selfish, but not as selfish as she was. There was no way I was going to let him feed her this poison just so we had her testimony for my trial. The price was too high, and it was wrong. I was trying to live right. I couldn't expect God to bless me when I was doing stuff like this.

The doorbell rang, and I opened it to a certified letter. The *Coincidence God* again. It was paperwork from Hightower, and it included my court summons. He'd called and given me a heads-up. Jury selection was starting in six weeks, earlier than he'd thought it would happen. The anticipated start date of my trial was a week after. In seven weeks I would be in court. Mekhi and I would be getting married just in time for me to be a married, pregnant defendant. Hightower said that would look better, but the timing was eerie. How had Mekhi known to move the wedding up? Instinct? I sighed. It didn't even matter. In seven weeks, my fate would be in the hands of Hightower, a judge, and twelve strangers. I'd have to see Nadine, the nasty undercover GBI agent who stung me, my coworkers, the media, and God knew who else. Tears streamed down my face. I closed the door and leaned against it.

"God," I looked upward, "is there any way I can get out of this? I'm so scared."

I cried some more, sank down to my knees, rubbed my belly, and continued to sob. If only I thought about the consequences when I was stealing those pills I wouldn't be in this situation now. I had been so reckless with my life. I'd gambled with it, and now I was going to pay. And it wasn't just me who had to pay; so did my baby. My precious, innocent baby deserved better than a mother who was locked up.

I groaned from the pain in my soul. I whispered, "I'm sorry, little baby." Then I felt it, a tapping on my belly from the inside. My breath caught. My heart stopped. I'd had fluttering and tickling feelings, but I'd never had an actual kicking feeling. I rubbed my belly some more. More kicking. "Oh God!" This is what it felt like? It was incredible.

"Hey in there, little baby." I raised my hand to wipe the tears from my eyes. I rubbed my belly some more. "Are you trying to tell Mama to stop all that crying?" I felt another kick. I couldn't believe my baby was talking to me. I sat there on the floor for a few minutes, enjoying kick after kick. I cried and laughed, but mostly I felt like everything was going to work out.

Chapter 26

Mekhi

The situation with Samaria was messed up. That's basically what the meeting after the meeting with the attorney had concluded. Bernard Hightower and I had a "Let's keep it one hundred, lay it on the line, tell it like it is, no lawyer bull crap, tell me the real deal." lunch and the man admitted he was pretty sure Samaria was going to have to do some time.

"The GBI wants to make examples out of all the nurses who were arrested. Apparently hospital drug thefts are up, and these cases were highly publicized as a deterrent. The conclusion has to be jail for each and every one of the women for it to work."

I fought to remain composed. "So you're telling me I can't throw money at this problem and make it go away." I'd thrown a whole heap of cash in this brother's bank account.

Hightower squinted like he wasn't sure what I was asking, but then thought he might. "No, you can't. Money can't fix this. I sent Samaria a copy of the court docket. You should get it in the mail today. We have a tough judge. Kinchen. He's fairly young. Early forties. He's trying to make a name for himself. He's being tough on everything from crime to immigration to traffic court."

I placed my elbow on the table and clenched a fist. "Does he have a family?"

Hightower squinted again. It was that same Negro-what-you-thinking-about type of look he'd just given me. "Of course, but—"

I opened my palm to halt him. "Don't trip, man. I'm not about to put out a hit. I'm just trying to know who the man is that's got my life in his hands."

Hightower sat back, and so did I. He continued to talk like he needed to convince me that he had been worth the money I gave him, but I could care less about that. He was courtroom eye candy. I was going to have to pay somebody to show up and yak lawyer-speak, and he was just as good as any other suited-up monkey. I'd already left him and his failure to deliver behind. The wheels in my head were turning. I had to come up with a plan. I nodded like I was listening to Hightower and reached for my drink, but I hadn't heard a word he'd said. You don't tell somebody like me that money won't fix it. Money fixes everything. It's timing that messes you up.

I left Hightower's office and jumped in my car. *Timing.* I couldn't shake the thought. We wouldn't even be in this mess if mine were better. If I'd done better, worked faster with getting information, we wouldn't have this mess.

Samaria had asked him to look into the suspicious nurse she'd been working with, and his boy, Rufus, part-time bondsman, part-time private investigator, part-time bodyguard, full-time whatever the heck he needed a brother to do, had found out the nurse was no ordinary nurse. She was with the GBI, but Mekhi got that call too late. Two minutes too late, because when he called Samaria to let her know what was going down, the call dropped. She stepped off the elevator to handcuffs.

I banged my fist on the steering wheel and cursed. Two minutes late. But even if Samaria wasn't lucky, I was. I'd evaded the police for every criminal thing I'd ever done, which included stealing everything from cars to clothing and swinging a little "X" to rich college boys. I'd even run an illegal gambling circle for a while. I, Mekhi Johnson, had risen from the stank of the worst housing project in Atlanta completely unblemished and with a spotless record; even my FICO score was good. Some would call me lucky, but I didn't think of it as luck. Luck was for suckers who didn't know how to plan. I was a doer—a beast. I made the thing happen; like signing Benxi. No way should a low-rent, unfunded label like mine have picked up the biggest, hottest R&B singer in the business, but I had. A miracle, *VIBE* magazine called it. They were right. I was in the business of making miracles happen, and I was going to make this one happen for my woman.

I pulled my car over to the shoulder of the road and placed a phone call. When I got an answer on the other end I said, "Rufus, I have a job for you. I need you to check out a judge."

Chapter 27

Greg

Every time I thought about Samaria carrying my baby my heart stopped. I had been certain it wasn't mine. I'd assumed with all the lying she was doing that she had to be sleeping with other men. The news reporters said Mekhi Johnson was a longtime boyfriend, so she'd been kicking it with both of us. I tried to be sure of that. But what if she wasn't? What if I had had a fertile month?

Angelina wasn't going to take me back until after Samaria's baby was born, and that was too long to wait. As angry as she was, she could fall out of love with me. I couldn't risk it. Besides, I wanted my life back. The fast-food meals thing had gotten old. Doing my own laundry had gotten old. The no-sex thing had definitely gotten old. I needed my wife. I wanted my lover. I wanted everything that I'd lost.

I checked my watch and reached for my Starbucks cup. Over the lid I saw my attorney, Philip Madden, enter the store, place an order, and beeline for the table I was hunched over.

We fist bumped like we always did when we weren't in a formal setting, and Philip claimed a chair. "You look like crap."

"Thanks, I actually feel worse than I look."

Philip and I had both gone to Morehouse and both pledged Omega Psi Phi. I'd known him more than twenty years, and aside from being a great lawyer, he tended to be a good friend when I needed one.

"I've got drama." I emptied my cup and tossed it into a nearby receptacle.

"Angelina want more money?"

"No. Angelina is wonderful. Angelina is a perfectly sane woman who I can't believe I've been stupid enough to mess up on," I continued. "As a matter of fact, Angelina's pregnant."

Philip threw a thumbs-up and smiled. "Hey, now, that's great. It's yours, right?"

"What, you got jokes this morning? Of course, it's mine."

Philip punched me in the shoulder. "I'm teasing. Old dude still got it."

"Yeah, but I don't have her."

Philip frowned. "She wants to move forward with the divorce?"

"There's a complication." I paused while the clerk delivered Philip's coffee. "You can't tell anybody this."

"Come on, man, you know me better than that," Philip smirked. "I'm your lawyer first."

"Yeah, but this is almost too good to keep."

Philip removed the lid from his coffee, blew on it a bit, and took a sip. "I've heard it all."

"Oh, yeah? What about prestigious neurosurgeon becomes a single father while his baby mama goes to prison for drugs?" I could tell my boy was dumbfounded. He didn't say a word. "I know, not a good look, and definitely not the look I wanted at this age."

"Dude," Philip laughed. It was one of those I-don't-mean-to-laugh-but-I-can't-stop roars. Philip knew about Samaria, because I filled him in on the details of why Angelina and I were getting divorced. He chuckled a few more times and shook his head. I couldn't even be annoyed with him; because it was so bad it was almost funny. "Dang, man, not pregnant."

I sighed. "There's hope. It might not be mine." I covered my face with both my hands, took a deep breath, and dropped my hands in my lap. "Might not."

Philip raised an eyebrow. I knew my might wasn't mighty.

"Angelina won't consider taking me back until we know for sure, and even then, she might not. If it's mine and Samaria goes to prison, I'll have to make arrangements for the baby until she gets out."

Philip whistled low and hard. "I didn't even think about that. You're right. You've got drama."

"I've got drama, but I'm going to fix what I can. First off, I want you to pull back the divorce papers."

Philip raised his coffee cup again. "I can try, but it's been a minute. Depending on the judge, they might be signed and already in the mail."

"Well, do what you do and let me know," I said. "The other thing is, if this is my baby, what do I do? What are my rights? Is she going to bankrupt me? You know she's a gold digger."

Philip threw his hands up. "Greg, let me give you some advice as a friend. Lawyer hat off. Take one day at a time, brother. Wait until you're sure it's yours."

I let out a deep breath. "You're right, but that's hard to do, Phil. I mean, I'm out of my house. My wife is not being my wife if you know what I mean."

We sat in silence for a minute while Philip finished his coffee. "I know what you mean, but you're strong. Men don't act like boys about sex. Go to the gym."

I smirked. "That's easy for you to say."

A beat of silence passed, and then Philip eyed me curiously. "You back in church? I mean, are you praying about all this mess? Praying for Angelina and Samaria?"

If I had more coffee I would have spit it across the room. "Praying for Samaria?"

Phillip nodded. "She might be carrying your baby, man. You best be praying she's not as psycho as you make her out to be or you could have a crazy kid."

My shoulders slumped. "Thanks, Phil, just what I needed to hear."

"Look, Greg, man, you got more than drama. You got the devil riding your back, and the only way you're going to get him off is with prayer. Now, I know you don't do the 'church thing,' as you like to call it, but you need to connect with God. That's your help. Not me. Not the law. I talked to Angelina a few months back. She loves you, dude. I can still hear it in her voice, but she wants more from you."

"What, so you a marriage counselor now?"

"You're offended because you know I'm right, and yes, I do some counseling in the marriage ministry at my church." Phillip stood. "Get yourself together. Stop trippin' on God. He's going to get you on your knees one way or another. Trust me, I know, and you know I know."

"Is that some new Christian cliché?"

Philip looked perplexed.

"God will get you on your knees one way or another. My mother said the same thing."

Philip poked his lips out and shook his head. "No, brother, just the truth. It's the way He has to work it out sometimes, especially with those hard-to-crack cases like you."

I chuckled. I couldn't dispute Philip's understanding of God's ways. Cancer had almost taken his life a few years back, so if anyone could push the "Trust God" envelope with me, it was him. He stood and tossed his cup in the trash.

"Think about what I'm saying, man."

I agreed I would, and Philip left. I continued to mull over his message and others I had recently heard. *Get right with God, connect with God, choose life.* Good God almighty. Was that all anyone had to say these days? How do I get right with God in the middle of drama? I had no idea, but I did know I needed another shot of espresso to deal with what I was about to try to get right. I looked at the time on my phone. I figured I had ten more minutes until my next meeting, but before I could stand to my feet, Samaria entered the coffee shop, spotted me, and was on her way to the table.

Chapter 28

Samaria

Greg was already here. I hadn't expected him to be early. As a married lover, his habit was to slip in and out. Time was limited, so he usually arrived on the dot for our meetings. I was disappointed. I thought I could sit, have a cup of tea, and calm my nerves before our chat.

He stood, pulled out the chair for me, and I slipped in. Greg was looking good. I could tell he was a little tired, but the two-day-old beard was sexy. In this light, his hazel eyes were more than a little seductive. I didn't want his baby, but Lord, those were some high quality genes.

"Thanks for coming," he said.

"I'm glad you called. I didn't expect to hear from you so quickly," I replied. That wasn't true. I figured he and Angelina would have it out and he'd call, just as he had. Plan C had worked.

He cupped his hands on the table. "So, how have you been? How's the pregnancy going?"

I chuckled and removed the dark sunglasses I'd been wearing. The paparazzi followed me sometimes. They liked talking up my despair over my pending prison term, but I was alone today. I was sure of it, so I felt comfortable discarding my disguise for a few minutes. I didn't know Greg well, but I knew him some. The look in his eyes said he wanted something. "You don't have to make small talk. What do you want?"

He leaned forward, and I saw his chest heave up and down from the hard sigh I heard before he spoke. "I want to know a couple of things. Why do you think this is my baby? Why if you thought it was my baby you couldn't just pin it on your man? And why did you go to see Angelina? In particular, I want to know the answer to that last one."

"The last question is the easiest. You wouldn't talk to me." My voice was as cool sheet of ice. Greg swallowed. I knew it was regret over being so nasty that day in his office. His regret gave me a surge of satisfaction. I continued. "In all honesty, I can't say I thought she'd tell you she saw me," I lied. "I told her it wasn't your baby. I swore to her it wasn't, so if she didn't believe me and you fessed up, then she punked you."

"Angelina doesn't play games."

I giggled sarcastically. "All women play games when they're desperate." I didn't blink. I could tell by the way he was squeezing his fingers that he wanted to put his hands around my throat.

"How far along are you?"

"I'm twenty weeks." I knew what he wanted to know, so I went ahead and gave him his answers. "The window of opportunity on this pregnancy had two men climbing in it. You the week before I was arrested, and Mekhi after I got out of jail. It's too close. I can't call it, but I am hoping it's Mekhi's."

"Did you use protection with him?"

"Yes."

Greg banged a fist on the table. "And I don't suppose he broke a condom."

"No."

"You aren't . . . weren't on the pill or something?"

"No."

Greg's head dropped back. "How irresponsible is that?"

"Condoms are a very effective form of birth control. You thought they were good enough at the time."

He leaned forward again. Our eyes caught, and I couldn't help but have a flashback to the last time. I could tell Greg did the same because his eyes got a warm cast. Angelina had moved. I was pretty sure without him, so they were still separated, which meant he probably wasn't getting any. I laughed at the thought, because he loved him some sex.

"What could possibly be funny?" Greg asked. Bitterness laced the question.

I shook my head. "Nothing. I need to know if you'll take the baby if it's yours. Seriously, I might be going to prison. I have to plan."

"What am I going to do with a baby?"

"Hire a good nanny and keep it until I get out."

"Don't you have somebody who can take care of it for you? I can pay for the childcare and stuff, but I can't have a baby. Angelina . . . She won't take me back if that's my baby, so she can't know if it is."

So, they were definitely still separated, and now I knew why he'd called. He was plotting a cover-up. "I really don't have anybody. I mean, I have a cousin, but she has four kids already." I thought about Ebony, I'd thought about her a lot lately, but she and her family were already on top of each other. She had her hands full. They'd recently taken in one of her husband's nephews. That boy was not well. Killing neighborhood pets, acting out in school, getting arrested—no way. "She can't do it."

"She could do it if I paid her enough."

"I'm telling you she's a no. I don't have family like that. You'd have to take him."

Greg raised his head. I saw the first glimmer of light in his eyes. "Him?"

I put a hand up to stop his burgeoning pride. "I'm not sure yet."

Greg let out a breath and scowled. A chill of emptiness cut through me, removing the sense that he'd been excited about the idea that he was having a son.

He hesitated a bit before asking. "When will you know the sex?"

"I'm not sure. I don't think I want to know until I deliver."

He seemed annoyed by my statement. I wondered if it was possible that the sex of the baby would play a factor in whether he was willing to take it. He and Angelina had lost a daughter. Was he afraid of having another girl? I wondered.

"It's ridiculous for you not to know the sex."

"Maybe it is. But it's my decision, and I just don't want to know right now."

"Well, I don't have the luxury of time. I've got to know," he said. "I've got to know if it's my baby, and I can't wait for you to deliver. I need you to take a DNA test."

Chapter 29

Greg

Samaria looked at me like I was out of my mind for suggesting she take an in utero paternity test. "It would the solve problem," I said.

"I'm not doing that."

"Why not?"

"There are risks."

"You're a healthy twenty-nine year old. There are no risks."

"I could go into preterm labor."

"You won't." I slammed a fist on the table. Our words were like tennis balls being batted across a net. I was tired of the banter with her. "You won't. You'll be fine." I said it like I was an expert. I actually knew very little about paternity tests.

Samaria put her hands over her mouth, and then smoothed her hair. She was considering it. I could tell, but she was scared. "You can't be sure I won't go into labor."

"I'll pay for you to take the test."

She reached for her sunglasses and stood. I grabbed her arm. "Sit down."

"I'm not going to talk about this."

I finally snapped. "Yes, you are!" Fear filled her eyes. She looked around like she was making sure the place hadn't emptied out and she had backup if I went berserk. Then she eased back into her chair. I released my grip on her arm. "You like money. I'll give you $15,000 to take the test."

She laughed. "What makes you think I need a measly $15,000?"

"You'll need a whole lot more than that if it's not Mr. Music's baby, and he finds out you're a scheming liar."

A vein popped out on her forehead. She was thinking hard about that. "If it's not his baby, I'll get it from you in child support," she said.

"You can't get child support if you don't have a child." Samaria's eyes widened. Terror. Just the reaction I was looking for. "If I lose my family over this and you go to jail, I'm keeping the baby." The ice water I felt running through my veins came out in my tone. "I'll make sure you never see it when you get out. I'm thinking your prison record will help with that."

Her eyes narrowed. "You can't be serious."

"I want you to have the DNA test. It can't wait." I reached into my pocket and pulled out a card. "This is the best lab in the city. I've already been there to check it out. We could know in two days."

She hesitated, but then took the card. She looked at it for a minute and raised her eyes to meet mine. "Greg, this test isn't a good idea."

"I'm a doctor. I researched it. They do them every day."

She shook her head. "You can't take my baby."

"I don't want your baby. I want my wife back." I felt a tiny bit guilty, but then reminded myself that I wouldn't even be in this mess if she hadn't tracked down Angelina. She didn't deserve mercy. I had to play hardball with a schemer like her. "Give me your bank account number. I'll put the money in as soon as you schedule it, but you have to do it immediately. It's almost too late for you to have it."

"What if I don't do this?"

"I'm going to be pissed, and you don't want that."

She didn't say anything, but I knew she was thinking—hard—on her next words. "I want twenty-five."

I blinked a few times. "Are you insane? Benxi's not
singing for me."

"You've got a whole lot more than $25,000, Greg.
If you want me to do this, you're going to have to pay
for it, especially now that you've threatened me. I may
need it to fight you in court." I could tell she wasn't
really as confident as she was coming across, but we
both wanted something, so I had to negotiate with her.
Besides, I knew she wasn't going to do squat for fifteen
thousand. I was expecting her to go up.

"Look," she continued, "if it's not your baby, I'll give
you your money back."

I still didn't respond.

"If you want, I'll sign a contract agreeing to give it
back to you."

I raised my hand and scratched my chin. We didn't
have time for all that and I didn't even want Philip to
know I was doing this. "Mr. Music Producer, he thinks
it's his kid?"

"Of course."

"Well, then, we don't need a contract."

She raised an eyebrow, opened her handbag, and
removed a checkbook.

"If you screw me, I'll make sure he knows about the
test, and I'll throw it out there that maybe there's a
third guy who should be giving up some blood or sa-
liva."

"You wouldn't dare," she hissed.

"For $25,000, I wouldn't not dare," I said. "Besides,
I'd love nothing more than to get even with you."

With force fueled by anger, Samaria made a mess of the first two deposit slips as she tried to rip them from her bankbook. "I love how you blame me for your problems. You are such an idiot that you can't even see that I'm not really your issue. If you would take the time to focus on yourself, you'd figure out what your wife wants."

I noticed we had gotten the attention of the people at the tables around us, so I swallowed my rebuke. "Don't mess with me, Samaria." The warning in my voice matched the fire in her eyes. "I'm not the nice guy you think I am."

She threw her hair over her shoulder and chuckled bitterly. "You know, I don't actually happen to think you're a nice guy." She tossed the slip of paper in my direction.

"Well, good. That means we understand each other." I slid her deposit slip in the pocket of my shirt. "Let me know when it's scheduled." I stood and walked out of Starbucks.

Chapter 30

Samaria

I decided to let Greg sweat it out. I was getting married, and that was happening before I put myself through the physical discomfort of an in utero paternity test. I could have cramping and fluid leaks after. I also needed to rest for at least twenty-four hours, and sex was out of the question for a couple of days. It would be easier to deal with all that when I got back, because I knew Mekhi was flying to New York the day after we returned for a meeting with the execs from UMC. The timing of that couldn't be more perfect.

I also wasn't going to let Greg run my life. Even though I'd consented to do the test, and true, I was getting very close to the deadline for being able to have it, it was still my body. This was *my* baby. I didn't care that Greg's life was in the toilet, because it was a toilet he'd filled with his own crap. I hated that Angelina was hurt, but Greg—I didn't care if that troll ever saw sunlight again. Threatening to take a baby he didn't want was lower than I ever would have thought he'd stoop. The things men did to protect a marriage they hadn't had the foresight to care about beforehand. It amazed me.

I smoothed the front of my dress and stepped through the fitting room door. Tanisha's face lit up. "Oh my God, you look amazing."

Ebony came from the back of the store, stopped, and gasped. "Sam, you're beautiful!"

I took a few steps, stood in front of the mirror, and took in my reflection. I had been a late bloomer, but my belly had popped out, literally overnight, and announced to the entire world that I was pregnant. But today, I didn't care what the world was thinking. I was wearing my wedding dress. I was getting married, and I was marrying a man I actually wanted to be with.

I turned a bit to get a better view of the side, and the room spun. I stepped back and leaned against a rack. I heard Tanisha's and Ebony's voices calling my name, asking me if I was okay. I continued to lean. I felt hands on my arms, and I was pushed down into a chair.

"My dress," I whispered. I was a little off, but I was coherent enough to know I didn't want it damaged.

"Dang, the dress," Ebony said. "Are you okay?"

I came out of the spin and accepted the glass of water the shop owner offered me. "I just got a little dizzy."

"It's the stress," Tanisha said. "All brides get to a point where they feel overwhelmed. With all the buzz on Twitter and Facebook about you being pregnant and going to court I know you're stressed."

Ebony nodded at Tanisha's words. "Yeah, that's it. Plus, you know, it's so hot out today. You need to go home and put your feet up for the rest of this week. Don't move until the second we get on the plane."

I agreed. I was tired, but it wasn't wedding stress. If anything was making me dizzy it was the whirlwind of drama I'd gotten myself caught in. "I'm better, so let's finish this." Ebony and Tanisha helped me to my feet, and I took a few steps to get to the mirror again.

The seamstress ran to us with her pin box. "We're going to hurry and get you out of here." She began pulling and pinning. "Not much to do. This is a perfect fit."

Within fifteen minutes we were out of the shop and on the street. The dress would be sent directly to the hotel in Puerto Rico.

"I think my assistant and I can handle the rest of the list," Tanisha said. "You're fitted; you have your jewelry and shoes. That's the most important thing."

John, the driver and undercover bodyguard Mekhi had hired to chauffer me, opened the car door, and I stepped in. "I trust you with the details, Tanisha."

"Get some rest," she and Ebony both said, and we all laughed a little.

I promised I would, and John pulled away from the curb.

Puerto Rico was breathtaking. White sandy beaches, crystalline blue water, majestic palm trees, gorgeous, colorful flowers, and lush greenery everywhere. I'd only been out of the United States once, when I'd gone to the Bahamas many years ago on a gambling ship with a man I had been dating. It was raining, and I was seasick, so the trip was an absolute disaster. This, however, was paradise.

Tanisha had arranged for us to stay at an exclusive resort in the cliffs with private villas that included twenty-four-hour butler service. The place had a Miami swag type of feel—very modern, very posh, very Latin, and very expensive. It was perfect for the wedding, and because of the video shoot, we billed a lot of the expenses to UMC.

"Are you almost done?" My patience was wearing thin. The makeup artist and hair stylist had been hovering over me for nearly an hour. Their collective body heat was making me hot. The stylists, the same chicks who'd been hired to do Benxi and the dancers for the video shoot, leaned back and in unison sang, "Perfection." The photographer took a few pictures. When he was done, the women stepped out of the view of the mirror and I looked at myself. I had to agree. I looked perfect. Like a royal princess.

"Mekhi's going to know he made the right choice," makeup chick said.

"No doubt, everybody will know that," the hairstylist added. "Even if they don't wanna know."

I rolled my neck. No, this hired help did not . . . I gave her the evil eye. "What is that supposed to mean?"

She threw her hands up. "Oh, no, my bad. I'm just saying your future hubby is a hottie. You know that. Single ladies hate to see the good ones get snatched up. That's all. I didn't mean no disrespect. I really think you're lucky."

Her explanation was plausible, but then I caught a look they exchanged and wondered for a second if they knew something about Benxi and Mekhi. Perspiration dotted my upper lip. Was I being made a fool of? Was it possible he was still sleeping with her? I reached for a tissue and dabbed at my sweat. I let out a long breath and took a few deep ones. Then I rolled my eyes at the twin idiots and said, "I'd like to be alone."

They gathered their cell phones and water bottles and left. The photographer took a few more pictures and followed them out.

I stood. *Mehki sleeping with Benxi*, I thought. *No.* Mekhi wasn't like that. He loved me. I was the sneaky one. *He's a man*, the voice in my head said. Before I could continue the argument I heard a knock at the door, and then Ebony's face appeared.

"I know you're nervous." She entered the room. "I thought I'd come pray with you, especially since you done got saved, and I know I won't be wasting my breath."

I cracked a smile and returned to a seat they'd transformed into a throne for my special day. Tanisha's idea.

"You look amazing." Ebony reached for my hands and squeezed them. "Your parents aren't here, so I'm representing for them." Ebony's eyes became wet. "I'm so proud of you."

I blinked back tears. "Proud?"

"Sammie, you were a mess. Running around with married men and scheming, trippin' on history with Mekhi, but you finally decided to follow your heart. You're trusting God, and that's the best decision you ever could make."

I smiled again, but this time, my lips trembled from nervousness. "I'm trying."

"You're succeeding," she said.

"But, Ebony, how do you trust them? How do you know a man's got your back? How do you know he's not cheating?"

Ebony paused and twisted her face like she was thinking about it. "You just let go and trust the love you have. You can't worry about a man twenty-four. You just can't do that. And then you have to weigh the pros and cons, because we all mess up. Does the good outweigh the bad? That's what you gotta do when it's tight, when things aren't good. 'Cause trust, I know about things not being good, but you can't give up on what you have."

I dropped my head back. "Girl, I don't know if I'm woman enough for all that."

Ebony sucked her teeth. "You trippin'. Mekhi is the truth. He's here for you in the worst possible situation. I mean, I know you're pregnant, but what does that mean to men these days? It means they got a bill to pay, not that they gotta get married. Not only are you pregnant, but you know you done caught a case."

I couldn't help but laugh. The grimace on Ebony's face said a mouthful about how messed up I was. She laughed with me. We both reached for tissues and dotted the corners of our carefully airbrushed eyes.

"I don't know." I sighed again and shook my head. I was scared, and I wasn't even sure what I was afraid of. Could I really still be that eighteen-year-old girl who Mekhi abandoned and left in jail? Was it our past? Or was it the fact that I was pregnant and didn't know if he was the father? Was it the future? Was it all of it?

"Sammie, relax. Stop being afraid of life. You can't control it anyway, boo. God has control."

I nodded. She was right. *God was in control. God was in control. God was in control.* I chanted that in my mind. It was the Christian mantra, and I needed to remember it.

"You have five minutes to be downstairs. Tanisha is not going to have a late bride on her watch, so let's lift up this day and this marriage." Ebony smiled and took my hands. We closed our eyes and she prayed.

Chapter 31

Samaria

I was doing it. I was going to walk down the aisle and marry this man when I wasn't even sure if I was carrying his baby, and I wasn't sure if he was sleeping with the heifer glaring at me from the third row, and I wasn't sure if I was going to prison. *This* didn't make sense, not even to me, and it was my drama.

We had decided not to do the "Wedding March," and since I really didn't have anyone to give me away, I decided to walk down the aisle by myself. The intro to "Love" came over the speaker, and the live voice of Musiq Soulchild followed it. The singer was on a small stage set up next to the band. I wanted to cry. Mekhi knew he was my favorite of all time.

Tanisha handed me my bouquet. "It's showtime." She pulled my veil over my face, fanned out my train, and nudged me forward.

The ceremony decor was gorgeous. The vision Tanisha had tried to recount to me hundreds of times was crystal clear now. I walked barefoot on a blanket of pink and yellow rose petals. White silk organza blew in the breeze as I passed through each of three arched canopies in my fifty-foot journey to the altar. Tropical flowers of every kind were interlaced through a beautiful wooden gazebo where Mekhi, Ebony, Wang, and the minister waited for me.

It was early evening. The sun was still high, but even still, lights flashed as cameras from our photographer, *Essence, Jet,* and other magazines went on and off. Benxi's back was turned, but just as I reached her row, she looked at me. She didn't even try to smile, and her lack of effort offended me. Was she sleeping with my man? I hated that I had to ask myself that. I hated that I cared.

I fought to keep my lips parted—to keep showing my pearly whites as I finished the procession. I noted the empty seat where my mother should have been sitting. She'd chickened out on flying at the last minute and opted not to attend her only child's wedding. That saddened me. So many emotions coursed through me—anxiety, relief, regret, excitement, and fear, all of them at the same time.

I was five feet from the altar when I got a really good look at Mekhi. He was fine as fine could be in his white tux. Seeing him caused another surge of emotion to come over me. Mekhi winked, and I realized I loved him. I really, really loved this man, and not just for what he could do for me. I loved his heart, his soul, and his mind.

Who, including me, would have ever thought I'd be marrying anyone for anything other than what Mekhi was going to have, and that was money? But here I was completely surrendered to the one thing I swore I'd never give in to: *love.* The thought overwhelmed me, engulfed me like a tidal wave from the ocean. I felt like I was suffocating. I stopped walking. The minister frowned. Mekhi extended his hand. I tried to take another step, but I felt myself slip away.

Minutes had passed. How many, I didn't know.

"I'm okay." I fought to sit up. "It was the heat." Tanisha put a cold cloth on my forehead, and I pushed it back. "You'll ruin my makeup."

"Then drink this water." She practically poured it in my mouth. I felt strong arms around my waist. I hadn't realized I was leaning against Mekhi until I smelled his cologne. I turned to his face. "I'm sorry."

He chuckled. "Are you sure you wanna marry me?"

I looked into his chestnut-brown eyes; my mouth fell open from the sheer magnetism of them, and I nodded. "I'm positive. Let's finish before you come to your senses and change your mind."

He laughed again. Wang helped me to my feet. Mekhi stood and the minister began.

Mekhi wouldn't stop kissing me, and I didn't want him to let me go. We took a million pictures against the gorgeous greenery that made up the backdrop of the cliffs. Then we went down the hill for pictures on the beach. The patio where the reception for our thirty-five guests was held was unbelievably gorgeous. Tanisha's decorator had turned it into a bride's dream.

Our guests drank liquor, but Mekhi and I toasted with nonalcoholic champagne and ate decadent foods that we couldn't even name. Brian McKnight made an appearance, and he and Benxi sang, "Love Is," my all-time favorite ballad. Mekhi swept me on the dance floor, and we swayed to one Brian McKnight song after another. It was perfect. Everything was beautiful until I entered the ladies' room and overheard Benxi on the telephone.

"I gotta get a flight out of here." She was standing near one of the stalls. "This is too much. I mean, he actually married her."

I held my breath. I was afraid if I breathed she'd hear me.

"Girl, I don't think I can face them. Instead of singing to them, I should have been the one in the dress. I should have his ring." Benxi paused. I presumed the other caller was speaking. "I know, I know. I shoulda told him . . . But I'm sayin', I thought he knew." More silence on Benxi's end. "We was cool, and then this chick comes from left field or from jail. Yeah, yeah, and it's probably not even his baby."

The door to the restroom burst open and two hotel guests startled Benxi and me when they came in laughing.

"I gotta go." She ended the call and walked to the area where I had been standing. Her eyes were wet with freshly shed tears.

"Samaria." I could tell she was shocked to see me. She looked from side to side like she was trying to figure out how long I'd been standing there. It was an awkward moment. She wanted my man. I wanted to cuss her out. I was *his* wife. *She* was his business. Our positions put us both in check. "I'm sorry I didn't get a chance to tell you how great you look. The ceremony was incredible," Benxi said, the quality of her voice high with nervousness.

"Thanks. I really enjoyed the song. I appreciate you staying after the video shoot and singing for us." I could lie just as good as she could.

She shrugged. "Anything for Mekhi." Her eyes got big. "I mean, and you, of course. Anything for love."

I nodded. "Well, I need to use the restroom."

"Oh, yeah . . . That's what this spot is for." Benxi walked toward one of the mirrors and played with her hair.

That and calling our friends, I thought. I swept past her and walked down to one of the larger, handicapped stalls to gain more room.

"Samaria," she said, "tell Mekhi I'm going. You guys enjoy the rest of your party."

"I will," I replied. She pulled the door and disappeared behind it. I walked into the stall, closed it, and leaned back against the door. She was not going to go away easily. I knew that look in her eyes. I'd seen it in mine just this morning. She wasn't in lust with Mekhi. She was in love, and that was a problem our marriage wasn't going to solve.

Chapter 32

Mekhi

"I've got a report."

I sat up and glanced at Samaria's sleeping form. I was glad the low beep of my phone hadn't awakened her. "Hold on," I whispered. I stood, left the bedroom, and made quiet steps out to the balcony of our suite. "Ruf, go ahead."

"Sorry, I know it's early, and you honeymooning, but you said not to waste a second," Rufus said.

"No, it's cool." I slipped into a chair.

"Look, I don't have much, but I've done all the digging I can do. The judge is clean. No extravagant living, no gambling debts, no drugs. Dude don't even have a woman he jumping off."

I let out a breath. This wasn't what I wanted to hear.

"The wife is a problem for him. She's the second misses. The first died of cancer eight years ago. He and wifey number two have been married for five years. She's a drunk. She spends more than half the year in the Turks and Caicos bingeing. She's there now. He's pretty much raising his kid by himself."

"One child."

"A teenage daughter. I'm e-mailing you the file with the pictures. She's a Facebook and Twitter junkie. I've been reading her page for a week trying to get some leads on some stuff, but she don't talk about nothing but her Sweet Sixteen party and Benxi."

"Benxi?"

"Yeah, this girl is the ultimate fan. Makes videos of herself singing Benxi's songs and everything."

"They all love Benxi."

"Well, I'm sorry, boss. I really got nothing. I'm not sure what you looking for. I assume leverage. I'll keep digging, but he looks like the last Boy Scout."

"Thanks, Ruf. Stay on it." I ended the phone call just as Samaria pulled the sliding glass door open.

She came toward me. I pulled her into my lap. The gentle breeze from the ocean swept her hair off her shoulders. Like the milk chocolate color it was, her makeup-free skin looked good enough to eat. My nostrils flared when the coconut body lotion she wore drifted into my nostrils. She looked and smelled incredible. She had an aura that I assumed had to be the glow pregnant women got. Our baby was making her look better and better by the month. I had been feeling like a lucky man, until I got that phone call.

"I felt you get of out bed." She wiggled around like she and her newly bulging belly were trying to get comfortable.

"Business." That one word always sufficed for my disruptive phone calls.

"On our honeymoon and at this hour?" She wrapped her arms around my neck.

"You don't think I'm creeping, do you?" I was teasing, but the light left her eyes.

"I don't think about that at all, Mekhi."

"That doesn't answer the question of trust."

"What are you talking about? I just said I don't think about that."

"That's what I mean. You don't think about us at a level that's deep enough to wonder about that. Not that I can tell. Every time I try to get you to open up to me, you shut down and give me the 'let's deal with today.'"

She sighed. "How did we get here? I just asked you why you got out of bed."

"Sam, I want to know why we get to *stop* every time I try to talk to you. To this place where you shut down on me."

She didn't answer. She tried to rise up from my lap, but I stopped her. "All men are not the same. I'm not like your mama's boyfriends or even the busters who cheated on their wives with you. I'm not saying I'm perfect, but I need to know you believe in me."

"Mekhi, please, let's go back to bed. It's too early for us to be up."

"No, Sammie. I want to talk about your cracked heart, because it's eventually going to leak some poison into this marriage."

Samaria didn't respond.

I shook my head. "I love you, but sometimes I wonder."

"Wonder what?"

"Wonder if you love me." I held my breath, scared I'd see she didn't in her eyes, but when she spoke, they revealed nothing.

"That's ridiculous. I just married you."

I laughed. "Come on, girl, I'm not stupid. That doesn't mean you love me. Don't let me remind you how you passed out at the altar."

Samaria punched me playfully. "You wrong for that."

"But you still not answering my question. You haven't said it. I'm not sure if you've ever said it."

"Mekhi, you know how I feel."

I shook my head. That wasn't good enough. "I want to hear you say it."

"I just did."

"No, you didn't, but I'm putting you on notice. Work out whatever's got you twisted, Sammie. I want this marriage to be built on trust."

She stood. "I'm going back to bed." She let her gown fall off her shoulders and shimmed a little. "Join me." I didn't respond. She smirked annoyance and went back into the room.

I shook my head. She was trying not to think about us, and I was trying not to think about us. I slammed my hand down on the table because there's an *us*, and I wanted *us* to be the real deal.

"I'm not going to sweat it," I whispered, knowing full well it was not leaving my thoughts that easily. I loved that girl. Flaws and all. I wanted to believe I knew what was in her heart, that I could trust her with mine. But I didn't know. I just couldn't be sure.

I picked up my cell and swiped the screen. I tapped until I found the file I was looking for and watched the video clip from the filming we'd done. It was hot. The album was almost ready, and the project was early. I nodded. I was getting something right. The music—no problems. My professional life was tight, even with the mess Miss Jacobs caused with the drug bust, but the personal . . . I wasn't sure. The more I tried to take a hold of it, the more it felt like it was spiraling out of control.

Chapter 33

Samaria

I dreaded seeing Hartsfield Jackson Airport. It meant the honeymoon was over and my real life was crawling up my back. The paternity test was tomorrow, and I don't think I dreaded anything more, not even my prior stints in jail; and jail was pretty bad. I wasn't sure if it was the idea of the long needle they used for the procedure or the idea of the short time it took to get the results. What had I gotten myself into? I should have never pushed Greg, because he pushed back—hard. I don't know what made me think I could bring Angelina into this without there being repercussions. I'd underestimated him, big time.

Mekhi was sitting next to me, but he was asleep, mouth open, knocked out kinda sleeping. I shoved my e-reader in my handbag and closed the window shade. Sherri Lewis's new novel was going to have to wait. I had real-life drama to contend with, and no matter how much I wished things would have a storybook ending, I wasn't assured that would happen.

Greg had put the money in my bank account. I received a banking text message alert advising me of the deposit. He'd also given a DNA sample at one of the lab drop-off sites. He'd kept his end of the deal, but I still wasn't ready to keep mine. Mine was more difficult, more invasive, and no matter how stressed he was about his separation from Angelina, mine had more consequences.

Although Dr. Cotter had told me the test was pretty safe, she was clear that there were still risks. What if I was one of the women who cramped her way to preterm labor or worse, my placenta ruptured? Even though I never worked maternity when I was a nurse, I knew how dangerous placenta-related complications were. I'd convinced myself that the risks were the reason I didn't have a good feeling about this, but if I was honest, the results were really what had me scared.

I looked at Mekhi. I was no longer his girlfriend, his chick, his Samich-on-the-side as he liked to call me. I was his wife. He had to stick with me through thick and thin, but did he have to put up with a lie. *Truth.* That's what we said we'd give each other. I'd made the promise, but I hadn't kept it, because the truth was, I'd convinced myself he didn't need to know it. I'd convinced myself that he wouldn't benefit from knowing whose baby it was. If it wasn't his, it would just make him angry. But how far was I willing to take it? If the DNA test revealed that it wasn't his, did my new prayer become, "Lord, let it look like me?" Or "Lord, please don't let it have hazel eyes." Or "Lord, let it have my blood type." If it wasn't his baby, when did the truth come out? After I got out of jail, when the child was five, before college, or at the child's wedding? When did I tell it?

I could end all this foolishness if I just sat Mekhi down and told him the truth, but I was terrified he might not understand. I'd been lying since Dr. Cotter told me how far along I was. Mekhi had touched my belly and talked to his child every day. He'd attended doctor's visits, run out to the store for my ice-cream cravings. He'd lie in bed at night throwing out baby names. He'd done everything an excited father should do. He wouldn't understand, and he might never look at me the same. He might hate me for it. I couldn't bear that.

I groaned and threw my head back against the seat. The sudden movement woke Mekhi. His bloodshot eyes did a sweep of the cabin like he wasn't sure where he was. After about sixty seconds, he grabbed my hand and squeezed it. "Just a few more months to go." I was puzzled, and my expression had to show it. With whispery kisses, his lips met mine. "Just a few more months 'til you get that cake out of the oven." He backed away a bit and smiled. "I can't wait to meet 'em." He rubbed my belly. "I just had a dream. Dreamt it was a boy."

"Really?"

"Yeah, and he looked just like me."

I rolled my eyes. If I could have climbed out of the tiny window next to my seat, I would have jumped off this plane.

Chapter 34

Samaria

"Slide a little to the right," Dr. Cotter's lab tech said, and I did as I was told. "Don't be nervous. We do these all the time. Although you're a little young to have an amnio, the good news is that being young works to your advantage."

I smiled nervously. Dr. Cotter had told me that the reason for the amnio was never disclosed to staff. She had my record in a highly secure safe. She and the office manager were the only people with the key. I was the wife of a celebrity, so the confidentiality of my record was protected at a higher level than most. Even the most loyal staff could be swayed to give up copies from a medical record for the right price, and tabloids wrote hefty checks.

Dr. Cotter entered the room. Her yellow-framed glasses made her look like she was filming an episode of *Sesame Street* rather than wielding a needle for an amnio. "This won't take long. Most of the time is spent doing the scan to find the fluid. Extraction of the fluid takes less than thirty seconds," she said, washing her hands.

The ultrasound machine was already on. The tech removed a tube of gel from the table, pulled back my sheet, and rubbed it on my belly. I winced at her touch. I winced at the cold gel. I winced from my fear.

Dr. Cotter handled the transducer herself. She rolled it back and forth across my protruding belly for what seemed like forever. The more she rolled, the more anxious I became.

"How are you getting home?" she asked.

"I have a driver," I said, looking at the black and white screen.

"Still don't want to know the sex?"

I shook my head. "No, I, maybe next week after—" I looked at the lab tech who at this point was just watching. "Mekhi and I want to be surprised."

"Rare, but nice," she smiled. "How was the wedding?"

I knew she was trying to distract me. My body was tensing up every time she stopped and started again. "It was amazing. Really beautiful."

"I got married in Antigua." Dr. Cotter smiled again. "Fifteen years ago. Seems like yesterday."

I nodded.

"Okay, I've got the spot."

"The spot?" my voice rose an octave.

"Where the most amniotic fluid is and the furthest from the fetus."

The lab tech took control of the transducer, and Dr. Cotter stood and reached for the needle. "Remember, I said this was going to pinch a little."

Inhale, exhale.

Dr. Cotter looked at the monitor. "Try to relax. You're as tight as a drum."

Breathe.

Dr. Cotter positioned the needle. I closed my eyes. I felt her hands on my belly, then a prick on my flesh.

"Stop!" I yelled.

Dr. Cotter bolted upright.

I burst into tears. "I can't. I can't."

Dr. Cotter looked at her tech and said, "Give us a minute." The tech had turned as white as Casper the Ghost. She didn't hesitate to jet from the room.

"I can't. I just—I can't." I reached for a towel and tried to wipe the gel from my belly. "I can't do this."

Dr. Cotter seemed unmoved by my drama. She acted as if it was common for her to have patients screaming when they weren't in labor. She took the towel from my hand and wiped for me. Then she helped me sit up and told me to get dressed.

A few minutes later, I entered her office. Dr. Cotter had been standing, but she took a seat behind the desk. Her happy glasses were no longer on her face. They hung on a chain around her neck. I still hadn't stopped crying. "Samaria, please tell me what's going on."

"I don't think it's Mekhi's baby, and I'm terrified, because everything will be wrong if it's not. Everything!"

"But he already knows about the possibility of that. He's prepared for it."

"No," I shook my head. "He has no idea. I told you after the sonogram, but I never told him."

"But, how are—?"

I knew where she was going so I answered. "Mekhi's not the man giving the sample to the lab. It's the other man, the other potential father."

Dr. Cotter sat back and a drawn out "Oh" escaped her lips.

"Yes, oh." I choked back a sob. "I'm almost certain it's not Mekhi's. We used condoms, and me and the other man had a broken condom. What are the chances it's my husband's?"

Dr. Cotter nodded. "Slimmer than the other man's."

"Slimmer like as in zero chance?" I dropped my head in my hands. "Mekhi's going to be furious."

"Tell him, Samaria. You're really making this worse by not telling him now."

"He'll think I waited until after the wedding."

Dr. Cotter shrugged. "You did, but it doesn't matter now because the wedding is over. You have to move forward. Tell him before he finds out on his own."

I nodded. She was right. I had made a mess, and it was time to clean it up. "Thanks. Hearing it from another person . . ." I stalled. "I appreciate it."

"Let me know if I can help."

I thanked her again and stepped out of her office.

Tell him now. Her voice came back to me as I walked down the hall and left the office. *Tell him before he finds out.*

I walked out into the parking lot, spotted my driver sitting in the car, and walked to it. I felt a sharp pain low in my uterus. I doubled over for a moment and slowed my pace. I was moving too fast. Sometimes I think I forgot I was pregnant, probably because subconsciously, I wished I wasn't. That thought always made me feel guilty. It wasn't my baby's fault I didn't know who the father was. It was mine. I just needed to come up with a new plan, one that included the scenario where I was honest with my husband.

Chapter 35

Samaria

I had a plan. Mekhi came in from New York at 4:00 P.M. I'd meet his plane. We'd go to dinner and be home by seven. I'd serve up some welcome home lovin', and then, while he was still weak in the knees, I'd tell him. I was going to get this out before I lost my nerve, before I went one more day caught up in my lies and deceit. Before Greg found out I hadn't submitted my sample and did who knows what.

But the plan got slippery. Mekhi's flight was delayed. He wasn't getting back to Atlanta until almost 11:00 P.M. He had to be at the studio early. I'd have to wait. Greg had texted me three times. He wanted confirmation that I'd done the test. I ignored him. I wasn't having another conversation with him until I spoke to my husband. No matter what, both men were going to have to wait until this baby made it into the world to find out who the daddy was because on Monday, I would be officially twenty-four weeks pregnant. It would be too late for a paternity test.

I had to keep myself busy. The wedding DVD arrived by courier. I decided to take it to Ebony's house so I could watch it with her. I stopped for enough takeout to feed a small army, which Ebony had, and relaxed in her living room while she piled plates for both us. The kids were at school. Her husband, Tyrone, worked for Mekhi, doing what I had no idea, because I'd rarely seen him in the studio. They were friends from elementary school, so I think Mekhi just had him on the payroll so their family could eat. That was just like Mekhi. He was always looking out.

Ebony handed me a plate and plopped down in a chair next to me. "Girl, I'm so glad you called. I was hungry. Y'all got me spoiled in Puerto Rico. My food is not chef quality."

"Neither is my takeout," I chuckled. "I was dying to watch the video, and I know Mekhi is going to be home late. Besides, I needed to relax today. I'm still recovering from all the running I did before the wedding. I don't think my little somebody likes it," I said, looking down at my belly.

"Little somebody," Ebony waved a hand at me. "Girl, in this day and age you don't know the sex of a baby . . . That's crazy."

"Yeah, well, Mekhi and I are fine with waiting." I reached for my water and took a long sip.

"Mekhi ain't fine with jack. He said he wanna know and you don't, so don't go throwing 'we' on it."

I smirked. "You've been married long enough to know that 'we' means I."

Ebony raised her fist, and I bumped it. "You got that right, girl. You ain't been married but a minute and figured that one out."

We laughed, ate, talked about the wedding, her kids, her crazy nephew, and then got to the subject of my baby shower.

"When you wanna do it? Before or after the trial starts?"

I sighed. "I don't think I want one."

"Oh, come on, Sam. You can't deny me the chance to give my only cousin on my mama's side a baby shower."

"Ebony, I don't have any friends. Who's going to come?"

Ebony bit her lip. "Oh."

I put my fork down and sighed. "Girl, you just don't know. I've made such a mess out of my life." I shook my head and a river of tears streamed down my face.

Ebony rose from her seat to pat me on the back. "Sammie, we all make mistakes."

"I don't make mistakes," I choked. "A mistake would be bouncing a check. A mistake is dropping out of college or buying the wrong car. I make disasters. Huge messes that tear up my entire life. I've been so foolish."

"Sammie, a mistake is still a mistake, no matter how big or small. I know you scared about the trial, but I'm praying for you every day. My entire prayer group has you on the list. You have to trust God to make a way out of this for you."

I raised an elbow to the table and pressed my head against my fist. *God is in control, God is in control.* I'd already stopped believing that. I had to find a way to believe that again.

Ebony reached for my hand. "All this stress isn't good for the baby, Sammie."

I looked into my cousin's eyes. Her concern for me was all over her face. She didn't know it all. She was believing God, but she didn't have all the information.

"I know I used to be really hard on you when you was sleeping around for money, but you're not that girl anymore. You don't scheme and lie and cheat, and you're not hurting other women."

I thought about the money I'd taken from Greg and shook my head. "You've never done anything wrong in your life, so you don't know what I'm going through."

"I'm no angel."

"Yes, you are, compared to the devil!" I sobbed again.

"Samaria, let's pray about this," Ebony pulled my hand tighter.

"Praying is not going to help me!" I snatched my hand away. "You don't know what I've done."

Ebony's mouth fell open.

"You keep telling me that God is going to work it out for me, but what if I have to pay, Ebony? What if I have to pay for my past sins?"

I shook my head and continued to sob.

Chapter 36

Mekhi

"You pay me for ideas, and I have one." Rufus climbed in the passenger side of my SUV. "It's light, but it's all you can do and keep it legal, but first, do me a favor. Drive down that way and head toward Covington for me. I'm trying to serve this fool, and he knows what my ride looks like."

I didn't like the idea of Rufus using my car as his cover while he worked for someone else, but I was not trying to appear as if I wasn't down. Rufus had covered up a lot of stuff for me in my life, and as long as he stayed sharp, he would stay on my payroll.

"Look, the man's daughter is in love with Benxi, right? So use Benxi to help you out. The girl got a Sweet Sixteen party Saturday. She talking about it twenty-four-seven. Benxi should go sing at the party. Sing 'Happy Birthday' or something. She'll be so happy that Daddy will be grateful to you."

I didn't respond. I knew Rufus had to have more to say.

"You go with Benxi. Make sure you introduce yourself to Daddy. Make sure Benxi takes a lot of pictures with the girl and you, and he'll show his appreciation with the sentence."

"But he'll know that's why I showed up."

"He'll take it a few ways, dog. He'll know that you trying to make him go soft. He'll know that it may appear highly irregular, you know, Benxi showing up. But I think he'll play it cool. All business is give and take. You give him something he wants, and he gives you something you want."

My brain couldn't process that this was my solution. It was too simple, and it wasn't concrete. I liked a plan to be more foolproof than this.

"Oh, and he'll also know that you know how to find him and his precious spoiled-behind baby girl." Rufus's voice had a sinister edge. He gave me more directions. "Turn right here and it's that first house on the left."

I pulled in front of the house that had a sign on the gate that read *Beware of dog*.

Rufus hopped out, pulled the door open to the fence like he was a bigger dog, and jogged up the walk to the door. He knocked a few times.

I thought about what he'd suggested. Was he telling me to try to get the guy to owe me? I can't say I was convinced that it would work. He could just enjoy the party and still stick Samaria with the toughest sentence he had.

I heard cussin' outside my window and saw a dude standing on his porch waving papers. Rufus came back through the gate, opened the door, and hopped in. "I'm done. Let's flow."

I put the car in drive and pulled away. "How'd you know the dog wasn't gonna eat you?"

Rufus chuckled. "Ain't no dog, dude. I been over here three times. No evidence of a dog. Just a sign. That's what I'm talking about with the judge. Bluff him. You deliver Benxi, and you let the threat of 'where this could go if you don't hook me up' hang in the air. It's a legal blackmail. It's a legal threat. You ain't did nothing wrong. He gonna know where you coming from, trust a brother on that."

I gave Rufus the side eye. An ex-wannabe rapper, he could be pretty metaphorical at times, a little too lyrical when I wanted straight talk. "I was thinking he could go hard on Samaria."

"And then you nail his behind with the pictures and make up stories to the press that he pressured you for Benxi and all that. At the minimum, if it went that far, the case would be thrown out. If Samaria's already sentenced, she might get a pardon. Dude is a Republican, like the governor."

Rufus was the master of some drama. A pardon? Where did he come up with this stuff?

"I'm telling you, Mekhi, he's gonna wash your back to keep the possibility of backlash down. He's gonna accept your kind gift and give you what you want. Just keep it on the low that Benxi is coming. No prepublicity, so he can't stop it."

I drove back to the studio, pulled alongside Rufus's Jag, and he opened the door.

"You don't have nothing to lose. All you gotta do is talk Benxi into doing it."

I had been looking straight-ahead, but I turned to catch Rufus's eye. "I think I can do that."

"Yeah," Rufus smiled slyly. "I'm sure you can. I'll text you the location. Time is five."

I nodded. Rufus climbed into his car and sped away.

I let myself into the studio. I could hear the commotion coming from the viewing room, so I went straight there. This was the spot where we watched videos. It had a 150-inch plasma and six rows of reclining leather theater seats. It was tricked out with a black and white marble floor and art deco lighting fixtures on the walls. If that wasn't enough, a vintage popcorn machine was stationed alongside the far wall. Diddy himself would be impressed with the layout at Airamas, even if it was UMC's money.

"We were waiting for you," Benxi said. She hadn't looked back and seen me, which bugged me. The chick had eyes in the back of her head or she was connected to me in a way that I was not connected to her. I slid into the empty chair to her left.

"I watched it in New York with the UMC folks."

Benxi nudged me. "I know, but still, I wanted to see it with you first." Benxi pushed the PLAY button on the remote.

What did that mean?

The video opened with Benxi and a team of dancers playing around in the sand as she sang. There were clips of her singing in front of the Statue of Liberty, the Eiffel Tower, the Grand Canyon, and other well-known spots. Almost all the backgrounds were computer-assisted add-ins. The beauty of technology was that filming didn't have to take place on location. By the time the song ended, she was making snow angels and had frozen snowflakes for tears. The video was hot. Benxi was in love with the camera, and it was in love with her.

When the video closed, she turned off the power, someone clapped, and the lights came on. There was a collective round of fist bumps and high fives with "that's fancy," "that's the bizness," "that's what's up," and "straight to number one."

Benxi and I stood and joined in the celebration. She reached for me and grabbed me around the neck. "You are the best. If you hadn't been there to help with the creative direction of the video, it wouldn't have been this good."

"I'm glad you don't regret leaving Coco Records."

"No, it's like I told you. Those busters at Coco were trying to keep me in a box with the same old song, same old video. This is my next level. An artist has to push it up a notch or they're just a performer."

"Benxi, let's go celebrate!" one of the women from her entourage yelled. "We holding VIP at Club Seasons."

"A'ight," Benxi smiled. She turned back to me. "You wanna join us?"

I was tired. I wanted to go home and climb into bed with my wife, but I needed to talk to her, so . . . "Yeah, I'm in a celebrating mood." Everyone got hyped that I said yes, especially Benxi.

I didn't do as much of the party and club scene as I needed too because the studio work had taken a lot out of me. Being seen was a part of the business, and I knew I'd have to up my game with that as soon as the album hit. We left the building. Benxi rode with me, and her girls piled into her limo.

"Let me tell Sammie where I'm going so she can update Facebook and Twitter," I said.

I sent Samaria a text with the details and told her not to wait up. Then I started the car, and we rolled out.

Club Seasons was not that far, so I had to say something right away. I was waiting for Benxi to break the ice, but she was quiet, almost solemn, so I rushed in. "Benx, I need a favor."

Through my peripheral vision I could see she was looking at me, so I turned for a second and caught her eye. "I need you to sing at a birthday party."

I heard a noise come from her. It was part chuckle, part sigh, and all *Are you kidding?* "A birthday party?"

"Yeah, it's a Sweet Sixteen, Saturday at five at a spot in Alpharetta. I need you to go, sing and take pictures, and be out. Just two songs, and one of them is 'Happy Birthday.'"

"Saturday?" She careened her neck. "As in the day after tomorrow?"

I nodded.

"Is this promo for the album?"

"No. As a matter of fact, it's got to be a surprise. No tweets—nothing."

"Who's it for?"

"Like I said, it's a Sweet Sixteen," I replied, clearing my throat to disguise my nervousness.

Through my peripheral vision, I could see she was staring at me hard. "You gonna have to do better than that. I was planning to go to Vegas tomorrow."

We came to a red light, so I gave her eye contact. "It's the daughter of a business associate."

She laughed, but there was no humor in her voice. "Are you serious?"

I swallowed the knot of desperation lodged in my throat. "I am." I paused a few seconds. "I know I owe you more of an explanation, but I think it would be better if you didn't have the details."

"No." She raised her index finger. "I don't let anybody make that decision for me, and I don't do anything without the details, Mekhi. Not something like show up at a birthday party and sing. This is my career."

I swung my head in her direction for a second and caught her eye. "You trust me?"

"Of course I do, but I still need to know."

I sighed. "It's Samaria. It's the judge assigned to her case. His daughter's party."

She laughed, but again, no humor.

The light turned green, and I was glad to be able to focus on the road again. "I'm hoping he'll feel like he owes me for hooking up his only child with her favorite artist."

I could feel the heat of Benxi's stare on the side of my head. "So, this is for her?"

"It's for me. She's my wife and the mother of my child."

"You sure about that, Mekhi? I'm not trying to get in your—"

"It's my baby."

Benxi let out a long breath. "Okay. I'll do it, but you're going to have to do something for me."

Relief washed over me, and I smiled. I pulled into the parking lot of Club Seasons. "I got you. Just let me know what you need."

She turned to me. The car was in a stopped position as we were waiting in a valet parking line. "I want you, Mekhi."

I squinted and my lips fell apart. Benxi leaned closer and kissed me on them. "My birthday is coming up, and I want you as a present. Just one last time, so I can get you out of my system and move on."

I tightened my grip on the steering wheel. "Benx, I'm married."

"Newly married and married because she's pregnant." She leaned across the seat again, took my chin in her hand, and turned my face to hers. "The ink is hardly dry on your certificate."

I moved my face away from her hand and shook my head. "Benx, I didn't marry her because she was pregnant. I know you want to believe that, but . . . I love her."

Benxi sucked in her cheeks and let out a long plume of air. She waited a few seconds. I thought she was considering my words, but then . . . "I sing, and afterward, you come to my place. That's the deal."

Benxi's door opened. Her girls and security detail had crowded around waiting for her. She slipped her hand into mine and squeezed. "Let me know if you cool with that, otherwise, I'm going to Vegas."

She stepped out of the car leaving me stupefied. Women. I would never figure them out. How could a young, gorgeous, hella-fancified chick like Benxi gonna play herself by begging for some sex? I banged on the steering wheel.

The valet pulled the handle to open my door. I stepped out and joined them. Benxi slipped her arm through mine like I was her man, and we left the cars behind.

The paparazzi was in full force. The lights of digital cameras flashed on and off like Christmas tree lights. I should have been elated. The album was done, P.R. 'bout to be popping, but with Samaria's future on the line and Benxi's demand on the table, the only thing I felt as I passed under the door of Club Seasons was that I was entering a season of purgatory.

Chapter 37

Samaria

I was in hell. Physically and emotionally. Both woke me up this morning. The physical being Braxton Hicks contractions. Dr. Cotter said they were like practice contractions. The uterus is stretching to accommodate the baby, but accommodating the baby or not, I hated them. They were getting stronger and stronger as this baby got bigger. In particular, the last round I'd just had wore me out. I was glad they had stopped.

On the emotional front, I was scared to death. I decided I was telling Mekhi about the baby this morning. Two days had gone by since he'd returned from New York, and his work kept getting in the way, but it was Saturday, he was off, so I wasn't going to let anything stop me.

Greg had already sent me a text message. This time leaving a threat that if he didn't hear from me he was going to tell Mekhi. I threw my phone across the room to the chaise on the other side. I was sick of his threats. Who did he think he was dealing with? He had a lot to lose too. He was just going to have to wait.

"Sammie!" I heard Mekhi yell my name from the shower. I walked to the bathroom. "I need a bar of soap."

"You can't use anything in there?" I asked, opening the linen closet and removing his soap.

Mekhi slid the shower door open. "I'm not trying to smell like peaches, or coconuts, or let's see what's this one—lavender," he laughed.

I stuck a hand through the opening and gave him the bar. He got a hungry look in his eyes, and I could tell he was not thinking about soap. "Join me."

I smirked. "I took a shower while you were out running."

"You can never be too clean. Besides, I want to see if I can still get you up on this wall in here."

I blushed. "I've gotten too heavy for that."

"I've got a strong back, baby."

I smiled at his teasing and slipped off my robe. I wasn't really in the mood, but I hadn't forgotten, sex was in the plan. I was delayed, not derailed. I was supposed to get him weak in the knees before I told him about the baby. I could still do that. I stepped into the shower. Mekhi pushed me against the wall with a kiss so potent I was the one who got dizzy.

We played around in the shower, but began to make serious love on the bed. He lowered his head to my neck, buried his face, and nibbled.

I love this man.

Mekhi lowered his head and continued to assault me with his tongue.

He loves me.

I didn't want that to change, but I had to—"Khi," I interrupted him. "I have to tell you something important later. Remind me, okay?" I needed accountability. He'd hold me to it.

"Sure, baby." He would not be distracted. He raised his head and kissed me on the mouth again. His tongue explored my face. I wrapped my arms around his back and surrendered to our passion.

This might be the last time, I thought. The last time he looks at me with love in his eyes. But I had to tell him. I had to tell him before the love turned to hate.

Chapter 38

Mekhi

Samaria was looking worn out and complaining about those Braxton Hicks contractions again. I was thinking the sex might have started them up. "Maybe we shouldn't have," I said.

"It's okay. They come and go, you know. They weren't coming when we were—well, you know." She smiled, and my guilt over the aggressive way I'd handled her subsided, but nothing would squash the guilt I was feeling about my upcoming evening with Benxi.

I'd decided to take her deal. I didn't really think I had a choice. Hightower was sounding like a loser. I had nothing on the judge, so getting on his good side was all I had. Still, I knew it was messed up. Aside from the fact that I was stepping into the lion's den with Benxi, I was cheating on my wife. That's why I think I tried to give Samaria everything I had, so Benxi would get me running on empty. I mentally and physically had to make this date a big nothing, or I'd never be able to keep up my end of the deal. Where would that leave my wife and my baby? I was not willing to accept separated by bars.

I removed a long tee shirt out of Samaria's drawer and slid it over her head. Then I pulled on a pair of sweats and a tee shirt. "The baby is probably hungry," I said. "It's eleven o'clock." I picked her up. "Let's go eat."

Samaria giggled. "Let me walk."

"No. You ain't got to walk. I'm your slave this morning."

I carried her down the stairs, put her in a chair on our deck, and walked back into the kitchen to prepare a quick breakfast. I placed glasses of water and orange juice in front of her. "Drink both. I read those contraction things can come from dehydration."

I served sausage, eggs, and toast, and we enjoyed a nice breakfast in the fresh morning air. This was the life I wanted, the life I was working for—big house, gorgeous wife, respectability. Once Benxi's album hit and the trial was behind us, I'd have it all.

Samaria put her feet up on an ottoman and closed her eyes against the midday sun. She looked so beautiful, so perfect, so at peace. All those years I thought about us hooking back up and being just like this, I can't say for sure that I'd ever thought it would happen. Samaria had moved on with her life, held out for so many years that I was starting to assume I'd really lost her forever. So now, I couldn't lose her again, not when I'd waited all that time; not when she was having my child. I had to do what I had to do, so I wasn't going to feel guilty about Benxi. Sleeping with her was business. Folks pimped themselves every day for a dollar. It wasn't even about money for me. I had a higher purpose. I was trying to keep my wife out of prison.

"What are you thinking about?" Samaria's voice broke through my thoughts.

The house phone rang and saved me from having to lie. I stood. "I'm expecting a call. We have this thing to do later, and I have to coordinate the time with everybody."

Samaria pouted. "Another club?"

I leaned over and kissed her. "Something like that, but don't sweat it. You can join us after you have the baby."

I went inside and checked the caller ID. It wasn't a familiar number, so I let it ring to voice mail. Most of my business contacts called me on my cell, which I'd left in the bedroom. I needed to get it just in case someone was trying to reach me. "I'm running upstairs for a minute. When I come back, you can tell me whatever it was you needed reminding about," I yelled, and then I took the stairs two at a time.

I entered the bedroom to a ringing phone, not mine, but Samaria's. I followed the sound and found it under a cushion on the chaise. I accidently hit a button which caused the call to be accepted. "Hello, hello," I heard the voice on the other end.

"Hello," I returned.

"May I speak with Ms. Jacobs."

"She's not available right now. Can I take a message?"

"It's a personal matter. What would be a good time for me to call back, sir?"

"This is her husband." I think that was the first time I'd said those words to anyone. They felt good. "You can give me the message."

"We'll call back." The woman hung up on me.

I thought that was strange. A local Atlanta number. A personal matter. What was up? I pushed the call log and redialed.

"Testing Center of Atlanta." It wasn't the same voice as the caller who had hung up on me. *Testing Center. What kind of test?* "How can I help you?"

"I—I need to take a test," I said.

"Are you looking for a collection site, sir?"

Collection site? Now I was more than curious, so I played along. "Yeah, I guess so."

"Do we already have a sample from the other parties involved?"

Samples?—Parties?—What kind of place is this? "What kind of tests do you do?"

"Sir, do you have the wrong number?"

"No, I have a number I just pulled off my wife's cell phone. What kind of tests do you do?"

"I'm not at liberty to discuss the nature of our services." She ended the call.

"What the—?"

I sat down. Samaria was keeping something from me. Testing center. Collection sites. Was something wrong with the baby? I scrolled through her call log. She hadn't made many, but she had three missed calls from the same number. I dialed it.

"It's about time!" an angry male voice said. "Didn't you get my text messages? Did you take the test?"

I snatched my head back, looked at the phone, and put it back against my ear. "Dude, who are you?"

The call ended. I dialed him back. He hung up. I dialed him back. He hung up again. I heard Samaria yelling for me from the bottom of the stairs. "Khi, what are you doing?"

I called the number again. This time it went to voice mail. *You've reached Gregory Preston. Leave a message.*

Truth. We said we'd keep the truth between us, but whatever this was . . . It was a lie.

I remembered dude had said he'd been texting her. I opened the inbox for the messages—scanned through each and every one that she'd received in the last few days. Samaria entered the bedroom. She looked at the phone in my hand and terror filled her eyes.

"Let me explain."

"Explain?" I shook my head. "Go ahead. Do your best explainin' about who Gregory Preston is, what test he wants you to take, and why he gave you $25,000."

Chapter 39

Greg

I know Samaria had some serious explaining to do. I wanted to get even, but who knew karma would come back so strong. My thought was that it couldn't have happened to a nicer person. The only problem was now that he knew, I had no leverage. I had nothing to hold over her head. She wasn't going to take the DNA test. I was stuck with waiting and was probably out of $25,000.

I pulled into Angelina's driveway and hopped out of the car. Before I could ring the bell, Angelina pulled the door open and stepped out.

"Good morning." I looked her up and down. She was freshly showered. I could smell her body wash and her hair was still damp and curly from being washed and gelled. I liked when she wore it like that. It made her look younger. Coupled with the sunshine yellow sundress, she had taken off ten years. "You look fantastic."

"Thank you," she replied. "You're early."

"Gotta get every second I can." I looked toward the door. "I was going to say hello to Katrice."

"I told you I'm not trying to confuse her," Angelina replied. "She's in the backyard with the sitter."

"Confuse her by saying hello?"

"With you, period."

I leaned close to her. Close enough to smell the orange juice on her breath. "Are you sure you're not the one who's confused?"

She smirked and gave me a gentle shove away from her. "Don't make me regret calling you."

I waved my hand toward the car. "I don't want to do that. Your chariot, ma'am." We climbed inside.

"Sorry, it looks like you won't learn the sex today." The ultrasound technician had been trying to get a picture of the front of our baby for more than twenty minutes, but he or she had been extremely stubborn.

"Learning everything else is intact is good enough for me right now." Angelina sat up and put her weight on her elbows.

"We can repeat in a month if you'd like. Maybe your little one will turn for us."

She escorted Angelina to the restroom and me to the waiting room. After about ten minutes, Angelina came out with the DVD and pictures of the ultrasound and we left. I offered to take her to lunch. She tried to turn me down by insisting she needed to get home, but I wasn't having it. "Come on, Lena. We need to talk. I have something to tell you." She agreed with someplace quick, so I found a cafeteria-style restaurant and within minutes we were seated.

"So, what did you have to tell me?" she asked between sips of water.

"I told Phil to stop the divorce, and he called back yesterday and said the papers had been pulled." To my surprise she didn't complain. She just nodded and picked up her fork. A brother had made some progress. This pregnancy was working to my advantage.

We ate in silence for a few minutes. She brought me up to date on the IRS investigation which basically amounted to nothing. The IRS was still reviewing documents. It would probably be a few more months before they had any information for her.

"I can't worry about it," she said. "I haven't done anything wrong. I know I never signed anything without reading it, so Don won't have my signature on some dirty paperwork."

"The fact that he's missing and you're not should add to your credibility."

"You would think so. All I know is I'm going to be out of money soon. I've got no donations coming in."

"Well, let me give you something to carry you through."

She shook her head. "I don't think there's any point. I'd need too much. Even when they clear me, I don't know that I can go back to it. It's almost impossible for a charity to recover from this type of thing. Being cleared won't be in the paper or on the television. If I'm lucky, they'll run one story and that'll be it, whereas the suspicion of my guilt was headline news for more than a week." She shrugged. "I've been thinking that maybe I should give it up and focus on my children."

"But you love it."

"I do, but what can I do? Don has destroyed it. What's more important to me is getting back on the DYFS board before they fill my seat. Being a liaison to the counties was so rewarding. I wouldn't have Katrice if I hadn't been involved at that level."

"So, you looking to build a tribe of foster children?" I asked, teasing her.

She half-smiled and waved me off. "No, I'm good with her and this little one." Then her smile disappeared. "Speaking of foster children, have you talked to Samaria?"

I didn't see that coming. Here it goes, the wonderful lunch was about to turn sour in both our stomachs. I stopped chewing. "I have. I saw her a couple weeks ago."

Angelina raised an eyebrow. I guess talking to her and seeing her were two different things. She picked up her glass and took a short sip of water, looking at me suspiciously over the rim of the glass. "I thought I saw on the news that she was in Puerto Rico."

"I met with her before that."

Another raised eyebrow.

"I asked her to take a paternity test."

Angelina picked up her fork and swirled it around in her pasta. "A paternity test? Don't those happen after the baby is born?"

"They have prenatal ones. They use amnio fluid."

Angelina put her fork down. "What? You asked her to take a test that required an amniocentesis?"

"Yes. It's not that big of a deal. They're pretty routine now."

Her scowl told me she did not approve. "An amnio is always a big deal. I'm thirty-nine, and I'm not even having one."

I wiped the corners of my mouth with a napkin. "Well, I asked her. I was trying to get this baby stuff behind us."

Angelina stiffened. "And is it?"

"I called the lab and found out she didn't do it yet, and what's worse is her husband answered the phone today when I called her to find out why."

"He didn't know about you?"

"No. You know what a deceitful person she is."

Angelina laughed sarcastically. "She had help being deceitful. Amazing how you completely blame her for your infidelity. Like she gave you the darn date rape drug. You were carrying on with her for six months, so don't act like a victim."

I swallowed a huge lump of remorse. "I'm not blaming her, but how many mistresses try to meet their lover's wives. That's the part I'm talking about."

Angelina didn't respond. She wasn't going to let me have that point.

"Well, like I said, she's probably in hot water with him. He was plenty angry on the phone."

"What did he say?"

"Nothing. I hung up on him. I'd sent her some text messages, so if he had her phone he probably saw them. They were about the paternity test." I didn't add that one of the messages referenced the $25,000. "He called back, but I didn't answer the phone."

"What do you mean you didn't answer the phone? It might have been her. She could have been in trouble."

"She's not going to call me if she's in trouble. Besides, her trouble is not my problem."

"Greg, she's pregnant, and you leave her alone with an angry husband. Anything could happen. He could have a temper."

"I repeat, not my problem."

Angelina shook her head. "How could you? She's a woman who could be in danger."

I threw my hands up. "Look, I hear you on that, but Samaria has made this messed up situation all by herself. I'm not responsible for her. She should have told him before she married him." I knew I wasn't scoring any points with Angelina, but the mere thought of Samaria got me steamed. "Anyway, I didn't think it was cool for me to call. Her husband might get more pissed."

"Well, I met him. He doesn't strike me as a man with a short fuse. I'll call her later and make sure she's okay."

"Don't."

Angelina reached into her purse. She was not hearing me. "Let me have her number."

There was no point in telling her that I didn't want her talking to Samaria, that she shouldn't care about her, because my wife cared about everyone, even my ex-mistress. I pulled out my phone and read the numbers off.

"I'll check on her when I get home, which will be in a few minutes, because I'd like to go."

"So now you're angry with me because I don't care about Samaria."

"I'm not angry. I'm just tired of all of this. You have no idea."

We sat in silence for a few more minutes, and then Angelina dropped her fork. Then she dropped her head in her hands. "Seriously, I've lost my appetite. I want to go."

I sighed. Things were going so well. She was enjoying my company. It was like the good old days until Samaria came up. Angelina slid out of the booth, and I followed.

She tried not to talk to me on the drive home, but I wouldn't let it go down like that. I brought up the subject of baby names and teased her with suggestions like Shobama Michelle, Treybama, Michelle-Loubama, and many other messed up ghetto spins on Barack and Michelle Obama that had Angelina in tears by the time we pulled into the driveway.

I walked her to the door. We stood outside of it like two unsure teenagers after a first date. "I guess I can't come in."

"No," she said.

"I'm bored. I have absolutely nothing to do today."

"Go play golf. That's what you would have been do-ing if we were together." She turned to stick her key in the door, and I whipped her around. I leaned forward and kissed her on the lips with an intensity that showed her how much I missed her. She didn't fuss or rebuke me or even pull away; in fact, she looked heady from the experience. I know I was.

"Can we go get a room?" I asked, pulling her against me again.

Angelina twisted out of my grasp. "No."

"You sure? There's a Holiday Inn right—"

"No!" she laughed. Then she cleared her throat and got serious. "I appreciate you taking me today."

"I want to know about every doctor's appointment. Don't you dare go to another one without me."

"I won't."

"Call me any time, day or night, and I'm here."

She nodded. "I know."

"And please know I love you, and I love our baby, even if it is a stubborn little Baracka or Obamalita Preston."

Angelina laughed, and I felt like the heavens had opened. She put her key in the lock and went inside the house.

"Yes!" I yelled. I wasn't in yet, but the kiss was a good start. Angelina could say what she wanted about not taking me back. I was going to do what my sister said—redeem myself. No more words, no more begging. It was time to let my actions speak for me.

Chapter 40

Samaria

I opened my mouth and spoke, but there was no talking to him. No way to explain my deception. No way to make it right.

Mekhi exploded in a rage. He called me a liar and a cheat, said I married him for his money, and accused me of still sleeping with Greg.

I should have told him. That was all I could think as I watched him pace the room. He stopped and rubbed his hand across his head a few times. He only did that when he was thinking really hard, so I knew while he was processing what he found, his anger was building, and with it, his total distrust of me. He stopped moving and sank down on the bed. I wanted to touch him. If we connect physically, maybe I could hope . . .

"How long have you known it might not be my baby?"

Lie.

"I—I—"

Mekhi screamed. "How long?"

"Not long."

Mekhi raised a finger, shook his head, and said, "Samaria, don't play with me."

Lie the voice in my head said, but a lie wouldn't come. "Since the engagement party. I had an ultrasound that day, and Dr. Cotter told me I was eleven weeks."

Mekhi pounded his fist on the bed and stood. "I gotta get out of here. I can't look at you."

He went into his closet and came out with sneakers and socks.

"Mekhi, I was going to tell you. That's what I was going to talk to you about."

His head snapped up. "Do I look like a fool to you? You've got $25,000 in your bank account. It was just put in there, and you expect to tell me you were coming clean?"

"It's the truth. I was going to go have the test, but I decided not to have it. Not until I was honest with you, so I cancelled and—"

"What's the money for, Sam?"

The money. How could I explain the money?

He shook his head. "I don't even think I want to know." Mekhi walked out of the bedroom, stopped on the other side of the door, and then came back in. "Why did you marry me?"

I struggled to find my voice. "Love . . . I love you."

He shook his head. "No, love don't lie. Love don't keep secrets."

Tears ran down my face.

"If you just needed money, you could have asked me for it. You didn't have to make me think you cared about me." He pointed a finger at his chest. "You didn't have to take vows. I would've helped you no matter what, because even though you're playing me, I actually do love you. I've always loved you." He removed his wedding band and threw it against the wall.

I sank to the chaise, and then slid to the floor. I needed to get low. I wanted to disappear. I didn't want him looking at me the way he was looking. "I swear, I didn't mean to hurt you. I was just scared. I didn't know what to do."

Mekhi stepped to where I was sitting. He leaned close and whispered through grit teeth. "You didn't know what to do, so you tricked yourself out?" He punched the wall next to my head. I closed my eyes and covered my ears. Sheetrock crumbled around me. I jerked back.

"What did he get for twenty-five grand?"

I waited a beat before saying, "Mekhi, please, it could be your baby."

He shook his head and laughed bitterly. "I hope not. You ain't fit to be nobody's mother. A whore ain't good for nothing but selling herself." He walked out of the bedroom.

I screamed his name over and over and over again. A moment later, I heard the garage open, his sports car rev, and pull out. "Mekhi." My voice was a croaked whisper. "Mekhi."

I crawled across the room to the bed and pulled myself up on the mattress. The Braxton Hicks were worse, stronger, sharper. I lay on the bed for over an hour trying to tolerate them, but they were so painful I couldn't stand it. I drank so much at breakfast that my bladder was going to burst. I stood and grabbed furniture as I made my way to the restroom. Suddenly, I felt water gush. However, it didn't feel like it came from my bladder. Something was wrong. I looked at my legs. There was a mix of water and blood running down to my foot. I screamed and hobbled back into the bedroom, reached for my discarded phone, and dialed Mekhi's cell. Voice mail. A pain shot through my body. I dialed Ebony. Voice mail. *More pain.* I had to call 911. I was about to dial when a call came through. *Mekhi,* I thought. I looked at the number and saw that the caller was not Mekhi. It was Angelina.

Chapter 41

Angelina

I put Samaria on three-way with the 911 operator and stayed on the line until the EMTs broke into the house. The paramedic said she was definitely in labor. She'd given me the numbers for her husband and cousin, so I grabbed my other phone and tried them. Neither picked up. I left messages. The paramedic told me the hospital they were taking her to. I climbed in my car and rushed there. No woman should have to deliver a baby without family or friends. Not that I was either, but I decided I'd stand by her until someone could replace me. I'd wrestled with my decision about whether to go or stay home during the entire ride to the hospital. Once I entered the room, I was glad I had come. She was so upset that she didn't even look like herself.

Samaria was dilated five centimeters. Her water had broken at the house, so there was no going back. She was having this baby, and she was terrified, which she should have been. She was so early. I felt horrible that I hadn't called right when Greg told me about the situation with her husband, because then, they might have been able to give her medication to stop the labor.

"Thank you for coming." Samaria reached for my hand. I swallowed my hesitation and took hers.

"I've been trying to reach your family, but no one is available," I said.

"My cousin doesn't have a cell phone, and her family is probably at the county fair," she said. "I remember her telling me they were going this weekend."

"Well, hopefully your husband will answer soon."

Samaria didn't say anything. She just looked off like that statement had taken her a million miles away. She turned back to me. "I'm sorry I lied to you—about being sure it was Mekhi's baby."

I let go of her hand. I wanted to say, *You're always lying to me.* But, of course, I couldn't say it now. It would be cruel, even if it was true. "This is not the time."

Samaria adjusted her position on the bed. "It is the time, because you're likely to come to your senses after today and not call me again." Silence enveloped the room before she spoke again. "I already hurt you enough. I didn't want you thinking I'd gotten pregnant by Greg. I was hoping that it was Mekhi's."

"Could it be?" I asked, and I immediately regretted that I had. She could say no, and then I'd be here helping my husband's mistress deliver their child. That was too much.

Samaria raised her hand and wiped a tear. "I guess." She let out a long breath. "I don't know. Trifling, right? Not knowing who your child's father is." She shook her head. "I watched women do that all my life. Come up pregnant and not know who the father was. I swore that would never be me, but I guess if you're sleeping around—"

I cut her off by saying, "Don't beat yourself up about it." I had to stop her before she mentioned Greg. Did she think I was made out of iron? I sighed, closed my eyes, and tried to focus. I wanted to be bigger than my emotions were urging me to be. Samaria had disappointed me. She'd made me so angry that I could barely breathe, but one thing I was sure of was that there was no such thing as coincidences. God had arranged for me to be here with her today. There was something this woman needed from me, so it was time to heed His call, find some way to release my bitterness, and help her. "You have to be positive and strong through this delivery. The baby needs mommy to have her full strength no matter who the father is."

She began to sob. "I'm so scared."

I got closer to the bed and rubbed her back. "Don't be. It'll be okay. You have the best doctors here, and let's not forget that God is in control."

Samaria managed a weak smile.

"Why don't we pray?" I suggested.

A pain hit her. She worked through it. "Lord have mercy." She grabbed my hand. "I need a prayer before that happens again."

I prayed with her. Afterward, I made another attempt to reach Mekhi, but he would not answer his phone. "He doesn't recognize my number. I know I don't pick up strange calls. I should try from yours."

"He's not likely to answer that either, but you can try," she replied. "It's in my purse, and I think they put it in the closet."

I retrieved the phone, placed a call to Mekhi, and left another message.

A contraction came. Samaria moaned, low and hard. The nurse came in to check her and announced that she was dilated to six. We asked about the epidural she'd requested, and the nurse informed us that a lot of women had gone into labor and the anesthesia staff was behind. They had to take care of the emergency caesarean sections first.

We waited another twenty minutes and the anesthesiologist came in with a nurse and completed the epidural. Samaria quieted down instantly and fell asleep.

I called Chelsea and checked on Katrice. I gave her an update and told her I'd be here until some other relative was reached. She was fine with it. In fact, she was taking Katrice to the park down the street and maybe to the movies later to get her out of the house. After we hung up, I thought about calling Greg, but decided against it. I was jealous that another woman might be having his baby, and I didn't want him thinking about her and thinking about it. With the stank attitude he'd had this morning, he wasn't likely to come rushing to the hospital to see, but still, I thought holding off until the DNA results were in was for the best. Thinking that helped soothe my selfish ego.

I kept trying Samaria's husband and cousin. No one answered the phone. They'd hate themselves later for it, especially, Mekhi, because no matter how angry he was about the stuff that happened this morning, he still loved her. I knew that. I had seen it in his eyes when I'd met him.

I thought about how unfortunate it was that I couldn't call her mother. My mother was a pain in my neck, but she'd be here for me in a heartbeat. Samaria had told me earlier that her mother hadn't even come to the wedding. She was hooked on drugs so bad that she rarely left her neighborhood these days. She wouldn't come to the hospital unless she was coming to see a baby, and even then, she might not show.

I looked at her. She slept so peacefully, like she didn't have a care in the world, when, in fact, her entire world was turned upside down. I couldn't imagine having a baby, and then having to go to prison and leave it behind. I know she'd made this trouble for herself, but the mother in me was empathetic to the child and the mother in her.

A nurse entered the room. "I need to check her." She roused Samaria from her sleep and said, "Come on, Mommy, I need to see how far along you are."

Samaria shifted again and spread her legs for the examination. When the nurse left, she said, "Angelina, would you hand me my phone. I just thought of somebody who might be able to reach Mekhi."

Chapter 42

Mekhi

I drove around for hours. I'd been sitting in my car for more than thirty minutes outside the spot where Judge Kinchen's daughter's party was being held. I'd stopped at Macy's and picked up a change of clothes for the occasion and reengineered myself in the fitting room. I was moving on some bizarre form of autopilot, trying not to think about Samaria and the fact that the baby I'd spent months thinking was mine was not. I'd Googled Gregory Preston. He was some big-time neurosurgeon. He was also that woman's, Angelina Preston's, husband, which confirmed he was supposed to be an ex. Twenty-five grand in the bank said he wasn't.

What I couldn't understand was why. I wasn't gonna front. Dude was handsome if a chick liked that slick-haired, hazel-eyed type. He was the complete opposite of me, which I'd always thought was a pretty nice package. But one could never could tell with women, especially the type of women who traded themselves for money. Still, I felt bad about calling her a whore. I didn't have the facts. I hadn't waited for them, because no matter what she muttered out of her mouth, she wasn't going to be able to explain the money. No way should my wife have taken money from another man.

My phone was ringing again. I reached in the glove box, made sure it wasn't Benxi, turned down the volume, and shoved it in my pocket. I had a ton of missed calls, and I knew they were from Samaria. I wasn't ready to talk yet, so she'd have to save her story for later. Rufus pulled into the lot, and sixty seconds behind him rolled Benxi's Hummer. I left my car to greet them.

Benxi stepped out of her ride, greased and glittered up like she was going on stage at Madison Square Garden. Her eyes were filled with sexy confidence. I hadn't seen that look in months. I gave her a quick hug, bumped fists with my man Rufus, and we and Benxi's bodyguards walked into the venue.

Within seconds, teenage girl screams filled the air. They started panting and fanning like they were trying to keep themselves from fainting. Rufus and the judge's photographer went crazy taking pictures. Benxi approached the judge's little princess, identified by a blinged-out tiara, and no lie, a throne at the front of the room. The girl was swooning, and if she hadn't been sitting down, I swear she would have passed out. Benxi hugged her.

"I hear you got a birthday today!" She backed up, asked the lead singer of the band for his microphone, and said, "How about you guys play 'Happy Birthday' for me." They looked like they were going to faint too, but they pulled themselves together and began to play. Benxi sang and danced around like the star she was. That girl could perform to anything. If I hadn't felt the lock of the noose around my neck, I would have been glad to be here.

Rufus caught my eye and nodded in the direction of the judge who happened to be standing just to my right. I closed the distance between us and stuck out my hand. "Judge Kinchen, Mekhi Johnson, Airamas Records. I'm Benxi's producer." I saw the flash of Rufus's camera when our hands connected.

The judge was thrilled. His skin was bright red from smiling so much. He gave me a jovial handshake and asked, "How in the world did this come together?"

"Your daughter is Benxi's biggest fan. My wife, Samaria Jacobs-Johnson, handles social media for me, and she noticed how much your daughter tweeted and Facebooked about Benxi. We figured it would be a nice birthday present."

"Nice?" The judge rested a hand on his chest. "Nice would have been an autographed picture. This is amazing. Benxi's all she talks about."

"Well, surprise." Rufus joined us. He and the judge shook hands and Rufus added, "We can all be of help to each other. That's what life's about. I do something for you; you do something for me." Rufus grinned.

The judge got a funny look on his face, like he wasn't sure where Rufus was coming from, but then he nodded, smiled, and continued to watch the show.

Benxi's rendition of 'Happy Birthday' was done. She asked, "Would you like me to sing another song?"

The party guests roared hearty yeses.

"Y'all know I have a new album dropping next month. How about a song from my album?"

They screamed again.

"Okay, now, we have to ask the boss!" She pointed the microphone in my direction. The girls cheered and stomped and begged me to say yes. I nodded, and Benxi did an a cappella version of one of the first songs we'd recorded together. I was proud.

"That was actually fun. I should do it more often," Benxi said as we stepped out of the banquet hall.

"They seemed to enjoy it. Could be a way to get good, positive PR," I replied.

Benxi sexily tousled her hair before she stepped to me. I could tell she was done with business. "So," she put a hand on my chest, "we got a date?"

"We have a deal." I let out a long breath. I thought being angry with Samaria would make this easier, but it wasn't going to be. *This is not about sex. I don't even want her,* I told myself, but who was I kidding? I was wrong. I'd put a hole in my bedroom wall because I wanted my marriage to be about the truth. I was a hypocrite. Sleeping with Benxi was going to be a lie, no matter the reason.

"Good," she grabbed my hand like we were lovers, "because I haven't been able to think about anything but the—"

"Mekhi!" I heard Rufus yell. He had stopped in the restroom so he was just coming outside. "Samaria had to go to Perimeter Medical! She's in labor."

I let go of Benxi's hand. Without a word I flew to the car and jumped in. Once again, I was driving in a blur, but for a different reason. I'd listened to the messages Samaria and Angelina and even the hospital registrar staff had left for me. They had started leaving voice mails right after I'd left the house. More than five hours had gone by. I banged my fist on the steering wheel. *Irresponsible,* I thought. I had a pregnant wife.

I tossed my keys to the parking valet, dashed into the hospital, and rushed the folks trying to get in the elevator before me. I arrived on the sixth floor and grabbed the elbow of a nurse passing by. "Samaria Johnson. Which way is room 6032?" She pointed, and I flew in that direction.

I was scared to death. Samaria was way too early to be in labor. And then there was that Angelina chick— What was she doing here? Had she upset Samaria and caused her to go into labor? I raced down the hall. I was anxious for answers, but I was even more anxious to meet my son or daughter. Uneasiness settled in the pit of my stomach. I couldn't shake the feeling that this day, which had been pretty bad already, was going to get worse. The "why" of the worse I didn't know.

Chapter 43

Samaria

"Uhhh!" I felt like I was being ripped in two. "Oh, please, help me!" I screamed at the top of my lungs. Tears escaped my closed eyelids. A cool cloth touched my forehead and a warm hand squeezed mine. I looked at Angelina and through my agony I could see she was afraid; afraid for me, just like I was afraid for myself and my baby. I was glad she was here; otherwise, I might be alone. "I'm not going to make it," I whined. "This hurts so much."

Angelina wiped my head again. "You're going to be fine. Just breathe like I showed you. Breathe through the contractions."

"You're doing great, Samaria," Dr. Cotter said. "You're almost dilated. The epidural drip has been off for a while, and pretty soon you'll be ready to start pushing."

"I needed that epidural." I puffed like the women I'd seen on television. The breathing didn't seem to be helping. Who said breathing would help? All it did was make me tired. "Is my baby okay?"

"The baby is holding its own," Dr. Cotter said. "You just keep doing what you're doing."

I looked at Angelina. "Thank you for staying." I thrashed my head from side to side. "I know I've been horrible to you, but you're still here."

Angelina wiped my forehead again. "It's okay. Don't think about anything right now but that baby."

I felt another contraction starting up. I squeezed my eyes tight and bore down. I grunted and tried to fight the urge to push, but I was unable to.

"Wait, Samaria!" Dr. Cotter yelled.

Was she kidding? Had she done this before? I opened my eyes and saw Mekhi enter the room. My breath came quickly as my chest heaved up and down. The pain was growing. It grew and grew and grew until it finally started to subside. "Khi, thank God you're here," I whispered.

Mekhi was on the side of the bed opposite of Angelina. He took my other hand and leaned over and kissed my sweaty forehead. "Baby, I'm so sorry. Rufus just gave me the message."

God had answered my prayer. He was here. "Mekhi, I'm so sorry," I cried.

"I'm going to go wait outside," Angelina said.

I tightened my grip on her hand. "No," I whined. "Please, don't leave me."

Her voice was a whisper.

"But, Mekhi is here now."

I shook my head. "I want you both." Of that I was certain. Both provided me with a certain amount of strength. Both gave me something I needed that I couldn't get from the other. Mekhi, my husband, my lover, made me feel loved and safe. Angelina, my sister, made me feel strong, like I could do this being a mother thing. I looked into Angelina's eyes and squeezed her hand. "Please, I want you here." She looked at Mekhi. He tilted his head in a way that said, "Stay," and she squeezed my hand back.

I closed my eyes and rested for a moment, but then the pain was starting again; this time, it felt different.

***

"We'll have to do a Cesarean section," Dr. Cotter told the nurses. "Let's move into the OR!" she yelled, and the room shifted as everyone sprang into action. Then she came closer to me. "The baby is showing signs of distress, so we're going to deliver her now. We're doing a C-section," she said. "Remember, we talked about that."

I nodded understanding. "Just save my baby," I whispered and another contraction hit me in the back like someone was kicking me through the bed. Dr. Cotter squeezed my hand. "The anesthesiologist is going to have to put you under."

"But, I . . . I don't want to be out."

"It's routine for a C-section," Dr. Cotter said, and within seconds they were rolling me out of my room.

"Samaria, don't worry," I heard Angelina's voice in the distance. "I'm praying for you."

Mekhi walked with us. "Hold on, Sammie, it's going to be okay. Be brave, girl. It's going to be over in a few."

We entered the operating room. I heard one of the nurses say, "Her blood pressure is dropping." Even though I could see her standing over me, she sounded like she was a hundred miles away. Another nurse on the other side was rubbing a cold liquid across my belly.

I turned my head to the left and right, searching for Mekhi. I tried to open my mouth, but my lips were glued together. I couldn't get them apart. A man dressed like a doctor put a mask over my face. He wasn't Dr. Cotter. "I'm going to put you under now, Mrs. Johnson."

Under. I hated the thought. Why couldn't I have gotten to the part where they said push?

I turned my head and caught a glimpse of Mekhi. He was still here. He still cared about me. He came closer.

He was wearing a white paper gown, face mask, and head covering. He leaned in, telling me it was going to be all right, but I wasn't sure. I was in so much pain I could die, and I wanted him to know, so I said it, "I love you." Mekhi squeezed my hand. "I'm so sorry for what I did, but I married you because I love you."

"Mr. Johnson, please." He, the stranger who was putting me "under," said. Mekhi stepped back. A mask came down over the bottom half of my face. "Mrs. Johnson, I want you to count backward from ten."

I didn't think he expected me to count out loud since he had my mouth covered, so I counted in my head. Ten . . . nine . . . eight . . .

My eyes found Mekhi's again. He raised two fingers to his lips and blew me a kiss. I was drowsy, but my heart smiled, and then everything went black.

Joshua Malik Johnson came into the world screaming. I knew so because the video of his birth was playing on the television in the room. I held my little angel while I tried to avoid hitting my incision. He was beautiful, perfect, whiter looking than I would have expected, but those dark little ears foretold that he would be a nice chocolate brown, just like his parents, in no time.

My mother and cousins, June and Ebony, were pointing at the television. June was commenting about how nasty everything looked, and Ebony was bragging about how she'd pushed all four of her children out without drugs. My mother-in-law had come from Florida to see her first grandchild, and Uncle Wang-Wang was drinking champagne from the bottle.

There were flowers everywhere; on my table, the dresser, and on the windowsills. They were all white—

white carnations, orchids, roses, and calla lilies in beautiful arrangements. Someone opened the bathroom door and I saw flowers beyond it. The closet door fell open, and I saw that it held flowers instead of clothes. But then in an instant, as if a flash fire had swept through the room and struck only them, they all wilted and turned black and sooty.

I opened my eyes, gasped for my breath like I'd been submerged in water, and began to sob. I cried until I was empty and hoarse. I cried sometimes until they, the nurses, had to come and sedate me. I cried because that picture of the gathering of my family around my hospital bed was a dream. It was a dream I had every time I fell asleep.

I had not had a son. I'd had a daughter. She had not come into the world screaming. The little girl I'd carried for almost six months had not taken one breath.

Chapter 44

Samaria

"Sammie, we need to name her."

Mekhi stood next to my bed. I looked down and saw that he was holding my hand. I couldn't feel it. I couldn't feel anything. I was numb. Blood wasn't getting to any of my extremities, because my heart had stopped beating when the doctor said, "I'm sorry. She didn't make it."

"Baby." He tugged a little. I cut my eyes to his, warned him with a flash of my pain that I could not bear this agony. Mekhi was not my enemy, but he wanted something from me that I was incapable of giving him. Didn't he understand I couldn't move forward? Didn't he understand I was dead too? Couldn't he see me, not breathing, not living, dying a thousand times for the little girl who would never be? I tried to reason with myself. Mekhi still didn't know if this had been his baby. I'd insisted he submit to a DNA test, so that we would know for sure. *"It won't matter, Sammie,"* he'd said, but I didn't want the question to come up months or years from now. I didn't want him wondering if he'd actually fathered a child who had not lived.

The door to the room opened, and Dr. Cotter entered. She approached my bed with a slower gait than she usually carried herself with. She wasn't wearing her quirky, colored reading glasses. Those were meant to be fun. Her eyes did not have the cheer that usually danced around the irises. She'd left her "cheery" bedside manner downstairs on the maternity floor with the happy mothers who were holding their babies and nursing their babies and naming their babies names they would say a million times. Dr. Cotter made a lengthy show of looking at my vitals. I knew she had checked my chart at the desk before she came in, because that was the way it was done. But I suppose she had to do something since there was nothing her training could do to really fix what had happened. "Have you been resting?"

Mekhi's answer came before I could curse her out for asking. "She has on and off."

"Good. That's for the best." Dr. Cotter looked at him, not at me. "Samaria, I want to check your incision."

I didn't respond. I closed my eyes. I felt the blanket move. She poked and prodded, but I didn't feel it. I was numb there too. "Looks good." I opened my eyes. Dr. Cotter cleared her throat. "Mr. Johnson, may I speak with you outside?" She was already moving toward the door.

Mekhi let go of my hand and shifted to leave, but he stopped when I opened my mouth.

"I want to know."

An eerie stillness fell over the room. Neither Dr. Cotter nor Mekhi moved. I leaned forward, grabbed the handrails, and pulled myself higher on the bed. It was the first time she had heard my voice in two days, and she was noticeably shocked.

Dr. Cotter looked from me to Mekhi and retraced the steps she had just made and reclaimed the left side of the bed. Mekhi took my hand, raised it to his lips, and kissed it. Then he squeezed and covered it with his other hand, so they cupped mine completely.

"You requested a DNA test, and the result showed that Mr. Johnson was not the father."

I heard Mekhi take a deep breath. I turned my head to see if relief would paint its release on his face when he let it out, but it didn't. Worry lines filled his forehead and his sad eyes became sadder. How could I have doubted him? Mekhi wanted this baby. He still lost something. He'd lost his dream.

"You also commissioned a private autopsy, and it's been completed." Although Dr. Cotter attempted to keep her voice even and flat, I was aware of the slightest change in her tone, a high-pitched sound that I associated with nervousness.

I looked from Mekhi to her, then pushed the button to raise the back of the bed a little more. I waited in much the way I had been existing: without my heart beating, without my chest rising and falling.

"The autopsy was inconclusive."

I died.

A beat passed, and I heard Mekhi ask, "What does that mean?"

"It means that there was no cause of death that we could determine with certainty."

I died again.

"How could that happen?"

"She was only twenty-three weeks. Autopsies are often inconclusive at that age. I'm sorry."

I died again.

"There was no genetic thing? The cord wasn't wrapped around her neck or something like that?"

"No, not that we could determine, but the results of the genetic testing are not completed yet. Mr. Johnson, twenty-three weeks is extremely early. The rate of survival is less than 40 percent."

I died again.

"There isn't always—"

"Stop!" I shook my head. "Dr. Cotter, please leave."

She blinked rapidly. "Please let me know—"

"Now!" I reached for the flowers on my nightstand and hurled them across the room. The vase smashed into a mirror. It exploded, and both shattered into a million tiny shards of glass that flew everywhere.

Dr. Cotter escaped. I grabbed Mekhi's arm, and then his shirt. Tiny translucent buttons popped off, but still I pulled him to me as I reached up for his shoulders and his neck. He tried to comfort me with words my ears would not hear. If I could get out of this bed, I would climb inside him—make our bodies one. If I could become Mekhi, then I wouldn't feel the heartbreak. A sharp pain tore through my belly. Pain I wanted to feel. I wanted to punish myself, so I suffered as I pulled him closer and found tears that I thought had dried up the last time I cried. I heard a wounded animal scream in pain. I heard a human cry out like a savage. I heard both of them as if they were coming from inside of me, but I knew they hadn't, because I had died.

Chapter 45

Samaria

"Be not deceived; God is not mocked: for whatsoever a man soweth, that shall he also reap." I closed the Bible at the book of Galatians and returned it to the nightstand. Sowing and reaping—was that what this was about? I had been a bad girl, and now I had a dead baby. Before I could beat myself up with my latest theory, the door to my room opened and my new physician, Dr. Stanley, and a nurse walked in. It was time for my daily tummy check.

I had gotten rid of Dr. Cotter. On some level I blamed her; after all, she was the doctor. I needed to blame someone. I wanted to blame her, so, she couldn't continue my care. She had been one word away from having a hole stomped in her back, and I had enough legal trouble. There was no point adding "disabling a white woman" to the list of charges. Dr. Stanley was a serious man with no bedside manner, who never smiled. He was exactly what I needed.

"I believe we can get you discharged tomorrow," he said.

I was disappointed. My exaggerated sigh didn't mask it. "Why not today?"

"I've contacted a counselor to do an exit assessment. I won't be able to release you until you've had a chat with her. It's routine in these cases."

These cases. His clinical demeanor was stoic. Dr. Stanley had no cheer, no games, and no funny eyeglasses tucked in his pocket. It was a good match for my depressed state.

He reviewed my vitals, lifted the sheet to check for swelling in my legs and tummy. "Her visit won't happen until first thing tomorrow morning, so we'll keep you here, make sure the rupture in that incision continues to heal."

I nodded again.

"Are you comfortable?" he asked.

Are you from Mars? I thought.

"Medication-wise," he added as if he'd read my mind.

"I'm fine."

"Good." He used a stylus to make notes in his hand-held tablet. When he was done, he raised his head, looked into what had to be a very blank face, and said, "I'll see you in the morning. Don't hesitate to let me know if you need anything." He patted my blanketed shin and left the room.

I sighed, then pushed the button to raise my head. It was time for me to get out of this bed. If I could walk across the room, I just might put on my clothes and walk out of this God-forsaken hospital. I might figure out how to get to Mars.

The automated handrail went completely down, and I slowly moved my legs over the side until they touched the floor. In truth, I should have been walking before now. Normally, Cesarean patients walk within the first twenty-four hours, but I was not the typical patient. I had not had the typical Cesarean, so I wasn't going to comply with the protocol for care.

The door opened, and Mekhi walked in. I gripped the blanket, my back raised like a cornered cat.

"You're up. That's great." He joined me at the side of my bed, took my arm, and helped me stand up straight. "I just saw Dr. Stanley, and he told me you could go home tomorrow."

"I'm going home today," I replied, not looking at him. I could feel his disapproval.

"Sammie, you need to follow the doctor's orders. You want your body to heal."

I took slow steps across the floor. Mekhi assisted me. I felt amazingly well for someone who had her heart ripped out through her abdomen. Even with the stress of what I'd done yesterday, I was just sore.

"Sam." I heard pleading in Mekhi's voice.

I stopped moving, pieces of my long hair swung like a jungle vine in front of me. I know I looked like a wild animal. I'd scarcely touched myself since I'd come to this room. I looked into his eyes, saw what he wanted: a name. *We have to name her.* That was what he was going to say.

"As soon as we name her—"

I stopped breathing.

"We can have a service before you go home." Mekhi shifted from one foot to the other, as if he was afraid of how I would respond to what he said.

Why was he so willing to close the chapter on her life, to put her in a casket or a box or whatever they were going to do with her? Why was he pushing me to let her go? I dropped my head back. I was getting tired of fighting, and the truth was, I knew what I wanted to name her the first time I'd felt her kick. "Melia," I whispered, pushing the words through my throat. "Let's name her Melia."

Mekhi let out a heavy breath. He turned his body in front of mine, swept his hands up and down my arms a couple of times, and kissed me on the top of my head.

"Thank you." He raised my chin and pressed his forehead against mine. "Thank you," he repeated, and I knew what he meant. *Thank you for not making me ask you again, thank you for helping me to close this chapter, thank you, thank you, thank you for not losing your mind.* "I like it." Mekhi nodded. "It's a good cross between our names."

"I thought so." I appreciated him being okay with the "our" because we both knew I had not been carrying his seed and that this horror really belonged to me alone. I crept the rest of the way across the floor to the restroom and closed the door. Once inside, I turned the faucet to the on position, leaned back against the wall, and cried for the thousandth time since my Melia had died.

Chapter 46

Samaria

We held a service for Melia in the chapel. Mekhi had arranged for it to just be himself, the chaplain, and me. He'd also set up a private burial later this week when I was released from the hospital.

The chaplain, a retired local pastor, had to be close to ninety years old. He was a kind man, and he read several scriptures and said some words of consolation to us. When we were done, he handed me a small pamphlet about dealing with the death of an infant and we thanked him. I turned and to my surprise, Angelina was sitting in one of the chairs in the back. She stood, her slightly bulging belly unable to hide itself, shocked me, saddened me, and made me happy for her all at the same time. I hadn't noticed the other day. I remembered she had been wearing an empire waist sundress, but in this slimmer cut outfit it was obvious.

Mekhi was still talking to the pastor. Angelina made a timid approach. "I didn't want to invade your privacy. The nurse told me you were in here."

I reached for her. Hugged her around the neck. I'd missed those hugs. "You could never be unwelcome," I said as fresh tears welled in my eyes.

"I thought I should give you a little time, but I didn't want to wait so long that you thought I forgot you." Her nervous wringing of a linen handkerchief clued me into her emotions.

"Today was a good day. I managed to get out of bed," I said. "I'm going home tomorrow."

She opened her mouth, and then closed it, reducing her thoughts to a nod.

I wanted to acknowledge her pregnancy, but I couldn't. As much as I loved her, I couldn't think about anyone having a baby when I'd lost mine.

"Angelina." Mekhi joined us and we waited until the chaplain left the room. "It's good to see you."

I got into the wheelchair I had traveled in, and we made small talk in the elevator back to my room. Mekhi asked Angelina if she could stay for a little while. He needed to run to the studio, but didn't want to leave me alone. She agreed.

Although I didn't make much use of it when we initially got to my room, I was glad to have her company. I stared at the garden outside my window. It included waterfalls, tropical plants, and life-size and lifelike statues of indigenous creatures. A man-made rainforest outside of a hospital room in downtown Atlanta; it was amazing the things that money could buy, but the money that I'd always craved and always wanted could not replace the thing that meant the most to me. Melia was gone. I had to accept it.

We had been sitting in my room for more than five minutes in silence. Like a good listener, she was waiting for me to speak, and I had no words. My entire world had slid into an abyss. "I don't understand," I said.

"I don't know that you're supposed to," Angelina replied.

"I keep going over things I did in my head. Foods I ate or things I drank. Did I miss too many prenatal vitamins?" I slammed my fist down on the hard rubber armrest of the wheelchair. "What did I do wrong?"

Tears began to stream down my face. I looked at her. I wanted her, who was so smart and so wise, to have the answer. My eyes searched hers. Compassion, sympathy, and sadness were all there, but I could tell, the answers were not.

"Samaria, I doubt if you did anything wrong."

"But she was fine. I know she was early, but she was fine, and then she wasn't. I don't understand that. Why did she have to be so early?" I groaned. It was deep and long, and then I grunted. It was a new, guttural sound that I had been using to control the pain. I was trying to push the ache down into my belly so I wouldn't have to feel it in my heart. I burst into tears. Angelina stood from her seat and came to rub my back.

I groaned and grunted a few more times before I asked, "Am I reaping what I sowed?"

Angelina was silent for a moment. I thought she might be considering my question and trying to figure out how to say, *Yes, heifer, if you hadn't been running around with married men and stealing stuff, you might not have so much to reap.*

"Samaria, I don't believe you reaped what you sowed. I don't know why she—"

"Melia," I interrupted. "I named her Melia."

Angelina pulled the chair she had been sitting in closer to me and sat down. "Melia. It's beautiful." I knew the weight of her belly was heavy on her back and legs. I knew it well, because I'd just been carrying it. I sighed. I needed to congratulate her. I opened my mouth to try to get it out, but she spoke before I could speak the words.

"Did you take pictures of her?" Angelina asked.

"We did, but Mekhi took them home. He thought it best—" I paused and let a river of tears pour out of my soul. "She was a pretty baby. She was going to look just like . . ." I froze. I hadn't realized until just now that Melia looked like Greg. I was so upset about her death that when I held her I just thought she looked beautiful and peaceful, not about how much she didn't look like me or Mekhi.

"Just like who?" Angelina asked.

I raised my hand to my lips. *Lie,* I thought. *You have to lie to her.* But I couldn't lie. Not to her. Not anymore. Not about Melia. "She looked like her father." Our eyes met. I know mine were filled with sorrow, but soon I saw their image mirrored in Angelina's.

"Her father." Angelina repeated the words slowly, and then she didn't have a question on her face anymore. She stood. Fine worry lines had etched themselves across her forehead. "Excuse me. I need to use the restroom." She rushed out.

I sat there with my guilt covering me like a heavy cloak. Guilt about sowing and reaping, guilt about Greg being the father, guilt about Mekhi not being the father, and now guilt about Angelina's pain. I was the common denominator in all this sorrow. I had done so much to hurt the people I loved. "God forgive me," I croaked out the words, and then I cried some more.

Angelina returned looking better than she had before she'd left. "I'm sorry," she said, "the urge came over me quickly."

I could hear a slight tremor in her voice. She was disappointed, but no matter what, she was not going to disappoint me with attitude. I wondered if that's how "good" Christian women handled their issues. Superman changed in a phone booth. Did they excuse themselves to the restroom and come out stronger, faster Christians than they were before?

Angelina took a seat. "Samaria, I don't want you to beat yourself up about Melia. I did that. I know what it's like. I almost killed myself with what-ifs. What if I had been home, what if I hadn't needed to stop at the store, what if I had her when I was twenty-five instead of thirty-five, what if, what if, what if. Don't do it. This is not your fault."

"But why did she have to die? She was a baby. She was innocent."

"All I can tell you is the same thing I've been telling myself for years. There are some things we won't understand on this side of eternity."

More tears erupted. I began to sob and gasp and moan. Despair gripped me, but then so did Angelina. She took my hand that still held the residue of tears and did something no one else had done for me since I lost my daughter. She began to pray.

Chapter 47

Samaria

It was time to slay the dragon. I turned off the car's engine, stepped out, and walked to my mother's front door. I pushed the doorbell without hesitation for if I hesitated I might lose my nerve. I might go back to that dark place where I was reasoning away behavior that was unreasonable and let her manipulate me into doing what was wrong, again.

She didn't answer at first. It was early for her, 11:00 A.M., so I expected that I might be waking her. I rang the bell again, multiple times, and she finally opened the door.

"Whatchoo doing here so early?"

"Hello to you too."

She stepped back, and I ventured into the room.

My mother closed the door and claimed her seat on the recliner she loved to sit in. There was no place for me to sit. The sofa and armchair I'd purchased for her a few months ago were gone. I wondered where June lay his hulking body when they watched their menu of reality television shows, but then I saw a set of large pillows on the floor in the corner and reasoned that he pulled those out and hit the floor. I shook my head.

"What you trippin' for? The furniture was mine. It was a gift. I can do anything with a gift that I want." She lit a cigarette and blew a plume of smoke.

"You're right." I waved the smoke away. I did give new furniture to a drug addict. What did I expect?

"Your insides still healing. You should sit. Get a chair out of the kitchen."

"What I have to say won't take long. I'm just here to tell you that Mekhi isn't going to be supplying you with drugs anymore. We're willing to pay for you to go to a residential rehabilitation program, but no more drugs."

My mother blew smoke.

"There's a rehab center that's highly recommended. It's very nice. They have a bed and are willing to take you right away, but they usually have a waiting list, so you'd need to make a decision quickly."

My mother blew more smoke.

"I've decided to take a plea deal. A year in jail. I'll probably have to report to start serving my sentence in a month or so."

My mother blew more smoke.

"Don't you have anything to say?"

"What should I say? You got everything figured out."

"Mama, I'm just trying to help you and help me and save Mekhi from both of us."

"Girl, what in the devil is you talking about, save Mekhi?"

I dropped my head back. I wasn't going to listen to the "all men are dogs" rant from her when the only person hurting me right now was her. "I am saving Mekhi from our drama. Yours and mine. He doesn't need to spend another $30,000 trying to keep me out prison and I'm not . . ." Steam rose in my belly from an empty space that until recently had held my baby. "Mama, I'm not going to let Mekhi go to jail or lose his business over you. You who never, ever in all the years I've known you, done one thing for anyone other than yourself or June, and even what you do for him is self-serving."

"Now you wait a minute now. Who do you think raised you?"

"I raised myself!" I yelled. "That's what's wrong with me. You were never home unless you had some low-life man around, and even then you didn't take care of me. You let them stare at me and touch me."

"Yous a lie. Ain't nobody ever touched you."

"Yes, they did. You know it, Mama. So even when you were home you weren't looking out for me."

"Ain't nobody ever touched you, Samaria. Stop coming in here with those lies."

"Yes, they did, Mama. Roscoe did more than touch me."

My mother was silent. She took a deep breath, and then a few more puffs from her cigarette. She wouldn't look me in the eye.

"I thought you'd remember Roscoe."

"I barely remember Roscoe. You coming in here with all this old mess from almost twenty years ago."

"Fifteen years ago. I was fourteen. I remember how I had to let him feel it one afternoon so he would go pay the light bill and I could get my homework done. How'd you think the lights got back on?"

She stubbed the butt of the cigarette into the ashtray and lit another. "Well, I guess you was just earning your keep." This time she looked me right in the eyes.

"Earning my keep." I turned my head. I couldn't look at her. I swallowed, let out a wind of disgust, and met her eyes again. "I carried my daughter for less than six months. I would have done anything on the earth to protect her. I would have died in her place if she could have lived. So, I do not understand how you could abuse me for so many years." Tears I'd been fighting began to spill down my cheeks. "I'm going to jail because of you, because I always wanted to try to make you happy with me, but I've figured it out. I can't make you happy with me. You've got to start out being happy with yourself, and I have no control over that."

"You ain't going to jail because of me. You stole them pills. I didn't put no gun to your head."

"But you raised me to think it was okay to take things that didn't belong to me. You didn't instill any values or decent morals. That was your job."

My mother waved her hand. "I made sure you had some place to sleep, something to wear, and something to eat. That's all I had to do for you."

"That's all the law requires, but when you love someone, you want more than the bare minimum for them, more than just food, clothing, and shelter, and that's it. You failed me, and you can sit in that chair and convince yourself that it's okay, that you did the best you could or that it doesn't matter, but it does. You had one child, and you messed her up." I removed a tissue from my purse and wiped my eyes. "But I'm done with it. Losing Melia has taught me that life is precious. I'm not spending any more of my time on stuff or people who aren't going to make my life better."

I waited a beat and watched my mother roll her eyes and scrunch up her face. She did everything but make eye contact with me, because she was guilty. She knew I was right.

"If you decide not to go to rehab, we'll pay your rent every month, direct to the office, but that's it. No allowance." I reached into my purse and pulled out the brochure for the rehab center and placed it on the table next to her. She glanced at it, but did not pick it up. "Those are the terms."

I turned and walked the few steps it took to close the distance between where I had been standing and the door.

Then I heard the chair creak. "So that's it?" My mother had stood. "You gon' come in here and tell me you gonna pay $185 in rent for me. With all that money Mekhi making off of Benxi. You ungrateful heifer."

I flinched and turned to look at her. "Mekhi doesn't owe you anything."

"Yes, he does. He's my son-in-law."

"Yeah, and what a saint he was for marrying me in spite of you." I turned the knob, opened the door, stepped out of the apartment, and let out a deep breath. The dragon was dead.

The rest of my day was busy with errands. I went to the bank, withdrew $25,000 in a cashier's check, and mailed it to Greg's office. Next, I met with my attorney and the district attorney at the DA's office. The DA slid the necessary paperwork for the plea deal in front of me, and I picked up the pen they offered.

"Are you sure about this?" Hightower asked. "You've been through a lot. Is Mekhi in agreement?"

I met Hightower's eyes. He looked so sad for me. "I'll tell him tonight."

"He'll be very disappointed if you don't let him help you make this decision."

"My mind is made up. Sometimes when you do the crime, you gotta know when to do the time." I smiled. "It'll be okay. I'll help him understand." I pulled the papers closer, thought about reading them for a moment, but realized Hightower would not allow me to commit to anything that wasn't on the up-and-up and signed them.

The DA pulled the papers back, and we all stood. He shook Hightower's hand and said, "In light of Mrs. Johnson's recent surgery and pending medical release, we'll get back to you on the date she'll report." Then he turned to me. "Mrs. Johnson, our condolences to you and your husband. Thank you for saving the citizens of Fulton County the expense of a trial."

We all left the office. Hightower and I parted ways in the parking lot. I climbed in my car, put down the ragtop, and let the wind blow against my face, through my hair, and into my soul. Even though I'd just signed my physical freedom away for a year, dealing with my mother and Greg and adding closure to this situation had set my spirit free.

Chapter 48

Mekhi

I sat across the table from Samaria and thought I saw a glimmer of my old girl. She'd hooked up the table for romance—flowers, candles, wedding china. I figured she must be in the mood even though she was a week away from being released from her doctor's care. I wanted her, in a way I had never wanted her before. I wanted to heal all the broken, hurt places in her spirit. I wanted to fill her with the promise that no matter what, I was always going to love her, I had forgiven her, and I would protect her.

"We need to talk," Samaria said after I scooped the last bit of my ice-cream sundae from the dish. "I have some things to tell you."

I wiped my mouth, stood, and pulled my seat closer. I reached for her, kissed her fingers, and raised her hand to the side of my face. She was staring at me with those big brown eyes that I loved so much. I don't think I've ever seen her look so serious. "What's on your mind, baby?"

Samaria sighed. "You already know why I was having the paternity test, but I want to tell you about the money."

I wished I could tell her it was okay and say I didn't want to talk about it, but that was where I'd gone wrong months ago when I bailed Samaria out of jail. I told her that night that her past was her past and she didn't need to tell me any of it. I'd silenced her on more than one occasion when she'd said we should talk, because I didn't want to think of the woman I'd known to only want me from the time we were teenagers as a woman who'd been through many men over the eight years we were apart. My ego was in the way of the truth, and she'd paid for it by feeling forced to lie, so I nodded my head. "Tell me," and she did.

I sat back, but continued to hold her hand. "That was low-down of him to blackmail you."

"Greg's not that bad. I think he was desperate."

"Threatening my wife. I ought to break his jaw."

Samaria shook her head. "I returned his money today. Greg is behind us in more ways than one."

I heard her swallow hard, and her eyes got misty. I suppose thinking about him made her think about Melia. Then I felt horrible for letting my ego speak. "I'm sorry, Sammie. I should be more sensitive."

She sniffed, picked up a napkin, and wiped the corner of her eyes. "It's okay. You're just trying to protect me." She returned the napkin to the table. "I love that about you."

"I would have given you the money for a lawyer for custody court. I'd do anything for you. Don't you know I'm always going to have your back?"

"I should have known that, but I was too messed up with my issues to trust you. You know, the issues you told me that would bleed into this marriage."

"Well, I'm glad you trust me now, 'cause I got you, girl; always and forever." I stroked her face.

"Another thing," she paused. I could tell this was going to be harder to speak about than the last one. "I talked to my mother. I told her she was no longer getting drugs from you. Not anything unless she agrees to rehab."

I squinted, thought about the implications of that, but before I could open my mouth, she spoke words that broke my heart into a million little pieces.

"I signed a plea deal agreement today."

I stood, resisting the urge to put my fist through another wall by pacing in circles a few times. *A plea deal; guaranteed jail time. Why? How could you?* I fell back in my chair. I put my hands to my head and shook it. Tears welled up in my eyes.

"It's for the best, Khi. It's a year. I'm guaranteed to do the time in a county jail in the metro area. Hightower says I'll probably only do six months because with good behavior and overcrowding they'll cut my time."

I raised my eyes to hers. I tried hard to fight the tears that wanted to come, but I couldn't. They fell.

"We're not going to get a better deal than six months. I'm not going to let you go through a public trial. You've worked too hard to keep letting my reputation bring you down."

I wiped my eyes. "I wish you had talked to me, baby. I was working on something."

She reached for my chin and used a thumb to wipe a tear that had slid down my jawbone. "Not something that's legal or right, Khi, 'cause there's nothing legal or right that you could do to fix this. I don't want anyone else doing things that aren't right to help me. I got in this mess trying to right my mother's wrong. Bad behavior can only bring bad results."

I scratched the side of my head. I heard her, but I didn't want to believe I couldn't save her. I didn't want to believe I couldn't protect her. She was my woman. That was my job.

"Stop letting the wheels in your head turn. I just need you to visit me as often as possible and make sure I got money on my book at the commissary so I can shop." She smiled. I tried to smile with her, but I felt like I had a knife sticking in my heart. Samaria stood, slid on my lap, and rubbed her hands across my head. "It's time for me to make a sacrifice, to prove how I feel about you."

I let out a breath. She was right. Going to jail to keep me out of hot water with UMC was the ultimate proof. "I love you, baby."

"I love you too." She kissed me down to my soul. It removed thoughts of jail, the debt I owed UMC, the deal I'd made with Benxi that I knew I was not going to make good on no matter what went down. That kiss erased the entire world.

Samaria and I climbed the stairs, stripped off our clothes, and crawled into bed. We couldn't make love the way I wanted to, but it was all good. We talked. Really talked. I told her about my previous business dealings and history with Benxi. She told me about some dudes from her past and some scheming she'd done to get money. We were intimate in a way that we'd never been before. Sharing who we were, our faults and failures and our dreams was better than gettin' down. When we were done talking, when our souls were emotionally spent, we held each other until we both fell asleep.

Part IV
Angelina and Greg

"He that trusteth in his own heart is a fool: but whoso walketh wisely, he shall be delivered."
~ Proverbs 28:26

Chapter 49

Greg

"It's a boy."

I threw my hands up victoriously. *"That's* what I'm talking about."

The ultrasound tech continued to take pictures. "Yeah, he's a good size too." She took paper towels and wiped Angelina's belly.

Angelina sat up. "I thought we were never going to find out what this baby was," she said. "This is our third ultrasound."

"He's stubborn." I pulled Angelina to a sitting position. "Just like his mother."

She smirked and stepped down from the bed. "His mother needs to get all this water off her bladder." She wobbled out of the room, and I hung back for the pictures.

I was having a son. I wanted to shout it to the entire world. It would make up for the fact that Samaria's baby died. Although I hadn't wanted a baby with her, she was another daughter, gone, and the thought of that saddened me. It reminded me of Danielle.

We drove back to Angelina's house. She intercepted her mail and a letter from her lawyer, Hightower, stating that the IRS had requested her presence at a summation meeting, meaning the investigation was complete.

"I wonder what they'll say." Her big brown eyes focused on mine.

"They're going to say it's all over," I reassured her. "This mess has come to an end." The media had long moved on from the story. Angelina had told me the hate mail and phone calls had finally stopped. She'd temporarily closed the office, deciding, instead, to focus on her pregnancy and raising Katrice. I was glad. Angelina was making a lot of changes, but one of them wasn't letting me come back home. After Samaria's child was born I thought I would be in the clear, but it had been almost two months since Samaria delivered and still the answers from my wife's lips were *No, you can't come home. No, I'm not ready to reconcile. Greg, I'm not convinced you're any different.* I didn't know what I was supposed to do, so I enlisted the help of her best friend.

Felesia Sosa climbed onto a barstool next to me and ordered a virgin margarita. I'd known Felesia since college when she and Angelina were roommates. If there was anyone who could give me the inside scoop on what my wife was thinking, it was her best friend. "What's up, Daddy, 'cause I know this isn't about the baby shower?"

"What is up with Angelina? You know I want to reconcile, and her answer is 'no,' 'not yet,' 'stop asking.'"

Felesia laughed. I couldn't imagine what she found funny. "So, you want me to tell you? What does Angelina say?"

"She's not saying anything."

Felesia laughed again. "She saying something, but you're not listening."

"Well, help a brother out because if she's saying something, I'm not hearing."

"You sure you want me to tell you?"

"I'm desperate."

"Greg, I've talked to Angelina about taking you back. We've talked a few times. Not that you're my favorite person for cheating on her with that woman, but I know she loves you, and I know you love her, so I don't want her to give up on you."

"Okay, so—"

The bartender slid a glass in front of her. "She wants your heart in the right place."

"What do you mean? I'm never going to cheat again. I swear. This thing has been like a remake of *Fatal Attraction*. I learned my lesson."

"I think she wants your heart in the right place spiritually. She doesn't believe that you'll stay true to her if you aren't in a relationship with God."

"So, I gotta go to church every Sunday?"

"That's not what I said. I said a relationship. That's more than church, hombre."

I dropped my head back. "You don't just get like that with God."

"Yes, you do, if you want to, unless something's stopping you."

"Something like what?"

Felesia raised her glass to her lips and peered at me over the rim. "Something like a little anger or resentment."

I turned away from her. *Here we go again.*

"You ain't gotta look me in the eye. I know it's true. You want an answer to your question, but then again, you don't want it. Angelina wants you off the team with the backsliders and until you do that, you gonna stay in that little apartment."

I nodded. "You forgot lonely," I said.

Felesia looked confused.

"It's a lonely little apartment." I looked at her and smirked.

Felesia laughed. "Oh, poppy, so sorry for you." She pinched my cheek, then took a long sip to finish her drink. "I gotta go. My date is here." She stood. "You find the faith." She gave me a sympathetic pat on the hand and walked away.

My mother, Phil, and now Felesia. Everybody had the same thing to say. Team Backsliders. I admit I had been sitting on that bench, but it wasn't one you just got off. The coach had to put you in the game. If Angelina was expecting me to just get all holy, she was being unrealistic. It just didn't work that way.

"Is she coming back?" The voice, female and sexy, purred the words from my left.

I swallowed and looked. She had to be some kind of video vixen. I blinked, turned my head, and I looked straight-ahead.

"Is she?" Perfume made its way to my nostrils. Her body heat told me she'd stepped closer. Blood coursed through my veins. *You need some sex.* I was going to have to fight that message. I reached for my wallet and with shaky hands, I removed some bills.

"Are you trying to be a good boy?" Her hand was on my arm. She was not even attempting to be subtle. "You don't have to be good. I'm from out of town, and I won't tell."

I looked at her again, this time from head to toe. I took in her strappy shoes, shapely calves, big hips, tiny waist, and exposed chest. My heart started to pound. *It's just sex. You ain't had none in half a year,* the voice inside my head said. I wanted to scream, but instead, I took control. "I'm leaving."

She squeezed my arm. "You sure that's what you want to do?"

I cleared my throat and looked my demon in the eyes. "Yeah, so please, stop begging."

Anger flashed across her face, and she snatched her hand from my arm. I watched her take that small waist and big behind down to the other end of the bar. Then I stood and got the attention of the bartender. I handed him the bills and walked out of the bar. As much as my body was craving the release only a woman would give, I'd learned my lesson. Being with anyone other than Angelina was wrong.

Chapter 50

Angelina

"How much longer is this going to go on?" Felesia zoomed past me from the outside and turned, hand on hip in a feet tapping frenzy.

I closed the door and tilted my head toward her. "Do you mind clarifying what you're talking about?"

Felesia swung her long hair over her shoulder. "You know what I'm talking about, Angelina. How long are you going to keep up this stalling tactic with Greg?"

I shrugged a little. "I'm not stalling."

"Yes, you are." Felesia paused. "And if you don't stop you're going to lose him." Those words made my stomach drop. How could she know that just before she rang my phone, announcing that she was outside and demanding that I open the door, I had been sitting here in the dark thinking the exact same thing? I'd been thinking that I was going to lose Greg, baby or no baby, if I couldn't figure out how to find my way back to him, back to our lives, back to our marriage. Tears filled my eyes. That had been happening every night now. Crying about this, crying about that, crying about everything, crying about nothing. The moment Katrice's head hit the pillow, I was crying. "I don't know how to trust it."

"Trust it or him?" Felesia put down her purse and walked toward me. She grabbed my hands and tugged for her answer.

"It. Our future." My lip quivered. "I don't think I could breathe if he had another affair."

Felesia raised her hand and wiped the lone tear that slid down my face. "Mami, you're not breathing now."

I sobbed and wrapped my arms around her.

"Angelina, I love you. You know I'm on your side no matter what you do, but this stubbornness . . . It has to end. Ultimatums to get someone saved. It won't work. You know better than that." She pulled away from me and raised my lowered head with a hand under my chin. "You love him. He's your husband. Just take him back and trust God to do the rest of it."

I shook my head, moved out of her reach, and sat down on the sofa. "I don't have to live with a cheating husband."

"But you won't be happy without Greg." Felesia got on the floor in front of me. "You can't get a divorce to punish him. In the end, you'll be punishing yourself. He's sorry, Angelina. You know he is."

I was fighting to hold on to my position, to hold on to that safe place where Greg was hanging on the outskirts of my heart. The place where my sore spots had begun to scab over and thinking about his unfaithfulness didn't hurt so much. I looked into the pleading eyes of my best friend. I knew she wanted me to be happy, or she wouldn't be begging me on her knees.

"Angelina, forgive him," she said. "I know his anger with God is misplaced, but you can't expect Greg to forgive God, when you won't set an example and forgive him."

Those words forced me to swallow my anger and pride. "You're right. I keep telling myself that I've forgiven him, but I haven't," I cried. Felesia reached up and hugged me. I swiped at my tears and wordlessly asked God to forgive me.

***

I spent the night praying about Greg and the next day, I didn't feel well. At first I thought I was just sleepy, but then I realized it was more than that. My blood pressure was normal. I'd checked it twice, but still I was struggling to catch my breath. I didn't remember having this kind of trouble breathing with my first pregnancy.

"Mommy, can we go to the park?" Katrice startled me. I had dozed off.

I took a deep breath, coughed a few times, and adjusted myself on the sofa to a higher position. "No, sweetie. Not today."

"But, Mommy, you should go to the park and walk because your feet need to walk." I smiled. Those twisted up little sentences were adorable. "Look at your feet, Mommy. They need a walk."

I looked down at my feet and had to fight from gasping in horror. They were swollen up like sausages, and so were my hands. I struggled to get off the sofa. The skin on my feet was stretched so tight that it actually hurt to stand on them. I checked my blood pressure again and called Dr. Luke to let him know what was going on. His nurse took a note of my symptoms and told me she'd have the doctor get back to me when he returned from lunch.

I put a new video in the DVD player for Katrice. Once I was sure she would be entertained for thirty minutes, I went into the library, sat down, and opened my Bible. I read over the scriptures from Sunday's message, hoping they'd give me a sense of peace; then I closed my eyes and began to pray. I asked God to show me if something was wrong, because I didn't want to depend on a doctor. I wanted to depend on Him. I fought the urge to nod off.

"Mommy, Mommy, I didn't know where you was." I heard Katrice before I was fully conscious. "Mommy, you look like Barney. You need to go walk."

Something was wrong. I could hardly breathe. I touched my face, and I could tell it was swollen. I heard crackling in my lungs. My heart was racing so fast I thought it would pound right out of my chest.

"Katrice, baby, can you get Mama's cell phone?"

She nodded and disappeared. A minute later she returned with it, and I called Chelsea. She arrived before I got off the phone with Greg and the 911 operator. She looked at me like I was a freak. It didn't take long for the ambulance to come. They assessed me and decided I needed to go to the hospital immediately.

I don't know how he did it, but I think Greg beat us there. I was seen in the Emergency Room, given a diuretic for the edema, and a breathing treatment that helped some but not as much as I would have liked. The doctors were throwing around a bunch of medical terms and performing various tests. Through it all, Greg held my hand, asked, and answered questions quickly and efficiently. He explained everything they were doing and tried his very best to comfort me, but I could see fear in his eyes, which didn't help with my anxiety. As a colleague, he received the maximum possible amount of professional courtesy. I knew I was probably getting served a little more promptly than the average patient.

I was admitted. They managed to get some of the fluid off me, but not much, and I was wearing an oxygen mask to help improve my oxygen levels.

My obstetrician, Dr. Luke, entered the room. I'd seen so many strange doctors since I was admitted that I was glad to see a familiar face. "How are you doing?" he asked.

I nodded. "I don't think very well."

"We're running tests, and I'm consulting with a few specialists," Dr. Luke said.

I nodded understanding. "Do you have a preliminary diagnosis?"

"Greg can tell you. We really have to wait until we get the full battery of tests back." He put his stethoscope in his ears and examined me.

I decided to stop asking the question no one was going to answer for me. My husband looked scared. That unsettled me, because Greg was as cool as a cucumber most of the time. Did that mean I was in worse trouble than I was imagining?

I reached for Greg's hand, and he turned to look at me. "It's going to be okay. God's not going to let anything happen to me or the baby. You'll see."

Relief lit his eyes for a few seconds. He learned over and kissed my forehead. Then he wrapped his arms around my back and pulled me into an awkward embrace. I drew myself close to him and repeated my own words in my head. *God's not going to let anything happen to me or the baby.* I had to believe that. I was going to stand on those words.

Chapter 51

Greg

My phone vibrated, and I all but tiptoed out of the room and into the corridor to talk to my mother.

"How is Angelina?" she asked.

"Sleeping." I noted the time on the wall clock. A little after twelve, which meant it was after eleven in New Orleans. I could hear background sounds like a pot clattering and cupboards opening and closing. "It's late for you. What are you doing out of bed?"

"Praying," she replied. "And making a cup of tea. How are you holding up?"

I stretched and scratched the back of my neck. "I'm hanging in here, Mom. What else am I going to do?"

"Have you tried praying?"

I sighed. "I don't know." I shook my head. "I feel like I'd be a hypocrite. Praying when I'm in trouble. Does God listen to that?"

"I think you should be focused on what you believe, not what God believes."

I pushed the door to Angelina's room open and peeked at her. She was still sleeping. I let it close and walked down to the lounge. "Maybe I should pray. I'm pretty desperate at this point." I reached into my pocket for money and got some bottled water out of a vending machine.

"Gregory, don't you think it's time to make peace with God?"

"Don't you think if I'm talking to God it should be about my wife? Angelina is the one in the hospital bed." I shook my head. "And I don't mean to take nothing from the big guy upstairs' track record, but Angelina is a good person. She prays all the time. Why is this happening to her?"

"Maybe it's not happening to her."

I cocked my head away from the phone. "What do you mean?"

"Maybe Angelina's illness is about you."

I fell down into a chair near the vending machines. I didn't think I'd heard her correctly. I respected my mother. I respected what she believed, but this was too much. "So, are you saying she's sick because of me? That my child could die and my wife could die because I'm backslidden?"

"Do you remember me telling you that God was going to have His way . . . that He would get you on your knees one way or another?"

I didn't respond. I was seriously too busy fighting the urge to hang up the phone.

"Pray, son."

I started a slow count to ten in my head, got to five, and said, "I have to go."

"You go, but think about what I said. Don't be a fool, Gregory. You were raised to know better than what you're doing."

I closed my eyes. She ended the call. I stuck my phone in my pocket, stretched my legs out, and opened the water. I downed it in a couple of long swallows and threw the empty bottle against the recycling bin. Then I just sat there for a long time, thinking about my mother's words. The longer I sat, the less crazy they felt, because I remembered Philip saying the same thing.

Don't be a fool. Ironic that she had chosen to use that particular word when I thought God directed me to the scripture about a fool believing there is no God.

I leaned forward, perched my elbows on my knees, and dropped my head in my hands.

"God, I'm trying. But I need your help." I looked up at the ceiling. "I told you before that I believe in you. I believe you exist, but I just don't know that I'm sure you care. Show me you care. Heal my wife, and I'll never question you again."

Telling God what to do I was pretty sure that's not how it was supposed to work, but talking to God was a one-sided affair. All I had to say was what I wanted. What else was I going to come up with? I let out a frustrated groan, stood, walked back to Angelina's room, climbed on my uncomfortable chair bed, and tried to close my eyes. *Don't be a fool*, reverberated in my mind. I closed my eyes, but this time I didn't close my heart. I was hoping that in the morning, God might put the answer there.

Chapter 52

Greg

The news was bad. Dr. Choi was wearing it on his face. I knew that look. I knew that demeanor. We doctors were taught to be stoic, emotionless, and unpredictable when we had bad news to deliver.

I stood and walked to Angelina's bedside. She struggled to get higher on the bed. The tubing had to be uncomfortable because her hands were still swollen. I swallowed the knot of fear that was lodged in my throat and pushed the button to raise the bed for her.

"Good morning, Dr. Choi." I stared into his eyes. I was looking for something, begging him with my own. *Please don't tell us something terrible.*

"Good morning to you, Mr. and Mrs. Preston. I have the results from your test, and we have a diagnosis." He paused for a moment. "Mrs. Preston, you have a condition called peripartum cardiomyopathy." My breathing stopped. "It's a form of heart failure that develops late in pregnancy or postpartum." My heart stopped. Time stopped. I couldn't hear. He hadn't just said heart failure, had he? I reached for Angelina's hand and squeezed it. I tried to breathe; I wanted to speak, but I couldn't make words come.

"Peripartum cardiomyopathy, or PPCM, as we call it, affects the heart by not allowing it to contract forcefully enough to send blood throughout the body." He deadpanned. I squeezed Angelina's hand again and looked at her. She was silent, but I could see the fear. Like me, she was shocked and probably couldn't speak. I had to be the strong one. I had to ask the questions.

I cleared my throat. "The cause?"

"The cause, we're not certain, but research is increasingly pointing toward virus or some immune system dysfunction."

I cleared my throat again. "Treatment?"

"Medication—diuretics, ACE inhibitors, beta-blockers." Dr. Choi gave me his full attention, because he knew I would explain ACE inhibitors and beta-blockers to my wife in regular people terms. "Bed rest." He looked at Angelina. "We'll keep you here for a few more days, probably a week, and watch your heart function to determine if we can send you home."

Angelina found her voice. "I have to stay here?"

Dr. Choi nodded. "Mrs. Preston, I don't want to scare you, but I also don't want to give you the impression that this is not serious. We've made great advances in treating PPCM. Many return to completely normal heart function postpregnancy. Some take longer to reach full heart function than others, and then some never recover. Heart transplantation might be necessary and/or death could occur at any time."

"I don't understand." Angelina stuttered her words. "I take good care of myself. I eat right. I exercise."

"Dr. Choi, can we have a minute?" I asked.

He nodded. "I have a few other patients to see. I've ordered some medications to begin right away, but I'll be back before I leave the hospital to address your questions." He turned and left, left me to really answer the questions, left me to be strong.

Tears filled my wife's eyes. "Greg, what does heart failure mean? Is he saying my heart could stop working?"

"Honey, he's saying that your heart is weak, and they're going to treat you to strengthen it." I blinked back tears that wanted to flood my eyes. "It's going to be okay. It's not permanent heart failure, it's just pregnancy-related."

She looked at me. Desperation cracked her voice. "Are you sure?"

The look in her eyes made my heart feel as if it would fail. I raised a hand to her cheek. "I'm sure." I wasn't. I wasn't sure of anything.

I pulled the chair I'd been sitting in closer and reached into my jacket for my phone. "I'm going to log on to a medical site and do a little reading for you."

"No." Angelina shook her head. "First, we need to pray. I need to pray, and I can't do that with you reading." Her voice broke. Her breaths came hard. "So, if you need to read . . . please leave and do that, but right now . . . I need this room to be filled . . . with prayer. Because . . ." she stopped and began to gasp for air and sob. "I'm scared, and when I'm scared, I pray." I reached for her. She wrapped her free arm around my neck and cried.

I let her go on for a few minutes, but then I had to make this stop. "Angelina, please, you're upsetting yourself and your—" I stopped myself. I couldn't tell her what I wanted to say. I couldn't say, you're upsetting yourself and that's going to put more pressure on your heart. That would only upset her more. She was human. She deserved to cry. *Pray.* I heard a voice in my head. *Pray for her.* "Honey, let's go ahead and pray."

Angelina stopped crying. She found strength instantly in those words. I handed her some tissue and took her hand again and began to pray the best I knew how. "Lord, we need you. Please help my wife with her fear. Help her to depend on you like she always does. Help her to know you will not only take care of her while she's pregnant, but you will heal her after she has the baby. That she'll be okay. That you have her in your thoughts and in your care." I stopped. My breaths were coming as rapidly as the words I was speaking. "She trusts you. *We* trust you. Amen."

Angelina seemed calmer. She even smiled a little through her tears. "Thank you," she whispered, her voice small and frail. "That was good. That's what I needed."

"Me too," I lied. I only needed one thing, and that was not to have a pregnant wife with heart disease. "It's going to be okay, Lena. It's just a thing that happens, you know, and it's like you told me. Sometimes we go through things that make us stronger people. Things that give us a reason to need God. It's a challenge, because life isn't perfect."

Angelina nodded and smiled again. She squeezed my hand. She had to know I was throwing her own words back at her. Words she had said to me after the car accident.

"I know, and I need to be grateful right now, because I'm still pregnant and my heart is still working and . . ." she grabbled for the words to convince herself. "We just have to ride this out." She raised a hand to cover her face for a moment. A grimace showed through her fingers. I could tell she was fighting pain. Fighting breaking down again.

"God's not going to leave us. He's not going to take this baby, and He's not going to take you from it or me." I removed her hand from her face and looked in her eyes, willing her to see strength in mine, but I wasn't sure what she would see, because I was unconvinced. I didn't believe a word I'd said. Didn't believe the prayer. Didn't believe anything but the fact that I knew I had to be strong for her.

Angelina fixed her face. "Okay." Her voice cracked. Her heart was probably cracking too. "No more tears. I need to save my strength for the baby." She smiled.

A nurse swept into the room with medication. I was so glad she had come. I was glad I had a second to breathe. I turned away from my wife, rolled my eyes, and swallowed hard. *Heart failure.* I shook my head, shook those words out of it. I had to busy myself. "I'm going to send some text messages and let everybody know what's going on."

I heard Angelina say, "Okay."

I sent a message to Catherine, Felesia, and Angelina's mother. I instructed them to give her a few hours to rest before they called. Women—who knew if any of them would respect that, but I couldn't not tell them what was going on. I also texted Chelsea and asked her if she could keep Katrice overnight again. I'd already made up my mind I was staying with my wife.

I avoided the urge to go to the Internet and read about her condition. I decided I wasn't going to do it in front of Angelina. She'd practically be reading over my shoulder, and I knew she'd have questions. I didn't want to answer them with my doctor's brain. I didn't want to be a scientist. I needed to be a husband. I needed to be all heart.

It was more than an hour before Dr. Choi returned, which was good because it gave us time to think of our questions. We asked a lot of them, but we were strong when we got the answers. Angelina and I had resolved while he was gone that we would not let fear encroach and take over. We would remember God was in control.

I could tell Angelina was feeling better. That magical peace that she had in the tank of her soul had taken over and brought her to a relatively calm place, so much so that she had become sleepy and dozed off. I took that as my opportunity to leave. I had to get my head together.

I exited the room and told the nurses to let Angelina know I'd be back soon. I took the stairs rather than the elevator, because I knew no one would be using them. It was my first opportunity to be alone. I needed some time to myself. Time to think and process what was happening. I climbed into my car, pulled out of the lot, and into traffic. *Heart failure.*

"No, no, no, brain," I whispered. I wasn't going to go there yet.

I turned my Miles Davis CD on the highest possible volume. I didn't want to hear myself think. Traffic was a little thick, so it took me a little longer to get back to my apartment than it should have; still, I hadn't allowed myself to think. I walked in, dropped my keys, and peeled off my jacket. I downed a bottle of water, went to the extra bedroom where I kept the home gym, and lay down on my weight bench. *Heart failure.* I bench-pressed the weight bar up and down . . . ten repetitions, twenty-five repetitions, forty repetitions . . . weakened arms at sixty repetitions. *Heart failure.* I dropped the weights in their stand and sat up. *Heart failure.*

I stood, walked out into the living room, and reached into the bar for the vodka. *Heart failure.* I shook my head. *Heart failure!* the voice yelled in my head.

"No!" I hurled the bottle against the window. It crashed, shattered, and chunks of glass flew everywhere. Liquid spilled down the impenetrable window like a stream of rainwater.

That felt good.

I grabbed a nearby lamp and smashed it. An ashtray, a vase, a framed poster from the wall, books, everything I could get my hands on. I grabbed and smashed. Tears fell from my eyes; my chest heaved up and down as I gasped for air and sobbed. "No, no, no, no, no!" *Heart failure.* I fell to the floor and covered my ears. *Heart failure!* It wouldn't stop. I was going to lose my mind. I crawled to the kitchen, pulled more things down around me, and threw them until there was nothing else to grab, nothing else to break. *Heart failure!* I fell on my face and cried and cried. "God, why? Why? Why?"

I heard a doorbell in the distance. *Mine.* I couldn't answer it.

"Dr. Preston, this is the building super. I'm coming in!"

Heart failure. I shook my head.

"Gregory?"

Who was that? It wasn't the super.

"Gregory!"

I was imagining it. The voice of . . . I looked toward the entrance to the kitchen. Through tear-filled eyes I saw her. She ran to me, got on her knees, and pulled me into her arms. *Heart failure.* I rocked back and forth as she continued to hold me. I clutched her back so tight I thought I would break her. "Please, Mom, help me! Oh, God, I can't take this! I can't lose my wife! I can't lose my son!"

Chapter 53

Greg

My mother and sister were my salvation. They took care of so many things that Angelina needed that I hadn't thought about. They brought Angelina's clothing and toiletries to her. Catherine prepared casseroles and quick meals for Katrice. They called Reverend Hines, and he and some of the women from the church came and prayed for Angelina. They also delivered books and magazines and more food. All I'd thought to do was buy flowers. I was paralyzed.

Angelina agreed it was best for all of us to stay at the house. It was closer to the hospital, and it gave her comfort to know people were around Katrice. I brought her to visit every day, and every day the tiny little girl put her hand on Angelina's heart and said a prayer. "Jesus going to fix you, Mommy." I waited for the faith of a child to do what my lack of faith wouldn't: make my wife well.

I wanted to spend as much time as I could with my family, so I cut back on my work schedule for the next few months. My calendar was set so I only had to go in three times a week, and on those days I worked half days. Most of the appointments I kept for the next month were complex surgical procedures. There were only a few of us that could perform them in the metro area, so I couldn't go ghost completely. I made sure to pick Katrice up every day, and Catherine and I alternated taking her to the park like her mother would have.

Angelina was released after eight days. She was thrilled to go home, and I was more thrilled that the doctors thought she was well enough. I'd done a lot of reading about PPCM. It was potentially fatal, but 100 percent recovery was possible. I just had to keep believing that it would happen that way for her.

If prayer was going to do the trick, Angelina was a shoo-in. She had many people praying for her on a daily basis—my mother and sister, Felesia, her mother who was now in town, the church family, Katrice, and she prayed for herself. I had avoided praying. I had felt like anything I opened my mouth and said would be a joke because I was afraid. I was afraid that things would go wrong with my wife's heart during or after the delivery. I was afraid to jinx what everybody else was doing.

The thing I was most afraid of was my mother's words that God was trying to get to me through Angelina. I would never meet God's qualifications, so where did that leave Angelina? I was losing sleep about it so much that I'd become a walking zombie, staying up all night watching television, but hiding my sleeplessness from everyone until I couldn't hide it anymore.

"Dr. Preston, Dr. Preston?" I heard my name and snapped to attention. "Sir, are you all right?" I looked around and found myself in the OR with a scalpel in my hand. I had absolutely no idea who I was operating on or what I was supposed to be doing to their brain. My hand started trembling, and I became nauseated. I ran out of the OR and vomited just inside of the men's room. Never in my professional career had one of my colleagues had to take over a surgery for me. I was losing it, and I'd crack up if I had to wait until the delivery if I didn't get some help.

Shortly afterward, I wandered into the hospital chapel. After sitting in the rear of the room for more than an hour, I found myself looking at Reverend Hines.

"Brother Preston, good to see you." His kind eyes crinkled, and I was reminded of the African American Father Christmas figurine that my mother put out on the foyer table every year during the season.

"Reverend." It was all I could manage to say. I was still in a state of confusion over my inability to perform surgery. "I'm surprised to see you here."

"I have parishioners all over the city," he said. "I always stop in the chapel to see if anyone needs a cleric. How are Angelina and the baby?"

"She's good. We're waiting until she's thirty-seven weeks, and then they'll induce labor, so we're all just holding on and waiting." I tried to infuse confidence into my tone.

"I'd say barely holding on by the looks of you." Worry lines creased his forehead, and he looked at me harder, like he was assessing just how bad the damage was.

"It's been difficult." I looked down at my trembling hands, made a fist of them to hide the shaking, but even the fist would not be still.

Reverend Hines took my hands, held them firmly, and said, "I want to pray with you, son."

A rebellious tear fell down my face. I let out a breath and shook my head. "Pray for my wife. Pray for my baby."

"I'm not sure if they're the ones who really need it."

I swallowed and pulled back my hands to wipe my eyes.

"Brother Preston, you do believe God is here for you; otherwise, you wouldn't have stepped in here today."

I felt like an eight-year-old boy crying in front of a grown man, but I couldn't stop. I was breaking down and letting go. It was time. "My first child died. She was six months old. She died in her crib. I was with her."

"Angelina shared that with me."

"And then there was another child that died, not my wife's, a child I shouldn't have had, but . . . She was stillborn." Reverend Hines sat back. I could see only sorrow and sympathy, no judgment about the "outside baby," so I continued. "I'm starting to wonder if I'm cursed. If I lose this baby, or if I lose my wife, I just don't know if I'll be able to survive it. I need a miracle, but I don't deserve one, because I've been so angry with God for the last couple of years that I've cursed Him and laughed at Him and laughed at anyone who put their faith in Him, including Angelina."

"So, you're afraid it's time to pay for that."

"Might it be? I don't know."

Reverend Hines nodded, and then chuckled a bit. "Do you know about the Apostle Paul? Do you know his story?"

"He wrote most of the New Testament. He was a great teacher. He won souls for Christ."

"And . . ." he urged me to continue.

"He was the man that was knocked off his horse and went blind."

"Back up," Reverend Hines said. "Before he was knocked off his horse, what was his life about?"

I hesitated some, but I knew this story. I just didn't know where we were going with it. "His name was Saul, and he persecuted Christians," I replied.

"That's it. He persecuted Christians, but he became one of the most important men in our church's history." Reverend Hines paused, and then continued. "Brother Preston, I don't think it's time for you to pay for your anger. I just think it's time for you to move forward. Forgive yourself and ask God to forgive you." He put his hand on my shoulder and said, "Son, it's time to stop letting this anger and regret destroy your life. We are going to pray, and we are going to pray until you are a new man."

And that's exactly what we did. Reverend Hines counseled me and prayed with me and forced me to talk about things I'd never told anyone. He helped me to peel back the layers of bitterness and hurt that surrounded my heart.

I went home, showered, and lay on my bed. I was no longer the zombie I had been. I was not the living dead. Reverend Hines had broken something in my spirit today. I honestly felt like a new person. In just that short span of time, my soul felt renewed and refreshed. Reverend Hines had told me with people, forgiveness is a process, but with God, it's just a decision. He releases us instantly and throws our sins into the sea of forgetfulness.

I had to pick up Katrice in a couple of hours, but I needed a nap. I had something to do, something that was going to be difficult, and I thought it might be easier once I had some rest, but sleep would not come. The Lord who had forgiven me would not let me rest. I sat up, picked up my phone, pulled a slip of paper from the desk, and placed a phone call. I got an answer on the other end—a soft-spoken, meek hello.

"Samaria, this is Greg," I said. "I'm sorry about the baby. I'm sorry about everything . . ."

Chapter 54

Angelina

The mess with the IRS was over, and it didn't wrap up the way I was expecting it to.

"No need for a summation hearing," Hightower said. "I'll be on them first thing in the morning to drop the charges."

"We need to celebrate!" My mother-in-law clapped her hands together. "It's not every day you watch your thieving accountant get arrested on national television."

"And trying to take his sawed-off self over the Mexican border," my mother added.

"With your receptionist!" Catherine laughed. "I thought we had drama in New Orleans."

We all laughed. I pushed the rewind button on the DVR to Don's close-up. "I'm sorry that I hurt the charity. It was my intention to return the money before anyone ever found out it was missing. Angelina, forgive me. Forgive me," he begged as they put handcuffs on him and pushed him into the police car.

"Liar," my mother said. "If he was planning to give it back, why was so much of it in that suitcase in the trunk of his car?"

The news footage cut to Portia. She was crying. Her green eyes were smeared black from running eyeliner. "I was kidnapped. I was taken against my will!" she screamed. Now I realized why she always had so many questions about Don. I thought it was concern. She was trying to find out if they were on to him. The thought of their betrayal gave me the shivers.

"She sounded like an idiot. How she gonna cry kidnapping when she got that passport less than a month ago?" My mother reached over and gave my knee a pat. "I'm glad that mess is over."

"We need to make a special dinner in honor of their stupidity," Catherine added. The women started tossing out suggestions for the meal that sounded like it was going to be a feast.

My cell phone rang, and I reached for it.

"Angelina." I recognized the thunder in the baritone voice. I pushed mute and raised my hands to shush the chatter in my house. "It's Dr. Adams from the DYFS Board." Everyone got quiet, and I pushed un-mute. "Hello, Dr. Adams, it's a pleasure to hear from you."

"It's a pleasure to be able to call you, Angelina. If you're still interested, I'd like to invite you back on the board for DYFS. You've been missed."

"I'd like that very much, Dr. Adams." My heart filled with joy. He said a few more things, and then we ended the call. If I hadn't been eight months pregnant I would have sprung from my seat.

"Oh, Angelina, I'm so happy," my mother-in-law said. "I know how much it meant to you."

"I know you've missed it, so even though I thought you were working too hard, I'm glad you didn't just get put out after all those years of service," my mother said.

Catherine stood. "It's getting late. Greg will be here with Katrice soon, so if we're going to make that celebration dinner, we'd better get on it."

All three of them stood and left the room. "Can I do something?" I called to them. Three distinct voices yelled, "No!" in unison. I knew that was coming.

"Well," I shrugged, "so much for that." I stood and walked out on the porch just in time to meet the postman. If the day hadn't already been exciting enough, a packet had arrived from my other attorney's office. Katrice's mother's rights had been severed. She was free for adoption, and the papers I'd completed would be filed right away. She was going to be mine. Tears filled my eyes, I was so misty and overcome with them that I hadn't noticed Greg's car pull into the driveway. He and Katrice got out. He took her hand, and they chatted on the way to the porch. There was a light in Katrice's eyes whenever she was around Greg. They'd grown really close over the last few weeks. She'd even taken to calling him Daddy, which I didn't mind, because my heart told me he would be just that.

Neither of them had seen me in the corner. When Katrice spotted me, she dropped Greg's hand, ran, and yelled, "Mommy!" She grabbed me tightly around my neck, and when she was done kissing my face, she rubbed my belly. It was a good thing I wasn't one of those pregnant women who didn't like to be touched, because this was the most rubbed, loved, unborn baby on the planet. "I wanna see the grandmas," Katrice said.

Greg climbed the steps, pushed the door open, and in she ran. "Nothing like those grandmas," he smiled.

"Nothing can top them," I remarked. He leaned over and kissed me on the forehead and joined me by taking a chair next to mine. He rubbed my belly, and then looked into my eyes. He looked tired, but there was something else—a glint of the happiness I hadn't seen in many, many months—maybe even years.

"How's my baby today?" he asked.

"Quiet again."

"Thirty-five weeks. He's about to make his debut."

I touched my own belly. "I'll be glad to meet him."

"Me, too," Greg said. "But before I do, I'd like to be worthy of him and worthy of you. I think I finally found out how to do that."

I tilted my head toward him. I hoped and prayed he had the answer my heart wanted to hear.

"I recommitted myself to Christ today."

I was stiff with shock. I held my breath, afraid that if I breathed I'd wake up from a dream. Greg took my hand, and I released the breath. He was really here. I swallowed a heart full of relief.

"I already know God will have me. We had a long talk this afternoon." He stopped. "But you, Angelina, what do I have to do to show you I'm committed to you?"

I raised his hand to my lips and kissed it. "You've already done it."

Greg smiled. "I was hoping you would say that." He reached into his pocket and pulled out a box from Tiffany's. "My father told me to buy you jewelry, but I told myself I'd only show it to you if I'd already won your heart back. No more bribes."

I swallowed any reservations I had about Greg and opened the box. It was a ring with a diamond so large that it was obscene. "This is incredible."

"Will you marry me again?" His voice was a husky whisper of desperation. "I know we're not divorced, but . . ."

"Shhh . . ." I put a finger to his lips. "I love you, Gregory Preston. Your days of begging me are over."

Our lips came together, and I felt like I'd gone straight to heaven.

Chapter 55

Angelina

Our relatives, friends, and my new church family from Steeple of Love sat in the backyard of my home. My mother and mother-in-law had tastefully decorated it with every pastel flower available in Atlanta. The women had cooked a feast. Greg's father had arrived with Miss Annie and a specially commissioned wedding cake from Greg's favorite bakery in New Orleans. I was so happy. It was a joy that I never thought I'd ever feel again. But I should have known better. My God had not forsaken me. The valleys in life are surrounded by hills. We just have to climb them to get back on top.

Reverend Hines stood with Greg, Felesia, Philip, and Katrice at a gazebo we'd rented for the occasion. All watched me waddle down the aisle in a beautiful satin A-line gown that made me look like a model. Those pregnant celebrities I saw on television hired professional stylists, but they had nothing on the handiwork of the women in my court. From the moment Greg and I announced we wanted to exchange our vows again, they got busy shopping for the perfect dress to make me shine. From the look in Greg's eyes, I knew they had accomplished their mission.

"You look amazing," he said. Those were the words I wanted to hear. I handed Felesia my bouquet. She squeezed my hand before letting it go, and I winked at her. She winked back. There was nothing like the love of a good sister-friend. I was so glad that I had someone to push me back on the path when I lost my way. We all need that.

Greg took my hand. Reverend Hines began with words about the wedding in Canaan and ended with what had become our new family motto, "Choose life." Then he said, "You may kiss your wife."

Greg took a step toward me and raised my chin. "Thank you for marrying me again," he said, his voice was husky with emotion.

"Thank you for not giving up on me," I whispered, and my eyes got wet with tears. When I thought about how my stubbornness had almost cost me this happiness I was feeling now, I was sick. Greg had made a horrible mistake, but so had I. I hadn't even tried to forgive him.

Greg leaned down and kissed me. His lips were so warm and inviting that I never wanted it to end. I melted under his touch. I loved this man, and now I knew without a doubt that he loved me.

When he released me from the kiss, our guests applauded. Katrice ran and jumped into Greg's arms. With his free hand he took mine, and we turned to face everyone. Flashes from cameras and cell phones lit up the backyard. I tried to keep smiling, but I felt a cramp. I squeezed Greg's hand, and he looked at me. I moaned. Greg grimaced. I moaned again, and then I felt a pop. Water trickled down my leg. I raised my gown. Greg's eyes followed mine to my wet shoes. "The good news is I don't have to be induced on Monday, but the bad news is I don't think we have time for cake," I giggled. "My water just broke."

We laughed. Greg kissed me again, turned to our guests, and said, "We'd like you all to stay and eat to your hearts' content. Angelina and I are going to go and have our baby."

Everyone gushed oohs and aahs. Reverend Hines said a quick prayer for a safe delivery. Then with the wedding party on our heels, Greg and I rushed to the car.

An hour later, Daniel Levitt Preston was born. I barely had time to get out of my wedding dress and onto the bed before I felt the first urge to push. Dr. Luke didn't make it to the hospital on time. But it didn't matter. Our beautiful, perfect son had made his arrival into the world with ease. I'd not had one complication or heart flutter along the way.

The rest of our family piled into the room. Each one took their turn staring into the face of our tiny new addition. My father-in-law took Daniel in his hands and raised him up in the air a bit. He said some words in Spanish, and Felesia told me that he was giving the baby a blessing. When he was done, he handed the baby to Greg and said, "He'll never see a day of trouble."

Greg's eyes got misty. He nodded and said, "I know." It was the kind of "I know" that came from deep inside the soul. An "I know" that held confidence in God. I knew it well, because it was the "I know" I felt in my soul when I thought about my recovery from PPCM. I "knew" my God was going to heal me completely. I had no doubt.

Greg placed Daniel in my arms. He leaned over, kissed me on the forehead, and said, "Thank you."

I pulled my baby high up on my chest and stared at him. I watched as his eyes slowly opened for the first time. With tears in my own eyes, I looked at Greg and thanked him back.

Epilogue

Samaria

I sat down at the table with the bag the guard had just given me. The store where I fulfilled my shopping addiction had been bumped down from Bergdorf's to the county jail's commissary, where they had an assortment of items like shampoo, deodorant, greeting cards, candy bars, and potato chips. I'd purchased paper and pens last week and was as excited as I could possibly be to receive them.

Mekhi made sure I had plenty of money on my book, which was a blessing, because most of the woman in this place had no one that cared enough to try to diminish their misery. My husband had a triple platinum hit album on his label, so I was a baller, even in the county jail. I could have told the guard an Afro comb and a round of donuts for everyone, on me. I'd actually thought about trying that one day, but realized it was better if I didn't. There were gangs in here that might not like the fact that I had a rich husband waiting for me. They could make it an uncomfortable stay. I knew some of the women knew who I was, but I kept it on the low-low. Inciting envy was not smart. I kept my mouth shut, so I could just do this time without any problems.

I turned my attention to my paper and pen. I wasn't much of a writer. My preference was e-mails, text messages, and tweets, but I had no access to such luxuries, so a simple letter would have to do.

I didn't want to be one of those prisoners who self-ishly sent letters to the people on the outside. They were selfish because their intention was to make them-selves feel better no matter how their words affected the receiver. Not cool. I was looking for absolution, but I also wanted to reach out in love to one of the few peo-ple in my life who had shown me love with no strings attached, so in my best penmanship and most heartfelt words, I began:

Dear Angelina,

I hope you don't mind my writing you. I know you said that I could, but if you were just be-ing kind, I'll understand and not write again. I wanted to thank you for being a friend to me. I know it wasn't easy to forgive me for my horrible behavior, but you did and that makes you an amazing woman; the kind of woman I pray I will be someday.

I am studying a book about the "greatness" of God. The lessons come from Romans. You told me to read that book, and well, now I am. My Bible Study teacher told me that the best way to embrace God as "The Father" was to accept His greatness, and His sovereign magnitude (her words), so I'm doing that. As a result, it occurred to me that God works in mysterious ways.

I never believed that Melia could die. Out of all the thoughts I had about my pregnancy and her paternity, I never thought that she wouldn't "be." At first, I thought her death was about sowing and reaping. I'd turned her into a burden with all my baby daddy drama. I stole men and drugs. I hurt people with my manipulation. You were not the first victim of my secrets and lies, so I thought I had gotten exactly what I deserved when I lost her. But then, I thought about your loss. We are as different as night and day, so this had to be something other than justice, because really, what evil seeds had you sown?

I don't want to presume to know His thoughts, but I think that I had to lose so you could gain. Losing my daughter was the only way that you and Greg could reconcile. The death of a child tore your marriage apart, and the death of another allowed you to come back together. You once told me that God loved us and that all things worked together for good, so I'm going to hide those words in my heart and believe that one day I'll see my baby again.

I know that you're busy with your family, but if you could make time to "mentor a sister," I'd appreciate it if you'd write me. Don't feel guilty if you choose not to. I will understand. You don't owe me anything.

Please love your children, love your husband, and pray for the woman you once considered a friend. I will be praying for you.

Love,
The Samaritan Woman

Readers' Group Guide Questions

1. Angelina refused to have sex with Greg even though she wanted to. Some people believe if two people are married that it's okay, even if they're separated. What are your thoughts about this?

2. Greg is tempted by three women in the story. The story shares his thoughts each time, and each time he decides to not take the women up on their offer for a different reason. Review his actions in Chapters 4, 9, and 49 and discuss his growth in this respect.

3. Have you ever experienced or considered the mental process involved in resisting sexual sin? Do you think it's different from other temptations? Why or why not?

4. It appears Greg's father may have passed down a legacy of infidelity. Discuss your thoughts about their marriage and the things Greg witnessed growing up.

5. Infidelity is a deal breaker for many relationships. Some believe a marriage can be restored. Do you agree or disagree? What would it take to restore it? Do you believe Greg deserved a second chance? Why or why not?

6. One of the biggest obstacles to Greg's faith in God was the difficult situations he'd had to endure and the lack of God's grace in the life of people he felt were strong believers (his mother and his wife). What are your thoughts about this? How do you minister to people who think the same way?

7. Samaria was in a precarious situation not knowing who the father of her unborn child was, and she handled it Samaria-style: deceptively. Discuss some of her choices.

8. At the end of Chapter 22, Angelina feels convicted about refusing to give Samaria a "church sister" hug. She reasoned that she didn't owe the woman anything. Think about Angelina's statement from the perspective of being a Christian. Did Angelina owe Samaria something? If yes, what?

9. Why do you think Samaria married Mekhi?

10. Benxi made Mekhi an offer he could refuse, but he decided to look at it as if it were business. Do you think he would have slept with Benxi? How would Samaria have responded to his logic? Finally, do you think sexual relations are different for men?

11. The loss of Samaria's child was tragic. Discuss how it affected her. What are your thoughts about the letter she wrote to Angelina?

12. What was the most memorable scene in the book? Did you have a favorite character? If so, who and why?

13. It's possible that I may write about some of these characters again. Take the time to think about what you'd like to see happen next. Have fun with it. Then e-mail me at Rhonda@rhondamcknight.net and share your thoughts. I'd love to hear from you.

About the Author

Rhonda McKnight is the author of the Black Expressions "Top 20" bestselling novel, *An Inconvenient Friend* (Aug. 2010) and the Black Expressions bestseller, *Secrets and Lies* (Dec. 2009). She is recipient of the 2010 EMMA Award for Favorite Debut Author, the 2010 SistahFriend's Book Club "Pink Diamond" Award, and the 2009 Shades of Romance Award for "Christian Fiction Author of the Year." She also owns Legacy Editing, a freelance editing service for fiction writers and Urban Christian Fiction Today, a popular Internet site that highlights African American Christian fiction. When she's not editing projects, teaching workshops about writing, or penning her next novel, she spends time with her family. Originally from a small, coastal town in New Jersey, she's called Atlanta, Georgia, home for thirteen years.

You may learn more about Rhonda and her novels at her Web site:
www.rhondamcknight.net

Contact her by e-mail at:
Rhonda@rhondamcknight.net.

UC HIS GLORY BOOK CLUB!

www.uchisglorybookclub.net

UC His Glory Book Club is the spirit-inspired brain-child of Joylynn Jossel, Author and Acquisitions Editor of Urban Christian, and Kendra Norman-Bellamy, Author for Urban Christian. This is an online book club that hosts authors of Urban Christian. We welcome as members all men and women who have a passion for reading Christian-based fiction.

UC His Glory Book Club pledges our commitment to provide support, positive feedback, encouragement, and a forum whereby members can openly discuss and review the literary works of Urban Christian authors.

There is no membership fee associated with UC His Glory Book Club; however, we do ask that you support the authors through purchasing, encouraging, providing book reviews, and of course, your prayers. We also ask that you respect our beliefs and follow the guidelines of the book club. We hope to receive your valuable input, opinions, and reviews that build up, rather than tear down our authors.

WHAT WE BELIEVE:

—We believe that Jesus is the Christ, Son of the Living God.

—We believe the Bible is the true, living Word of God.

—We believe all Urban Christian authors should use their God-given writing abilities to honor God and share the message of the written word God has given to each of them uniquely.

—We believe in supporting Urban Christian authors in their literary endeavors by reading, purchasing and sharing their titles with our online community.

—We believe that in everything we do in our literary arena should be done in a manner that will lead to God being glorified and honored.

—We look forward to the online fellowship with you. Please visit us often at *www.uchisglorybookclub.net.*

Many Blessings to You!

Shelia E. Lipsey,
President, UC His Glory Book Club

ORDER FORM
URBAN BOOKS, LLC
78 E. Industry Ct
Deer Park, NY 11729

Name: (please print):_____

Address: _____

City/State: _____

Zip: _____

QTY	TITLES	PRICE
	3:57 A.M Timing Is Everything	$14.95
	A Man's Worth	$14.95
	A Woman's Worth	$14.95
	Abundant Rain	$14.95
	After The Feeling	$14.95
	Amaryllis	$14.95
	An Inconvenient Friend	$14.95
	Battle of Jericho	$14.95
	Be Careful What You Pray For	$14.95
	Beautiful Ugly	$14.95
	Been There Prayed That:	$14.95
	Before Redemption	$14.95

Shipping and handling-add $3.50 for 1st book, then $1.75 for each additional book.

Please send a check payable to:

Urban Books, LLC

Please allow 4-6 weeks for delivery

ORDER FORM
URBAN BOOKS, LLC
78 E. Industry Ct
Deer Park, NY 11729

Name: (please print): _____

Address: _____

City/State: _____

Zip: _____

QTY	TITLES	PRICE
	By the Grace of God	$14.95
	Confessions Of A preachers Wife	$14.95
	Dance Into Destiny	$14.95
	Deliver Me From My Enemies	$14.95
	Desperate Decisions	$14.95
	Divorcing the Devil	$14.95
	Faith	$14.95
	First Comes Love	$14.95
	Flaws and All	$14.95
	Forgiven	$14.95
	Former Rain	$14.95
	Forsaken	$14.95

Shipping and handling-add $3.50 for 1st book, then $1.75 for each additional book.

Please send a check payable to:

Urban Books, LLC

Please allow 4-6 weeks for delivery